Abercynon

Spoken History

George Ewart Evans

Spoken History

faber and faber

LONDON · BOSTON

First published in 1987
by Faber and Faber Limited
3 Queen Square London WC1N 3AU

Photoset by Parker Typesetting Service Leicester
Printed in Great Britain by
Mackays of Chatham Kent
All rights reserved

British Library Cataloguing in Publication Data

Evans, George Ewart
Spoken history.
1. Oral history
907'.2   D16.14

ISBN 0-571-14982-0

Contents

Acknowledgements

During the past thirty or so years I have recorded many people on magnetic tape; and I have included these in the books published during this time. Their words are substantially the history that is within these nine volumes and the autobiography I wrote during those years. I wish to thank my numerous helpers for the implicit trust they gave to my project and to the assurance they gave me that I had transcribed their words faithfully.

From the first I have been fortunate that these books were handled by Faber and Faber who have always shown themselves understanding and imaginative publishers. Morley Kennerley, who managed my first book, came from America in the twenties, having a sound knowledge of country life and character in New England where he had been brought up. He very soon identified with East Anglia which he got to know fairly well, and was the subject of many of my books. When he retired, Peter du Sautoy the Chairman, took over their guidance; and later John Bodley had them in his charge.

About twenty years ago my books took on a new ambience, being illustrated by my son-in-law, David Gentleman, whose remarkable translation of the region and many of its people in his drawings gave the books a new distinction. Berthold Wolpe and Michael Wright both ensured they were excellently produced; and Elizabeth Renwick gave invaluable help with their editing. I am also very grateful to my neighbour David James for his careful reading of the proofs; and also to my next-door neighbour, Marjorie Sayer, who typed the manuscript, exchanging the copy through the *mardling* [gossip] *hole* in the hedge.

I wish to thank the following for permission to quote from

Acknowledgements

their work: Professor Colin Renfrew, Master of Jesus College, Cambridge; Michael Riviere for the nineteenth century family story of the well-known Paston Barn. Also 'a knowledgeable bystander' I have been unable to trace. He described the long and careful preparation, by a woman driver, of a team of eight Suffolk horses, prior to entering the Showring.

Finally, I would like to thank my wife for her constant support, and her forbearance at my frequent immurement in my room during the time this book was being completed.

Abbreviations

A.F.C.H.	*Ask the Fellows Who Cut the Hay*
H.I.F.	*The Horse in the Furrow*
P.U.P	*The Pattern under the Plough*
F.A.V.	*The Farm and the Village*
W.B.W.A.	*Where Beards Wag All*
T.L.H.	*The Leaping Hare* (with David Thomson)
D.T.W.H.S.	*The Days that We Have Seen*
F.M.M.	*From Mouths of Men*
H.P. & M.	*Horse Power and Magic*

Blaxhall

Introduction

In a series of books I have written since 1956 I have discussed
my involvement with what later became known as oral history. Although I had lived in East Anglia for over six years
before the last war my real knowledge of the region did not
begin until after the war when we all came as a family to the
Suffolk village of Blaxhall. My wife had been appointed as
head of the village school, and I began to know my neighbours who, almost to a man, were farm workers who had
reached retiring age. Then I laid down the foundation of the
work I have been doing ever since: getting history directly
from people, and going about introducing the technique to
schools, continuing education classes, and groups in universities all over Britain. Although I did not grasp this at the
time, the real proving-ground and forcing-bed of my work in
this field was laid down in my home valley in south Wales,
where most of my neighbours were miners. This was a thinking time in the late twenties and early thirties when the
community was in a perpetual state of crisis about the coal
industry and misgivings about the war that was threatening,
and which many of the more thinking miners were already
warning against. Preoccupied with the more selfish interests
of adolescence and my training as a teacher, about the only
escape from the restricted life in the valley, I had little contact

with my immediate neighbours. Yet when I finished at university in 1931 in the middle of a depression I found myself without a job and I experienced my first awakening. I was drawn more closely to my immediate neighbours, some of whom were in the same boat as myself: without a job and compelled to think day and night about their position. The main burden of my heavy thoughts was: What can I do to get out of this slough?

In my time-eating walks on the hills I met many of the miners, some still working and older ones who had retired. The older men had in their keeping the past of their people, and I got from them a lively sense of the scene before the opening up of the deep mines fifty or sixty years before. They gave me an arresting picture of the valley as it was then and told me that a squirrel could travel its whole length without coming to ground, so thickly was it forested. This was in contrast to the barrack-like streets that now thrust themselves uncompromisingly through these once beautiful hills where the streams that ran down had been full of trout not coal-dust. Many of my neighbours were avid readers and I was amazed by their political insight. But, indirectly, their reading was streamlined to a definite purpose: how to get out of the crisis we were in. They were all in accord about one thing: Hitler must be stopped. In the meantime I finally got a job in a pleasant environment on the other side of England.

After a few years I settled down and got married. Within a couple of years the war came, as my neighbours in Wales said it would. I was called up in 1941 and spent nearly five years in the Services. A short time after being demobilized we came to Blaxhall. I had been downgraded with increasing deafness during my war service, and decided to change to full-time freelance writing. I had already been writing for many years, starting from the time I left university and was without a job, and I had become marginally known. With a young family of four children and both of us with jobs, we were fully engaged; and for eight years we were actively involved with the villagers and shared some of their hopes and disappointments. The experience gave me my first acquaintance of a rural community of a very special nature, a village that had retained many of the marks and sinews of its long development from the most ancient times. For me, the people of Blaxhall helped to objectify a large and valuable sector of English history and to bring it to life in many small tableaux that will remain indelibly in my mind and I hope in some of my writings.

One of the first things that struck me was the speech of the natives of the village. It alerted me to the age of the community we had come to and gradually persuaded me that this dialect or *variety* of speech, as some scholars prefer to call it, avoiding the constricting associations of the word 'dialect' itself, was suitable as a vehicle for transferring the history of the East Anglian people to a new synthesis. As well as being signally appropriate to the description of East Anglian farming, it bears the accent of an older language and a much healthier one than current English, its unadorned purity being unpolluted by the numerous abstractions that have crept into our everyday discourse. It is the kind of language that could become a good corrective of much of modern speech. As far as oral history is concerned it helps to give some of it a lasting quality that is fitting to the material information conveyed. It gives it a proper and more durable clothing. The language of most of the respondents is much nearer to the soil and therefore does not smack of the muniment-room. And this applies to the Scottish and Welsh contributions as much as to the East Anglian. It is tied to the newest class of the population actively to reach the historical stage and for that reason has some of the vigour of youth and an ability to invigorate the discipline of history.

1

Blaxhall: *Where it Began*

My first acquaintance with the thoughts and opinions of ordinary people was well over half a century ago. I had recently finished a four-year course at university and came out at a critical point in the 1931 depression. I was therefore without a job; and there followed a crisis in my life when all my adolescent values went into the melting-pot, and I was compelled to think out a new course for myself. This influenced the rest of my life. At this period my contact with older miners, some of them unemployed, gave me an entirely new view of the common man whose judgement and opinions were far from being negligible as the events of that period – the middle thirties leading up to the last war – clearly showed. The thinking of some of the miners I was meeting then and their conviction of the crying need to face up to the Nazi threat was, as events proved, far superior to that of the nation's rulers.

It was then that I made my decision to become a writer, and

ever since in my writings I have shown my interest in the common man, believing that his history is a valuable component of a country's story, not only contributing to contemporary history but throwing a light – especially in the rural areas – on the people's way of living centuries before. He can demonstrate unself-consciously how his forefathers lived: their work, the tools they used, their beliefs and their customs, the whole complex of their pattern of living. A recent visit to western Ireland confirmed me in thinking that some of the oldest men I was meeting there had lived a life, at the beginning of this century before the big modern changes, that was essentially little different from the life their ancestors led in neolithic times when farming first started. They were people linked inextricably with the dawn of history, isolated by their way of life and their thinking which was only minimally affected by the town-based civilization. Casting my thoughts back to my own childhood and adolescence in the south Wales valleys I remembered, too, that I had met people like these on the hills above the industrialized valleys. When I was a boy some of them farmed as did their ancestors uninterruptedly over the long centuries, using the same equipment such as the primitive slide-car, in essentials an animal – an ox or a horse – drawing a long pair of shafts that trailed on the ground, an invention that pre-dated the coming of the wheel. Some of their beliefs were equally reminiscent of prehistoric times: they believed in fairies implicitly as I found out later from a fellow farmer who was younger than some of his neighbours. I also met people during the war, on the west coast of Scotland and Orkney, whose way of living had remained up to that time unchanged in its essentials from an earliest period.

During the early thirties when I first began writing I was drawn to short stories and verse. It took this form because they appeared to be the natural medium that offered themselves to a young writer groping to find his way. Then, too, little magazines were starting up spontaneously, offering encouragement to a young writer to see his work in print for the first time. The peak of my efforts came just before the war when a verse play I had written won the prize at the Denbigh National Eisteddfod in 1939. A short time later the war broke out, and all broadcasting except news was temporarily suspended; and the play never saw the light of day. I continued writing throughout the war when I spent four and a half years of it in the RAF. During this time I wrote verse and numerous short stories, and finally my first book of autobiographical fiction.

The end of the war precipitated a personal crisis. I had gone deaf during service and was advised to give up my pre-war job of teaching. We had lost our house at the beginning of the war, and Florence, my wife, and our family had been in temporary accommodation until after it had finished. The only course that presented itself to us was for Florence to continue with the teaching she had done occasionally during the war, and to take a full-time job. A job with a school house offered itself in Suffolk where her father's family had come from, and in 1948 we settled in Blaxhall near the Suffolk coast.

It was a kind of leap in the dark; but it worked in spite of the inevitable ups and downs of bringing up a family in circumstances that were far from ideal. I was writing whenever I could get release from the family chores. But now I was soon confronted with the question of what the subject of my writing should continue to be. Previously it had been almost entirely about Wales; but now the wealth of the material I was beginning to find in Suffolk gradually pressured me to relinquish my writing about Wales. I was reluctant at first to do this but I became aware that my knowledge of south Wales and its problems was already becoming outdated. I became deeply involved with my neighbours in Blaxhall, and decided in the middle fifties to write about the village. The result was my first East Anglian book. But by this time I had widened my interests by taking part in a conference about country and farming subjects at Barford in Warwickshire, the home of Joseph Arch, the founder of the farm workers' union. It was my first introduction to extra-mural work organized in this case, I believe, by the University of Birmingham. Through

the visit I got in contact with John Higgs the first Curator of
the Museum of English Rural Life at Reading. This led to my
attendance at the inaugural meeting of the British Agricultural History Society. One of the speakers was Sir Frank
Stenton, the historian, and I treasured a remark of his during
a lecture advising students of farming to go to working
farmers for material for farming history. This confirmed
what I was already doing at Blaxhall, including farm workers
as well as farmers in my researches. I was much encouraged
by the knowledge that other people were researching farming
history. I increased my reading of farming history and my
conversations with my neighbours who were retired farm
workers. Robert Savage, our nearest neighbour, was the chief
of these. Although he had started life as a shepherd's page
and had been with sheep all his life, he had a remarkable
overall knowledge of the arable farm-processes, and was a
very accurate instructor, conveying his information in pure
dialect which was almost as old as the processes he described.
Some of the material went into the book I was writing, along
with that I was getting from his wife Priscilla about her
domestic economy, the Three Bs as they came to be known:
bread-making, brewing and bacon-curing.

At this time the BBC set up an area station at Norwich,
administrated from Midland Region at Birmingham. The
head of the new Norwich station was David Bryson who came
down to Blaxhall and finally promised me the loan of a
Midget recording unit, and an engineer to instruct me in its
use. This portable tape-recorder caused a revolution in outside broadcasting. Previously, to record someone outside the
studio was an expensive exercise requiring a special van and
two or three personnel. A Midget was a very good machine,
comparatively simple to operate and with its own batteries so
that one could record anywhere. I had the loan of the
machine for three weeks and was able to record eight tapes of
my Blaxhall friends. I have the tapes in my desk now, and the
speech is as clear on them as when I recorded them thirty
years ago.

Unfortunately Robert Savage died early in that year before

I had access to the tape-recorder but I recorded his wife at that time and many years later. In spite of most of the faults of a beginner at interviewing, the tapes are valuable because they give both a true impression of the village at that period as it was before the mechanization of farming, and an account of the lives of some of the people who form the last generation to have been conditioned by the long historical continuity that has now been unceremoniously disrupted.

I have rarely used these Blaxhall tapes since I first recorded them in 1956. They were my first experiment at interviewing with the aid of a tape-recorder and are not good examples, being prentice work, of the technique. Yet they contain valuable material that has never been transcribed. The first of the eight tapes was of George Messenger, a seventy-nine-year-old neighbour who worked at the nearby Snape Maltings. He told me how he worked his *candy** or piece of common-yard, dividing it into two by a path, and growing wheat on one side and vegetables on the other, changing over the crops each year. He cut the wheat with a serrated sickle.

> I bound up the wheat in little bunches. Then when it was thrashed I had a straw bed laid down nice and thick on the barn floor. And I got a *frail* and thrashed that. Then I'd take all the straw off the floor. There lay the wheat. I put it in a basket whatever I'd got and then dress it with a 'blower' or dressing machine (if I could borrow one). This would blow the chaff away. I remember the first time I used the *frail* I got a clout o' the skull that I'd remember. An old chap that was there said: 'Never mind that, you'll get plenty o' those.'

George Messenger also told me how the family fared at Christmas when he was young:

> A man named Lord Rendlesham fatted a bullock every year. There was a pound for father and a pound for

---

*I have been unable to find this word in the dialect dictionaries. It may have been a corruption of *cansey*: a causeway or footpath across a common, an acre of which had been enclosed.

mother and half a pound for each of us children: we were seven. He gave us a pound of sugar and a pound of plums (raisins) and half a pound of beef suet, so we could have a pudding. We would have got no Christmas dinner but for that, unless we'd got a rabbit or two. That was at Christmas time: the other part of the time the poor old lady sometimes she ain't got much for us to eat. She'd get some bread, and she'd go to the fire and she'd get hold of the kittle, and cut the bread up and had some salt and pepper and she'd pour hot water on it. There you go! Kittle-broth. Sometimes we'd go to the shop for tea. Three pence an ounce it was then. We used to have an ounce of black tea and an ounce of green tea. Mix them together. That would last a week. If you fell short at the end of the week, you'd get some bread, put it before the fire and make it black; and put it in a big mug, pour hot water on it; and call it coffee. That's how we used to go on.

George Messenger worked on the barges at Snape Maltings and while he was there he must have had access to the smithy because he made himself a small sickle out of a smith's iron rasp – a tool made from the toughest steel. He gave it to me while we lived at Blaxhall. It is about the same size as one form of Roman sickle.

Mrs Celia Jay (born 1883) who lived about fifty yards along Mill Common from the Messengers, also told me about corn harvesting on the fields:

We used to go gleaning after they cut the wheat – cut and cart. They leave a shuff in the field after they'd drag-raked it; (This sheaf of corn was often called the *police-man*) until they'd properly drag-raked it. And when we knew it was carted and raked we asked the farmer could we go on the field. We had on our chob-bag which was made from hessian. It was like an apron only it was turned up at the bottom so that we'd got a place to put these ears of corn in. Then when we'd finished our gleaning we'd take handfuls of corn in the straw; and one of us would hold the straw end and then we could cut the chob off so that it dropped into our sack. We allus took a knife and a rub to sharpen it. There used to be some fun sharpening the knife. We gleaned nearly all day until we got tired; and we always reckoned to take a sack-full home. Our mothers used to go gleaning too.

We took the corn to the old barn and it stood there in the dry till my father was free to thrash it out.

At this point I asked her did her father use a *frail* for thrashing, the word George Messenger had used. I got taken up immediately by Mrs Jay who told me that her father had used a *flail*. And she followed this correction by explaining to me what a flail was, and how she had made a flail for her husband to take to work. But it didn't last because she had made the handles of rushes and omitted to cover them with leather. I kept my peace; and it was my first lesson in deferring to my informant. Mrs Jay was born in Tunstall, two miles away, and I noticed later on that many words used on the farms differed slightly from one district to another. Sometime a tool or a process had a different, usually dialect, name altogether. Mrs Jay was a very intelligent woman but she had left school early at twelve years of age after being examined and awarded the Labour Certificate by the schools inspector called Swinburne, who had some relation to the Victorian poet of that name. She was a school monitor for a period serving alternate weeks with another girl. They were paid two shillings a week. She won a prize in the needlework class, and was presented with a book. She took it home, and one day her mother caught her reading the book in her bedroom. She took it from her, hid it, and she never saw it again. This I found was not an unusual pattern at this period in this district. Parents discouraged education because it would make the child dissatisfied with her station in life. Mrs Jay said:

> We were very interested in Bible lessons. We all had this lesson about gleaning: Naomi going gleaning. And we used to have to say a proverb: I can remember one of them: Why take ye thought about raiment. Consider the

7

lilies of the field how they grow. They toil not neither do they spin. Yet Solomon in all his glory is not arrayed like one of these.

Nothing illustrates more graphically that this was the last generation of a line that had extended from Biblical times right to the threshold of the twentieth century. In the minds of people like Mrs Jay there was an unbroken continuity, and they were right. Their own experience was a telling argument for this continuity: in the farming of the land the basic skills were ancient hand-skills, practised right up to their time, and even when they had begun to be discarded on the farms the farm workers and their families still practised them on their common-yards, (what we would today call their allotments) as George Messenger and Mrs Jay illustrate. So that the Old Testament to a bright girl of the time was not simply some writing out of a book but something they knew intimately. They had felt the tiredness of a day's patient gleaning in the sun, the satisfaction of going home with a full sack of chobs; later they had the looking forward to seeing the thrashing, and watching the milling of the corn in the local windmill, and repeating as the sails revolved:

> Father, mother, sister, brother,
> All go round and can't catch each other.

And, finally, the satisfaction of seeing the loaves of bread fresh from the brick-oven and resplendent on their own table.

At the same time in 1956 I recorded a widow whose grand-daughter was a pupil in my wife's school. She was Mrs Drewery who was born in 1888. She remembered her school days in Blaxhall School under Mr Whitehead. She recalled:

When I first went to school I was laughed at because I wore hob-nail boots and had my hair cut short like a boy's. I wore long buttoned-gaiters that came right up to my knees, and in the place of gloves we had to wear a little muff tied round our neck with a piece of cord. We had to knit little things to put on our wrists to keep them warm. Our master was a very stern one. When we were taught things he would write them on the board and keep them there until we had thoroughly learned them. He wouldn't rub them off until we knew it by heart; and we would have to stay each day until we knew it.

We had cookery at Snape School which was three miles away: we had to walk that. I first of all had to chop beet (cattle-beet or mangel-wurzels) and put them into a skep; and then get the chaff-cutter out, fill it with hay, and cut chaff to put on top of the beet; and get it all ready for my father to feed the animals when he came home from ditching. Then I went and had my tea. After tea I had to go to help my mother, as we were very poor. I had to pick three bushels of stones off the field in one evening. That meant three or four pails of stones to each bushel. In the meantime my mother was classed as the best stone-picker in Blaxhall. She was a very hard worker.

It has been calculated that to make up a *load* of stones which the farmer sold to the surveyor of the highways, each heap of stones had to be twenty bushels.

I left school at the age of fourteen on the Friday. On the Monday I started work to seek my own living. We packed our little box and went by carrier cart. My first situation was at a doctor's house for three and a half years. My mother promised me if I stayed for a year she would buy me a bicycle. The first bicycle I'd ever had and at the age of fifteen. My mother brought me up very strictly. She was very stern. I always had to go to Church twice on Sunday as well as Sunday School in the afternoon. When we came out of school in the afternoon we were not allowed to go farther than the stile. My mother always told us never to look for the big things in life until we learned to value the little things.

All things connected with the farming work demonstrated to me how old was the community we had come to. My long talks with Robert Savage showed this when he described his job as a shepherd. I also recorded Abraham Ling (born 1887), Mrs Savage's brother, whose father was also a member of the Blaxhall company of 'clippers' or sheep-shearers:

I was eight year old when I used to go with them. The clipping season lasted about five to six weeks in May and June. They used to have their meetings on Sunday evenings in the Ship Inn to arrange where they would have to go during the following week. A man named Barker was the Captain and his job was to do the arranging. These farmers used to write to him; and he used to collect the clippers and arrange where they were to go on the Monday morning. They got at the farm at about half-past five to six, and then they used to take the barn doors off and put some bricks down and lay the doors all ready for shearing, and a little lime where each man sheared – underneath the board. The lime was in case they happened to nick a bit off the sheep – to stop the blood. That was called the shearing platform. There were nine or ten shearers on the job. They worked from six o'clock in the morning till as long as they could see, eight or nine o'clock. Later, if they wanted to finish the flock in one day. Those clippers would do a flock of 300 in a long day. If they hadn't finished they'd leave three or four men there and they'd finish and go to another farm. They'd sleep in the farm that night in the barn on the farm – tuck down in the hay or straw:

During the day they used to have breaks: *nineses*. A bit of food and a drop of gin and beer; and carry on until dinner, about eleven o'clock and another break about three; and they'd have a little bit of something then and carry on until tea-time. A drop of beer then – it was all home-brewed – and the Captain would say when they stopped; or when you've done your five sheep. Every five sheep they stopped for beer and gin. So many of the clippers brewed their own beer and took it with them. Sometimes one man brewed the beer for the company and they took a cask in the cart. They had a pony and cart, and one of them drew off the beer and carried it round to them. When one had done his sheep, he'd drop his shears and call out, 'Five'. Time was up. 'Pull up and sharp.' Sharpen the shears with a stone-rub that each man carried in his belt. Then he had his *horn* of beer, [a cup made from a sheep's horn which would travel better than a glass or a china mug]. The wrist was very sore after the first day, and all swollen up but they had to get used to it. They used to earn about five shillings a score. So if they clipped a flock of 300 in a day, with ten men clipping each would do three score and earn fifteen shillings. It was good going at that time, but you must do that because of the expenses of going about with horse and cart. And if they weren't very far from Blaxhall they used to come home of a night. But sometimes they used to go as far as Monk Soham or Earl Soham.

When I was collecting the material which Abraham Ling gave to me, and the history of the Blaxhall Company of sheep-shearers, I went back to the Shakespeare of *The Winter's Tale*, and Thomas Tusser and his 'land well-hearted with half of the flock', and this gave their description an extra dimension.

Aaron Ling, Abraham's father, was the village's unofficial barber. He used the same implement as barber as he did when he was sheep-shearing: a pair of sprung shears whose design had not changed since the Romans. One day he was performing as barber on a Sunday morning, his usual time, and a young boy who was in the chair turned his head rather suddenly, and he clipped a bit off his ear. The man was alive when we lived at Blaxhall and the scar was still visible.

The band of bell-ringers at Blaxhall Church was still very strong in 1956 when I made my recordings. It was the only church in the vicinity where the ringers still kept the art – or science as its adherents preferred to call it – of bell-ringing still alive. That is, change-ringing, the *Method* as they proudly referred to it, 'musical mathematics' as it is sometimes known. It needed a long apprenticeship to become an expert change-ringer, able to 'read' the bells by their sound and not simply

by rope-sight. This was the practice by which a ringer concentrated on the *Sally*, the coloured hand-grip at the end of the rope, which by its movement up and down told the ringer the sequence of the bells and where he should come in. A good ringer used sound and not sight to tell him his place to strike. Such a man was Henry Puttock, an old ringer of over eighty who like Robert Savage died before I had access to a tape-recorder. He had a list of over 200 churches he had rung a peal in around the eastern counties. He was the man chiefly responsible for the healthy tradition of the ringing in the village and for recruiting young members. I met two of these the evening I recorded a practice ring from many parts of the village, finishing up in the steeple itself. Sheila Shaw and Mollie Mayhew, her cousin, were two beginners who were there that night, sixteen-year-old girls who had already been attending practices for two years. Sheila had rung her first peal on the night previous to my visit, a considerable physical feat since it meant manipulating the bell from a standing position for two hours forty-five minutes, ringing a total of 5,040 changes. Mollie had previously been ill and had to defer her first peal to a later date. Undoubtedly it was the patient coaching of young beginners by the older members that had enabled the Blaxhall band to persist for so long, and to keep to the Method and preserve their ancient discipline when all around them the churches had fallen into the unesteemed practice of *call-changes*: changes rung in an unscientific and monotonous manner by which one ringer at intervals of his own choice directs the others in what order their bells are to strike, each change being repeated several times till a fresh change is called for. The Blaxhall ringers dismissed this manner of ringing with good-humoured contempt calling it 'Turkey-Driving' or 'Churchyard Bob'.

The ringers were a cohesive force in the village, carrying on a tradition that had lasted for hundreds of years. James Smy the Clerk of the Parish Council had been a member for about forty years; his neighbour Frank Shaw, Sheila's father Aldeman Ling and his son, young Aldy, and Henry Puttock formed the lasting core of the band. The sad story is that it has not lasted: the young members got married and left the village and the remaining older ones are too old to carry on.

Mrs Priscilla Savage, who gave me a detailed account of how she dealt with the Three Bs, recorded a piece about an annual popular event that was usually one of the high days of the summer: the Whitsun Ash Wednesday Fair. This occurred in the lull in the farming year when the farm workers got the only two or three days' holiday they had in the year. It was held at the Ship Inn, so called probably because of its association with sheep and not with the sea. (Ship is the dialect word for sheep as in the proverb: To spoil the ship for a ha'porth o' tar.) John Hewitt was the licensee of the inn and he organized a sports event centred on the inn itself for men, women, and children. There was ten-pin bowling for men and women; an ounce of tobacco and a pint of beer for the men as prizes and a quarter of tea for the women. Racing was from the Ship to an oak tree along the Tunstall road, about a mile; and half the distance for the women. There was also a wheelbarrow race and a three-legged race. A competition for the women only was Drinking the Hottest Cup of Tea. Prissy's mother often won this:

> She had a *fake*. She'd have something to eat, bread and butter before she began and the inside of her mouth was greased so she finished her cup of tea before the others. They used to say she had a tin mouth.

Then there was step-dancing on two bricks for the men, a feat of balance as well as of *stepping*. The women had a dance of their own: the Candlestick Dance, a ceremony with a very long history.

> There were lighted candles in the middle of a ring and the women tucked their skirts between their legs. They danced over and around the candles. And the one that danced the longest without putting the candles out won the prize. The music was: 'Jack be nimble, Jack be quick. Jack jump over the candle stick.' Billy Salmon Prickett, a travelling man [a gypsy] played his fiddle, someone played an accordion and Walter Quinn used to play the tin whistle.

It is likely that there is here a vestige of an ancient custom of ceremony with fire; which was continued long after the original purpose was forgotten. Beltane fires were lit on May Day, and if there was a maypole it was afterwards burned; and there were fires that had a close connection with the corn harvest. In some places the midsummer fires were lit on St John's Day. It was thought that those who leaped over the fire would not suffer from backache at reaping. It was also thought that the higher you leaped over the flames the higher the corn would grow.

The next competition at the Ship Inn Fair is not likely to have such an ancient origin, but I remember seeing it advertised in an early nineteenth-century bill in a Cambridge museum. This was Sneering Through a Horse Collar, sneering or making the ugliest face:

14

Flinny Joe Ling nearly always used to win. He had a very long face, just like George Messenger, and curly hair.

The most popular contest with the children was Scrambling the Hot Pennies.

Mr Hewitt made the pence very hot in a frying-pan. He then went upstairs and threw them out of his bedroom window which is over the bar-kitchen door; and he threw on to the sandy knoll outside. The children kept picking them up and dropping them. It was amusing to watch.

About six o'clock the older children took the younger ones home and put them to bed. And then they stayed up there and would have bread and cheese and whatever was going, and a pint of beer and a sing-song. They used to be there for the rounding of the Whitsun Wednesday. There was a very old saying that said: 'We love Whitsun Monday, and we love Whitsun Tuesday because they should go to Framlingham Gate. And they loved Whitsun Wednesday because they could go to Blaxhall Ship. But *Damn* Whitsun Thursday!' Well, the Fair stopped. I couldn't tell you what year. Before the First World War. All those old customs dropped off then. I don't think that was picked up any more. John Hewitt got older and it stopped.

While we lived in Blaxhall and for some time afterwards the post was delivered by Cyril Herring who was postmaster at the adjoining village of Tunstall. I recorded him one afternoon when he was on his rounds in Blaxhall. The recording has never been transcribed. I do so now because this account supplements considerably the portrait of the village:

I've been postman here for the last twelve years, and I've been a cycling postman. I deliver the whole of Blaxhall which is a very scattered village – 120 dwellings that takes me five and a half hours, at two deliveries a day. This means twenty-five miles' cycling. I come in from the neighbouring village where I pick up the mail. I sign on there and sign off and by the time I've done the whole round that amounts to about that. Blaxhall is a difficult village for a postman, more difficult than most post rounds, the reason being that very few people leave Blaxhall and most families are intermarried. One family being related to another the whole way through the village. And again houses here are not numbered and very few with names. You have actually to know the people, know their names and their Christian names. A strange postman delivering letters in Blaxhall would find it an absolute Bedlam, to deliver among the forty Lings and twenty Smiths. I have to sort them out; I often getting two people with the same initials: two J.W. Ling's living in separate houses, both on the same Common. So it was J.W. Ling, Stone Common, Blaxhall, and it was difficult to know which was which. The way I manage is this: I know from experience one is a farmer and the other is a roadman. And I know where the letters come from (by the postmark) and which was which. On occasions I can't tell and have to try the first J.W. He looks at it first, if it's not his, it goes to the next one. And I don't like that; and often gets me in a bit of trouble. But we can't avoid that. We can't avoid it. We get them right in the end.

My grandfather farmed in Blaxhall several years ago. He was born in 1838 and he started in a small business way as a hawker and used to walk the countryside with a basket on his head filled with haberdashery, to the surrounding villages. One thing he was famed for was his very strong braces. He sold chiefly to the reapers in the harvest field. In fact they used to look forward to his visits just before harvest because with their very strenuous work they required very strong braces, using the scythe from side to side. By the time harvest came round again things were beginning to get a bit serious and they looked for old Charlie Wardley and his strong braces which at that time were only 6½d a pair. They had very strong leather ends. He sold the ends extra as well, and they were three inches wide, able to stand some very heavy pulls.

My grandfather managed to get a few pounds together, and he took over this Glebe Farm. He had quite a large family by present-day standards – he had six children. He took on this farm and he passed his haberdashery business to one of his sons who graduated to a four-wheeler; and he got quite an established hawker with his oils and paints and cans. His chief decorations were his chamber-pots which he hung all round the cart. He used to travel all the villages round about and he'd stop in each pub in the village. He used to reckon he'd do a lot of business there. He said that was his ration, and his due: to have a *John Turner* at each pub. And he used to go to about six pubs during the day; and this *John Turner* at that time used to be three ha'porth of gin and a ha'porth of beer which meant half a pint. And I remember him telling me that when he went to the merchants to replenish his stock they couldn't think however he could pay his way spending so much money on drink which was a shilling a day. The only drink he had besides was home-brewed beer; and another day always started with a quart of this home-brewed beer. I used to like it very much myself. They gave me a tiny glass. They brewed very good beer. It was food as well as drink. Every cottage brewed their own beer, and they had two pigs in the sty and made their own bacon.

On one of my rounds – this is a true yarn – I was asked by one of my friends if I could tell him what was the matter with his sow: 'Can you tell me, bor, what is up with my owd sow? She don't fare to be regular at all!'

I said: 'Well, let's have a look at it.'

So I had a look at this sow and I said:

'What is the matter with it?'

'Well, the first time she pigged she never had any, and the second time she pigged she had two and twenty and there were too many for her to look arter; and I don't know what to do with her.'

'Well,' I said, 'the best advice I can give you is to advertise and see if you can get her an adopted litter and get the number you want. And if she don't take them you'll have to turn them into sausages.'

When Charlie Wardley, Cyril Herring's uncle, retired he sold his business to James Smy who became the Clerk to the Parish Council. He also had a four-wheel cart and used to visit us but after a few years he sold his pony and bought a motor.

Robert Sherwood, a Blaxhall farmer, came from a long-established farming family. His father was one of the farmers Rider Haggard consulted when he wrote his book *Rural England* at the beginning of this century. Robert Sherwood made a contribution to a portrait of Blaxhall in 1956 and spoke about the changes in farming that had happened since we came to live in the village; an interval when farming was rapidly becoming mechanized, wiping out the hand-skills that preceded the tractor. One of these was:

The sowing of English wild white clover which we used to grow. Practically every farmer round here used to grow it at one time. Now [1956], I don't know anybody at all. Sowing it was a very skilful job. You were lucky if you had a man on the farm who could do it. You only sowed about two pints or half-a-peck at the outside – to the acre. And this had to be sown keeping in step sowing with two hands alternately. And the man had only to take a pinch between his thumb and forefinger at a time, and it was broadcast as he kept in step. He used a container, which was called a hod, hung on his chest with a strap around his head; and he dipped one of his hands into this alternately; and he took a pinch out and it was sown. And if when the crop came up he missed a foot in the whole field, he would never hear the last of it. His reputation would have been lost. Absolutely! It was a picture to see a man do it. If you had one man on the farm you were lucky. We sowed this as a nurse crop and depending on the season at the end of April or beginning of May. And the following Spring, if it got too advanced, as we thought, we used to run a flock of sheep over it to keep it down. In July we would harvest it. On my farm it wasn't scythed; it was cut with a clipper. It was so short we used to hand-rake it to get it. A wooden hand-rake, and rake it and cart it and stack it. And if we got a peck an acre we thought it was quite a good crop. I can say that my neighbour, the late Mr Harry Toller, adjoining this farm in Blaxhall, once grew three pecks an acre. That was a most extraordinary crop. For a time it was the talk of Suffolk.

Clover under the old system was highly esteemed as a crop to improve land, not only pasture land but arable as well. East Anglian farmers used to grow clover as a nurse crop (undersown in a corn crop); and it played an integral part in their rotation. A Scottish farmer, Robert Elliot,* in the late nineteenth century had made his system of using clover to improve soil the basis of his farming philosophy and this was eventually followed by many British farmers. It was developed, notably by Sir George Stapledon, who did out standing work at a critical time during the last war to improve farming, enabling it to cushion the effects of war and isolation. Without a doubt the present fashionable application of chemicals to the land did a great deal to make the sowing of clover neglected, much to the land's detriment. Robert Sherwood also recalled vividly the hand-bell bell-ringers coming round at Christmas time:

They used to visit all the farmhouses and places in Blaxhall, and I remember when they came up to mine at Lime Tree Farm. First of all, they'd ring outside in the porch one or two times; and then my wife and I used to ask them in. And they used to come into the dining-room and, I remember, we always had to put a very thick cloth on the table. They used to stand round the dining-room table and ring the hand-bells and occasionally they put them down on the cloth, and it used to change them in some way. The object was: the cloth was put there so the

*The Clifton Park System of Farming, Faber and Faber, 1943. (First published as Agricultural Changes, 1898, it went into three more editions in ten years.)

19

bells wouldn't vibrate. As soon as they put a bell down it
was dead. Of course, we knew them all personally and
when they finished they had mugs of beer. And of course
we always gave them something in the way of money-
kind. And it was a most enjoyable evening and an
occasion that was looked forward to. Absolutely! We
always expected them.

It was Lewis Poacher, a farm worker in his seventies, who
told me of a belief that the older generation, the core of the
village, held and were proud of in the second half of the
twentieth century. This concerns the Blaxhall Stone. It is
situated in the yard of Stone Farm but there is a tradition that
it was found on Stone Common, three quarters of a mile
away, and was transported to the farm where it now lies, a flat
boulder of five or six tons. While we lived there a geologist
from Ipswich Museum came to examine it. He identified it as
a glacial erratic. It is of Spilsby sandstone carried down from
Spilsby in Lincolnshire by the Ice Sheet, about 150,000 years
ago. Lewis Poacher told me of a different origin of the stone:

My father-in-law ploughed it out, so he told me, in his
time, ploughed it out and brought it up there and placed
it down there in the farmyard in Stone Farm. And it's still
there now. He brought it up and he reckoned it weighed
about half a hundredweight when he brought it up. It
weighs about five tons now.

My father-in-law was William Ling. He was a horseman
at Stone Farm in Mr Toller's time. That's some time ago.
He was a champion ploughman. He took any amount of
copper kettles for ploughing a stetch of land. He used to
take all those high prizes; copper kettles and so much
money. He worked until he was about seventy. He lived
along o' me after I married his daughter, and he used to
tell me all these little things, and I tell Cyril [his son] and
that's how he knows. But that stone has been there for
years. And that whoolly grew. I haven't seen it lately but
they tell me it's a huge size. That stone ha'grew, you see.
They say that stones don't grow. They do!

Another finding while we lived in Blaxhall confirmed me in
the belief of the age of the community. The Romans had been
there at least since the second century. I had, in fact, picked
up some potshards of that period in a field opposite the oldest
farm in the parish, near the site where Roman remains are
marked on the ordnance survey map. Yet I did not imagine
that a village dispute that occurred just before we came to the
village would take us back to the Romans as surely as the
shards they had left in the field. The dispute was about a right
of way across one of Blaxhall's commons. One of the inhabitants wanted, for his own purpose, to erect a fence across one
of the paths across the common. The village people objected
strongly and the dispute was taken to court. The contention
of those who opposed the erection of the fence was that a
corpse had been taken along the path in fairly recent years
therefore it would be illegal to close the path. There were
many witnesses of this fact who claimed that it should always
remain open. This was a surprising contention. What had a
corpse carried over a footpath to do with its legal status? It
appears there is nothing in law to support the villagers' case.
The law can step in if someone attempts to close a right of way
only if the path leads to a church or cemetery. It is simply an
old and once common belief that has persisted since Roman
times. The belief is linked with the founding of Rome itself.
The story is found in Plutarch's *Life of Romulus*:*

> As Romulus was casting up a ditch where he designed the
> foundation of the city wall, Remus turned some pieces of
> the work into ridicule and obstructed others. At last, as
> though he was in contempt leaping over it, some say
> Romulus himself struck him (others say one of his com-
> panions). He fell.

A Roman settlement or town was first marked out by a
religious ceremony. The important part of it was the plough-

*Quoted by Joseph Rykwert, *The Idea of a Town*, Faber and Faber, 1976,
p.27.

ing of the boundary of the settlement on a solemn religious occasion. The plough was a special bronze one drawn by one, or a pair, of bulls. The ploughman was the founder of the settlement himself. He drew the *sulcus primigenius – the first furrow* – inside which the walls were afterwards built. The founder set the plough aslant so that all the earth would fall inside the furrow. If any earth happened to fall outside, the founder's followers would pick it up and throw it inside the settlement's boundary. When he came to a spot where the gates were to be sited he took the plough out of the ground and carried it† over the span or width of the gate. The walls that were later built followed the line of the furrow cut by the founder's plough. They were sacred to the gods but the gates were subject to civil jurisdiction. We can, therefore, understand the reason why Romulus killed his brother Remus: he had committed sacrilege by laughing at the work and, most of all, by breaking a religious prohibition not to cross the furrow, invading the boundary which was sacred. The last part of the ceremony was giving the settlement a name, invoking a protective deity and, finally, lighting a fire on a hearth inside the walls.

But this is the point that concerns us here: one of the uses of the gate, when the inhabitants had settled in, was to allow the corpses of those who had died in the town to be carried out and buried outside. The walls, because of the religious sanction, were inviolable; but the gate was recognized as the only access or channel for passing in and out of them. Over the years it would become renewable as the route for taking a man to his last resting-place. And that is why it remained in the community's memory for so long, carried over the centuries by the oral tradition. What we call myths today were once the people's religion; and these myths still have a numinous pull on the collective mind. They were the beliefs of their forefathers who unquestionably had faith in them and the doctrine that lay behind them. They were not so very different in their manner of living from their remote ancestors

†According to some ancient writers this carrying (*portare*) is the root of *porta* – a gate.

as we saw when we read Mrs Celia Jay's contribution on the same district. This is understandable since the physical conditions and tools of their living had remained radically the same: their beliefs and their manner of thinking, therefore, tended to remain unchanged. Their thoughts and particular associations with their environment too remained unaltered and would continue to do so as long as the context of their living remained as it had been for generations.

The traditional ploughing of 'the first furrow' reminds me of a tradition I heard in Suffolk at a village called Battisford, near Needham Market, where there is a perfectly straight section of highway called Battisford Straight. Tradition has it that the finest ploughman in the district drew a furrow to mark out the course of the road. Whether or not it is true, the road is as straight as if it had been planned by a road-surveyor with a theodolite, and bears out the traditional use of the plough as a boundary-marker.

2

The Interview

I have transcribed these Blaxhall recordings rather fully as
they gave a picture of a critical period during the history of
this small community. Its characteristic shape after a history
of at least two thousand years was coming to an end: as the
recordings show, both men and women were doing jobs that
would have been familiar before the Romans landed in
Britain. During the first two or three years after our coming
the farming, which was almost solely arable, with each farm
having a few cattle, remained as it had been for centuries;
except that for some reason there was not a flock of sheep in
the parish for many years after the last war. Sheep had gone
from the coastal districts years before at the start of the
1914–18 war; for enemy activity, with Zeppelins and war-
ships, unsettled the sheep and they were moved inland to
quieter districts. After the war sheep were not kept in the
same numbers, possibly because there was a change in the

fashion of farming. And during the last war more cows and
bullocks were kept when East Anglian farmers, as farmers
elsewhere, were required to make the greatest contribution to
feeding the nation in the face of the U-boat campaign. Certainly, sheep were not an integral part of farming while we
were in east Suffolk for two decades after the war.

We eventually moved from Blaxhall when my wife was
offered a bigger school at Needham Market, a few miles
farther east, a small town by East Anglian standards. I left the
village with mixed feelings because I sensed that it was there I
had found my life's work, although I did not fully realize this
at the time. It was only some years after I left that I identified
the village as my second academy when I began to learn the
technique of what became later known as oral history. But
more importantly, I had then an experience which sank in
gradually and imperceptibly as though it was a natural
growth from the environment. It was undramatic and
ordinary, and hardly to be remarked upon in detail, in the
then subjectively eventful course of my life. It was here at this
time, and with the dressing and elaborating on it later, that I
transposed the Blaxhall community in my own mind into its
true place in an ancient historical sequence, keeping the continuity that was for ever changing, and for ever remaining the
same, until an irreparable break substituted the machines for
animal power, and put an end to a period that had lasted well
over two thousand years. Yet I learned from this experience
that the main components of history are not things but
people. This is to make a song of a discovery of the obvious;
but it is something that needs to be repeated now, especially at
this time of wonderfully ingenious discoveries and inventions
that have cascaded on people in an embarrassment of rich
promises.

After leaving Blaxhall I began researching into the farm
horse and the history of its use on the farm in Suffolk since
the twelfth century, and its eventual near-demise as a farm
animal in the years I was researching – 1950–60. Almost from
that time one could forecast the shape of the farms and the

size of the community that would work them. First the farmers cut down their hedges and engrossed the fields into bigger units. Very soon the smaller farmers sold out and took retirement; and more hedges came down. For it was clear that the tractor and the combine harvester would not be confined in fields that had been laid out two or three centuries before. When the machines took over peremptorily the horses soon became redundant and went off the farms. Yet the couple of hundred years that went into the careful breeding of the Suffolk horse, for instance, are not entirely lost. Some of the first-class stock is still flourishing and is fostered by the Suffolk Horse Society although a majority of the horses are not engaged in agriculture. At least they have not borne out the forecast of a Suffolk horseman who told me in the fifties that 'in thirty years' time if you want to see a Suffolk you'll have to go to the zoo'.

My experience of recording on tape was not repeated in my next village. I continued with my method of having a conversation with a horseman, making a few notes and immediately after I got home, expanding them in a fuller account. One has, however, to be sure of your man before taking out a notebook. It can well impede the flow of the conversation. I found this in my first attempt at Blaxhall when, in my first enthusiasm I flashed a notebook about. The word got around: 'A *chiel's* among you takin' notes. An' faith he'll prent it.' So I kept my notebook in my pocket until I got to know my friends better. Then I could use it without comment overt or otherwise. Once when I was talking to Robert Savage the shepherd, he leaned over while explaining the shape of a special ploughshare and said: 'Give me your copybook a moment, and I'll make a *draught* of the share.' Interviewing was not difficult then because I knew everybody. I had been around for a few years; and in fact I had no difficulty, and anyone I asked recorded willingly. Yet I learned one or two important lessons. When I played back the recordings in the BBC studio I saw that it was important to keep out of the recording as much as possible. The natural tendency is for an interviewer to say something encouraging to a nervous speaker or one who is just getting into his stride, such as: 'Yes, yes, that's right,' something just to reassure him. It is better to encourage him with a nod or a smile. When I heard some of my early tapes I realized my interjections were unnecessary and obtrusive. I also learned when I got my own tape-recorder and had more experience with it, especially with people that I was recording for the first time, that I had to communicate to them that *they* have to do the talking. They are going to tell me about their life or their job. And, if after a few introductory questions they don't get the message, it is a good device to vary the speed of the questions. Hang back, and in the silence that follows the speaker will grasp that he is intended to fill it. He will then usually get into his stride, and you will be able to interrupt without necessarily breaking his rhythm. As some of the old people were unfamiliar with a tape-recorder, I made a practice of getting to know them first by visiting them before taking it along. Invariably, before doing this I got permission from a man's friend, one who has usually recommended him, to use his name.

Sometimes an old person sees a tape-recorder for the first time, and an instinct tells him to have nothing to do with it. I approach a situation like this in this way. I tell him: 'You don't want to record, but perhaps you'd like to hear your own voice. Just a sentence or two; and then I'll wipe it out, and there's no harm done.' He usually agrees and I set up the apparatus. To his surprise his voice emerges in recognizable tones. He is secretly pleased. You say: 'It's come over well!' and he is by this time usually ready to participate. It is merely the over-caution of old age that makes him hesitate. Another point to watch is the position of the microphone. If I am using a hand microphone I hold it about ten inches from the speaker's mouth. We get a much clearer signal if the microphone is placed at the right distance from the person who is speaking.

When I lived at Needham Market, a retired farmer, George Garrard, told me of a horseman whom he knew living in the nearby village of Battisford. He hinted that this particular horseman was well known in the district for being skilled in his craft and for knowing some of the closely guarded secrets of horsemanry. I had heard during my researches of a special class of rare farm horsemen who were outstanding in that they possessed a rich lore of traditional material. They did not boast about it: on the contrary they kept it very secret. They were sometimes called 'Whisperers' for the reason that they were said to control a horse simply by whispering to him, standing close up against a horse's head and seeming to talk to him quietly. Although I was sceptical about what I had heard about the 'Whisperers', I determined to visit this horseman, who was called Arthur Chaplin. I walked over to Battisford and had an interesting talk with him. He was direct and knowledgeable, having been head horseman on a big farm. I was aware that it would be a wrong tactic to ask him anything about the secrets of his craft; and in any case he gave me such an absorbing account of his life as a horseman that I had as much as I could do to take in what he told me about his daily work. I stayed with him, going to visit him once a week for a whole winter. He outlined in detail, material which formed the basis of two chapters in the book I was writing.* He gave me an excellent account, that was accurate and rich in the dialect words that had been in continuous use since the Middle Ages when they were standard English. Yet when I had known him for three or four months and broached the subject of secret horse-material, which I was pretty sure he had, he simply denied that he knew anything about it at all; and when I let drop an occasional remark later on to convey to him that I was not entirely ignorant of the secret horse-lore he immediately challenged me: 'Who told you that? Did you get that from someone at Needham?'

But by this time I had got a little further in my search, enough to know that among East Anglian horsemen the frog's and toad's bone, a kind of fetish prepared in a certain way, were part of the horse-witches' ritual. Therefore, on another occasion I attempted to reason with Arthur Chaplin, saying that now the horses had effectively gone off the farm

H.I.F.

and were being replaced by tractors, the horse-secrets would be no longer used by him or any other horsemen. But it was of no avail. One night, however, I found the old horseman on his own. I had been going up the hill to see him once a week in the afternoon and for some reason or other I changed my time on one occasion. It was quite dark when I reached his house. He was on his own. His wife was in hospital, and he was more inclined to ruminate than usual. Then he launched into a mildly astringent homily, about the danger of wanting to know too much; before surprisingly opening up about the subject we had previously discussed. He told me all that he knew about horse-magic, which I shall return to later.

I mention this at this point because afterwards it struck me that the night must be a good time to interview anyone. Perhaps the horseman had thrown aside his scruples about secrecy at last, induced partly by his relaxation at the end of the day, or perhaps he was lonely as he had spent the nights and days on his own since his wife was in hospital. There are, however, obviously some more conducive times for holding an interview than others, and the night is a good time when there is less danger of interruption and the thoughts, in a relaxed state, have a tendency to turn inwards. I was reminded of this interview by a writer from Ireland who was researching into some aspects of the recent Troubles. He writes: 'I haven't worked on the book since the month of April though I have continued to think about it a lot. Somehow, I found that the clear evenings were not conducive to the kind of material I am in search of. But obviously the days are shortening and I hope that conversations will start in October.'

It is quite conceivable that there is an optimum time for interviewing, though in collecting oral history one has often to take the time that is offered. But whatever time one goes to an informant I find it does not pay to be too urgent or tidy-minded in an interview. If your man digresses it is better to let him have his head. If you pull him up it may probably be the last time you will hear about the subject to which he has digressed. During the years I have found that some digressions, if followed up, reveal valuable social history which may otherwise have been lost. It was through two informants mentioning Burton-on-Trent that, on the second occasion, I let them digress and eventually got an account of the seasonal migration of East Anglian farm workers to the maltings to help with the making of malt. This was valuable because otherwise unrecorded.

The first essential for a good interview is a friendly relation with the man or woman you talk to. I was fortunate when I started interviewing farm workers because the men who followed after them had no interest in the old farming, and did not seek their company for advice about problems they had met in their work. The work had changed so much after the horses had gone, and most of the old men's wise saws and maxims were no longer applicable so that the young men and the retired workers had very little in common. Therefore the old were glad of someone to talk to and to listen to their experiences.

During the time we lived in Needham Market there was an important development in the study of rural communities. This was the founding of the Society of Folk Life Studies in 1960. It was initiated by Dr Iorwerth Peate, Curator of The Welsh Folk Museum at St Fagans, Cardiff. I welcomed the new development as a movement in which the work I was doing could find a place. Through the new Society I also met people who were doing similar work in the Celtic countries and through its President, Iorwerth Peate, I straightaway got support and encouragement, ending the period of being isolated in East Anglia. Shortly after the initial conference I contacted James Delaney a full-time collector of the Irish Folk Lore Commission in Dublin. The meeting of the Society in the following year was in Dublin, and Florence, my wife, and I attended. We met James Delaney, and after the conference was over we accompanied him to his home at Hodson Bay, near Athlone. His collecting district was in the midlands of Ireland, with Athlone at its centre. It was the first time we had been to Ireland and enjoyed our visit, but going around with

Jim Delaney to call on some of his informants was an experience I would not have missed. Yet it is wrong to describe them
as his informants. The official-sounding term is inept, for
each of the men I visited with him was his friend. He saw
them regularly, and as most of them were retired, he rarely
went by appointment but turned up at any time of the day.
The ones we saw on our first visit were small farmers who
lived fairly near Athlone. He had been collecting material
from some of them for years, pursuing various topics such as
I had been doing: the hand-tool methods of farming before
the recent changes, customs, sayings, myths, stories. He was
bilingual and recorded English and Irish on tape, transcribing his own tapes before sending them with the transcripts up to Dublin where they went into the Commission's
archives.

My visits to Ireland and the time I spent with Jim Delaney
confirmed me in my approach to interviewing. He was a
professional and had been doing it for years, and I learned a
lot from him. Some time later, I returned to Ireland again
when I took part with David Thomson (when he was a Third
Programme producer with the BBC) in a programme on the
hare. Following the broadcasts we collaborated on a book, *The
Leaping Hare*, and I got an unbelievably rich selection of tapes.
They were not merely talk-friends of Jim's but long accepted
companions he had been visiting for years, never passing
their door if he was anywhere in the area. The tales about the
hare and the hare-witch we encountered were from the
deepest layer of historical tradition; and what is so remarkable is that they were recounted as facts – although not
overtly. An example of this is the tale of a hare being poached
by night and shot in the leg by a countryman, before escaping
into a lonely cottage. When the countryman, looking about
for the hare next morning, went into the cottage, he encountered an old woman with a bandaged leg. But the countryman
in recounting the tale, to protect his real belief from the
mockery of younger men, would not state openly that the
hare was a witch: he would, however, state categorically:
'That hare was not a *right* one!'

In summing up my thoughts about interviewing it is not difficult to come to the conclusion that the more deeply you know your source, the more likely you are able to give a full and circumstantial account.

3

Folk Life Studies

In the sixties while I was researching for my third book, *The Pattern under the Plough*, I was stimulated by contact with the two newly formed organizations: the British Agricultural History Society, and later the Society of Folk Life Studies. The journals and the conferences of both societies strengthened me in the belief that historical information could be collected from farmers and farm workers, in fact from country people in general. They were living in a historical environment that was being subjected to cataclysmic change which emphasized the importance of their evidence of what had recently become the old farming. History, myths and traditions were contained in the same complex of information they were giving me about their work. There was, in addition, an attractive bonus to it in the virile and often colourful language in which the older country people wrapped their thoughts. They were the last generation in a continuous line since farming began, between six and seven thousand years before. These old men and women were, in a sense, historical documents. The generation stood out, for in their lifetime in this arable area there had been a complete revolutionary change, a break in which virtually all the work in farming was now done by machines. As a result, it meant the break-up of the close country communities. For it is an axiom that once the character of the work is changed, inevitably you change the nature of the society where the work is performed. On farms where, a short time before, a dozen men were employed, there would be likely one man and the farmer himself running the farm. And the farm itself, say of 400 acres, is in constant threat of being bought up and included in a big factory type of holding.

It was about this stage in my research into the East Anglian communities that I was visited by Paul and Thea Thompson of the Social History Department of the University of Essex. They had been recommended to see me as someone who was 'doing oral history'. They had just come back from a conference in the USA. It was the first time I had heard the term 'oral history'. They told me of their experiences there, where Columbia University had become the disseminating centre of the new study. At that time I felt a bit like the Frenchman in Molière who had been speaking prose for most of his life without knowing it. Yet I chiefly remember their enthusiasm for the new approach they had become aware of on their visit to the United States, and how, they reported, it had become popular and was spreading to colleges and universities. They had themselves already started collecting oral history where they lived near Colchester; and they had brought some of their recordings and played them over to me. In spite of what I thought was an unsatisfactory title I was very interested to hear more about the movement in the States. The pioneer, of what came to be called 'oral history', was Allan Nevins of Columbia University. He began his work in 1948, although years before this he had 'proposed some organization which made a systematic attempt to obtain from the life and papers of living Americans, who have led significant lives, a record of their participation in the political, economic and cultural life of the last sixty years'.*

By a little later, 1972, the Oral History Association in the United States had a large membership, including 122

*D.T.W.H.S. pp.19–20.

institutional projects. It was during the following year that the Oral History Society was founded in Britain at a meeting at the University of York. It would, however, be wrong to assume that oral research into the past had not started until the sixties and seventies in Britain. The real founders of the technique of collecting information from the old people of a vanishing culture had begun more than a half-century before, and continued under the banner of Folk Life although its historical aspect was emphasized only incidentally.

The main pioneer in Britain was Seamus Delargy, born 1899. He was a student of University College, Dublin. He stayed on as a lecturer, later becoming Professor of Irish Folklore. He prevailed on De Valera, the President of the new Irish Republic, to establish the Irish Folklore Institute which was later merged in the Irish Folklore Commission. Delargy, in addition to collecting oral material himself in south-west Ireland, contacted scholars all over Europe as well as in Scotland and Wales. Iorwerth Peate, a close friend and helper of Delargy, set up the Welsh Folk Museum at St Fagans, Cardiff, and later became head of the Society of Folk Life Studies. Although the impetus and intense devotion to the culture of their respective countries gave the founders of these movements a nationalist flavour they were, in fact, decidedly international in their outlook having ceaseless contacts with folk life movements on the Continent.

If anyone at this time had asked me to state what I had been writing about in my books, I would have said it was an attempt at recording the folk life of a community, using the word *folk* as the Scandinavians did, to describe the whole people and not just a section of it; or alternatively – to refer to it in more academic terms – social anthropology. On the Continent many people had become conscious of the quickly changing conditions of living and of a quickly developing new society; and they began to set up rural museums to collect and study those aspects of it that had already become out-dated. Incidentally, it should be remembered that in these local rural museums there were often objects linked with myth, sometimes an integral part of the myth itself. An example is the well-known horse-myth, the Mari Lwyd, exhibited in the Welsh Folk Museum at St Fagans, Cardiff: a horse-skull draped with rosettes and ribbons, and with eyes of bottle glass: from Pentyrch in Glamorgan. The mark of most folklore research was principally oral, including a close documentation and preservation of the material culture that was quickly disappearing. Although I was well aware that what I had been doing was history I hesitated to proclaim it as such. For in the fifties the term 'history' was very self-conscious and exclusive in the universities; and departments were very loath to admit oral evidence into their canon, usually demoting it to *hearsay*.

It was while I was researching for this third book that it became apparent that just as tremendous visible changes were happening in farming, the switch-over to machines and the consequent changes in the units of farm size and ownership, a parallel process was happening among the older people who were made redundant by the development of the new techniques. The farm workers were now outside of production, cast aside like some of the horses and ploughs they had followed for so long. I talked to dozens of them about their farming and the old methods. It is true that this was for my own purpose of recording what had now become historical material with a long background. Yet this process of recording helped to some degree to cushion a few of the men against the loneliness and ultimate rejection in themselves. Moreover, their many skills, acquired over a long lifetime, were now useless and were no longer passed on to a younger generation. The devaluation of the old was complete. Vaguely realizing this, many of them willingly co-operated with me in compiling tape recordings of some of the most memorable of their skills. It was as though there had occurred a spontaneous phenomenon that is said to pass through the consciousness of a drowning man, when vignettes of his past life appear as in a film-scape where he is the main actor, a valedictory salute to his own life.

In the fifties, in my first East Anglian book,* I wrote:

*A.F.C.H.

At present, old people in this countryside are survivors from another era. They belong essentially to a culture that has extended in unbroken line since at least the early Middle Ages. They are in some respects the last repositories of this culture, and for this reason should have some of the respect given to any source of valuable information. Their knowledge of dialect, folk tales and songs, old customs and usages, and craft vocabularies, and their ability to identify and describe the use of farm implements that are now going into limbo after being used for centuries, are sufficient reasons why they should have the local historian's greatest attention.

This plea was not much heeded, and I carried on with my self-appointed task, continuing my work under the aegis of Folk Life. Now, however, some friends knowing that my writings did not alone support the research I was doing, suggested that I make application to a funding body for a grant-in-aid. I applied, over two or three years, to at least half a dozen organizations for financial aid for my researches. I had no success: I was not even granted an exploratory interview. Ultimately, I gave up trying and my reaction was: 'Don't bother, I'll finish it myself.'

For a time I had a foot in two camps: Folk Life and Oral History. But gradually Paul and Thea Thompson began to teach oral history at the University of Essex, and I was going down regularly to take part in seminars. My allegiance tended to gravitate to oral history because there was a teaching-centre close at hand. In spite of my reservations about the title 'oral history' and the expressed aims of the American founder, I could see that when the new departure from conventional history was heralded from America, only a bold and singleminded claim to place oral evidence in the forecourt of History would gain a sure entry. Yet my main difficulty in accepting unreservedly the American oral history approach, as this appeared from the evidence of their work that we saw over here, was the lack of historical depth in the subjects they investigated.

One of the main subjects of oral history has been the recent change in work techniques and the consequent social changes and strains that this has caused. It was possible to get first-class historical data from the old men who were made redundant by these changes; and study of the work, for instance in farming, has become a fruitful field for oral history. For a man who has spent most of his life in a particular job has become an authority on it, by virtue of his experience; and anything he has to say about it is accurate and convincing. If he is a craftsman and closely identified with his work in spirit it is an integral part of his life; and it would be an offence against his own person to retail anything about it that is not accurate. Moreover, what he says, if it is recorded in any form, is soon monitored by his coevals who did a similar job; and this makes him doubly careful that he gives an accurate account of it.

The other outstanding contribution that oral history makes is the demonstration of the long historical continuity that is found in almost any social activity, as I found in farming and its various stages from earliest times to the present-day revolutionary techniques. It may seem unequal to compare the two approaches: the long, comparatively uninterrupted history we have in Britain, learnt through both documentary evidence and archaeological discoveries, and the truncated evidence present in the United States, beginning only with the European settlements in the sixteenth century. Yet North America was inhabited before the Europeans arrived. The Red Indian natives were established well before Columbus, and the rather lesser known landings farther north. One example of relevant evidence is the work of Lewis H. Morgan* about a century ago. Morgan was an anthropologist who spent a great part of his life living among the Iroquois tribe of Indians whose home-ground was the present New York State. As a result of his study of the Iroquois, Morgan solved a problem that had baffled historians for centuries: the composition of the kinship system of the Greeks and the Romans. He found that the whole social organization of the primitive Greek and Roman *genea*, or *gens*

*Ancient Society, 1877.

and *tribe* had an exact parallel with that of the North American Indians. (I choose this example because after reading classics, I got no light on this problem until later, in the thirties, I read of Morgan's discoveries through Friedrich Engels' book.)* And I mention this as it is conceivable that echoes of the system that Morgan discovered could be found among the Indians still inhabiting the Reservations.

Here, as well as America, there appears to be an over-emphasis on the *oral* component of our title and a comparative neglect of the *history*. How else can we explain the almost total neglect of the mythical and non-rational elements we invariably come across while collecting oral evidence in the field? It is understandable that the more 'recent' sources of oral history, research arising out of technical changes and developments during this century, bad social conditions, economic depression, war, the position of women, should readily present themselves as topics for collection in the field of oral history. Yet the less immediate topics for the student such as family tradition, folk traditions, myths, even psychoanalysis (Jung particularly), which are not immediately on tap but require long preliminary research, are often neglected. This implies that the student should not translate *history* in its rigidly conventional sense but in its more human context as defined by Terence, the old Roman: I am a man and everything to do with men is my concern.

Very early in my writing I had to face the problem of what was irrational and 'folklorish', according to some critics, recorded in the middle of straight factual material. This was in my second book *The Horse in the Furrow* at a time when I came across, for the first time, the secret material about farm-horse control. The subject came up in my conversations with old horsemen who had recently retired. They made references to certain practices and occasionally to a very rare horseman who had *the know*. I listened to a great deal of it but I was very doubtful whether I should include it in the book I

*The Origin of the Family, 1891.

was writing: a straight account mainly describing this recently displaced method of farming in an arable area, with horses as almost the sole source of power. I was aware of the attitude of people who were researching the same subject, chiefly young academics who had joined the new Agricultural History Society, and I had sensed their 'simon-pure' view of what they considered as folklore which was almost a term of abuse among this class of scholar. As I planned the book I was in a dilemma: should I compromise the original rich material I had obtained through the oral tradition, mainly about the actual farming with methods and techniques dating back at least as far as Thomas Tusser, and in many respects as far as Virgil in his *Georgics*? Should I play safe and keep religiously to the soil, and not risk the book's acceptance by my publisher who would probably hand over the manuscript to one of the members of the Agricultural History Society to read? Yet this would mean that all the secret material about horse-control would be classed as folklore and down graded. After considering it briefly I felt it would be wrong, and against my better judgement, to leave the folk life element out of my manuscript, especially as I considered it held some of the book's most original writing. I trusted my own judgement; and it was one of my most fortunate decisions. I headed my last section of the book: 'Folklore Connected with the Horse'. The reader of my manuscript was Brian Vesey-Fitzgerald who was an authority on the horse and had recently edited an anthology which contained work by some of the best-known horse-writers of his day. He recommended the book to my publishers.

It was in this book that I recorded my first real introduction to the secret horse material that many tried unsuccessfully to uncover. A statement that encouraged me to include this – according to the temper of the time – way-out material was made by Marc Bloch, the famous French rural historian. He wrote: 'The study of popular rites and beliefs [in France] is barely sketching its first outlines.' I felt that if an historian of Bloch's calibre approved of this aspect of history and was willing to admit it into the canon, I should be more than

willing to write about it. I return, therefore, to the night when
Arthur Chaplin, the Suffolk horseman, told me of his experience of the secret material I had heard about in my various
talks with the old farm workers. It was always linked with a
special class of rare horsemen; and this was the first time I
actually got information from one of these. After I had sat
patiently through his lecture, he went on:

Someone round here has been telling you about the
horseman's business – about stuff and chemicals, the
frog's boon and all thet. Well, you don't want to believe
half on it. It's someone who's heard a bit of it and is
making the rest up. Now I'll tell you about the frog's
boon. First of all not one in ten thousand knows what
kind of a frog it comes from, or would be able to recognize the boon if they saw it – not one in ten thousand. I
knew only one man in this district who had one. The frog
you were after wasn't easy to come by: it were a rare kind.
It were a black frog with a star on its back; and you'd be
most likely to find one in a wood where they'd been
a-felling trees. You'd get one, maybe, under an owd
felled log or something like thet. After you'd caught it
you had to kill it and hang it up on a blackthorn tree to
dry. Then you took it down and treated it till it were all
broke up and dismembered. Or you could clean it by
putting it in an ant hill: the ants would pick all its flesh off
the boons. You then took it to a running stream at midnight and placed it in the water. Part of it would float
upstream; and that's the part you had to keep.'

So far the account was no different from the conventional
account of the frog's bone ritual, already given me by other
horsemen in the area. But what followed was the crux:

When you got the boon you next cured it. You got
umpteen different things and you cured the boon in this
mixture. After you had cured it and dried it again, it was
ready. You kept it in your pocket until you wanted to use
it. There were no charm about it. This is how it were

used. A farmer would tell a horseman just before 'knocking-off' time:

'There's a load of oil-cake to get from the railway station: will you take the tumbril down and get it?'

But when the farmer told another horseman to harness the horse and put him in the tumbril, the horseman found that he wouldn't come out of the stable. What you did was to rub the frog's boon on the horse's shoulder. Then whoever came to fetch him would straightway be in a muddle. The horse would go through the motions of moving but wouldn't shift an inch. To make that horse go you just had to take the frog's boon and rub it lightly on his rump.

One or two of these inner-ring horsemen used, instead of the frog, a toad of a special kind: the natterjack or walking-toad (*bufo calamita* or rush-toad) which has a bright yellow line running down the back. The real 'magic' in this was not the exotic type of toad or frog, the ritual at the stream or even the bone itself: these were incidental. It was the herbs and chemicals in which the horseman cured or steeped the bone that had the seemingly magical effect. The bone was steeped in substances not detectable by human smell; but they were so aggressive to the sense of smell of the horse that he was as though paralysed when the odour was anywhere near his nostrils. And it was these *jading* substances that were so closely guarded. They were the dynamic. The elaborate ceremony was merely part of the cover-up; yet it seemed to convince the operator that it was essential to a successful outcome. It was a part of the whole complex.

These horsemen, apart from the satisfaction of being the possessors of closely guarded secrets and the social kudos and satisfaction that this gave them, greatly valued the secrets as a jewel in their craft skills. A good horseman who *had the know* and was, so to speak, in the apostolic succession could always be certain of a job usually in the farm of his choice. They were invariably in a long line of horseman and most of the inner-ring horsemen, through their family, had been with horses for centuries, as a horseman's son told me.

The next outstanding horseman I met was when we moved to our next Suffolk village, Helmingham. He was W. Charles Rookyard (1889–1965). He had been born in a village in mid-Suffolk and had been a farm horseman until he was called up for service during the First World War, most of which he spent in Mesopotamia. He took the piano-accordion which he played with him on service; as he explained to me, 'to entertain my pals in the desert'. He brought his accordion to our house in Helmingham a fortnight before he died and gave me a tune or two which I recorded. He lived by himself as his wife had died and his family had grown up and left home. He was certainly the most colourful horseman I had met. He was tall, well over six feet, and well built; and he had a gypsy look about him, with his jet black hair that had kept its colour in spite of his being in his late seventies. In appearance and manner he could have been an old repertory actor who was used to telling a tale and to putting over his personality. He did this often in entertaining people with his tunes and songs in the pubs. He was also well known in the villages around Helmingham for he took gardening jobs for a couple of hours a day in places within cycling distance. A farmer recommended me to see him, and on my first visit he did not, at first, grasp my purpose. He had the idea that I had horses I wanted him to manage. His answer was a decided no! But when he realized that I only wanted him to *talk* about horses I had as definite a welcome. He turned out to be one of my best informants. He was highly valued by the Helmingham farmer he worked for; and on more than one occasion, unknown to him, he had refused to be enticed away by visiting farmers from *The Sheres* [Shires] in spite of their offer of higher wages.

Charles Rookyard was a good example of an all-round farm horseman who was a real craftsman. He was a first-class ploughman, and he managed his horses so expertly that he got the reputation of being the best farm horseman in the district. He was also well informed in the traditional secrets of the inner ring of horsemen, and, I discovered, believed in the toad's or frog's bone ritual completely. It was not something that was a marginal adjunct to his work: it was an integral part of it, as I learned from an experience he had. He once told me that the stallion which he led round the farms in the spring had one night appeared by the side of his bed, a huge horse of seventeen hands and weighing over a ton. The hallucination frightened him and he attributed it to his involvement with the ritual. He therefore resolved to give up practising *magic*! He told me:*

> Do you know the frog's boon is a funny thing; and also I must mention this; there ain't one man out of a hundred know what dragon's blood is, and they never will! Well, I was once at home one night and my horse come right to my bedside, and in a way I thought to myself: I don't know, you'll git into trouble on yourself. You're going to be crazed with your stuff, if you don't mind. My missus said: I don't know, Charlie – well, she said, you'll soon have to do suthen. No matter what I've got indoors, there's nothing don't bake right and I don't feel right. And you're the same, she said, you're awake and your hoss come to the side of the bed.
>
> All right, I said, the only thing I can do is to get rid of it. So I dug a huge hole down to the clay, put this tin with the powder [the cured frog's bone], filled it with milk and vinegar first; and put the milk, tin, bottle and everything, and covered it up. And I never knew no more. But I could niver get on so well with my hosses after then. So the next thing I had to use with my hosses was the circus cords† to keep them under control.

The bone ritual and the secret oils that would *draw* or attract a horse, and the *jading* oils that repel, *jade* or arrest a horse, both operating on the horse's acute sense of smell, were all and part of the same integral complex. The older horsemen would not distinguish the oils or substances from the ritual itself. For although the ritual was on the surface directed to

*D.T.W.H.S., p.34.
†H.P. & M., pp.147–8.

the fetish, that is the bone, and indirectly to the horse himself, the ceremony he went through was aimed at inducing absolute conviction in the horseman – although he was not perhaps aware of this. He came to believe that so armed he could tackle any situation involving a horse. That is why Charles Rookyard having lost his confidence, partly through his own experience and that of his wife, was forced to use mechanical means: the circus cords, of the same colour as the horse's coat so that they couldn't be detected except under close examination. There was a strong conviction among farm horsemen that anyone who got too involved with magic eventually lost their balance and went mad. I have come across three instances of breakdowns where a breakdown was attributed to a horseman being involved in *magic*.

In connection with the jading substances, I recorded an experience of Charles Rookyard* of which I was reminded recently. He was ploughing in a field with a pair of horses when they suddenly stopped for no apparent reason. Being an experienced horseman he looked around to see what had frightened them:

> My surprise was that there was a rabbit about forty yards away this rabbit started shrieking which upset my horses. So I got them into another *stetch* and watched. There was a stoat after the rabbit. The rabbit was mesmerized by the stoat. And it went round until it got right into the wind: as soon as it got into the wind that stoat approached the rabbit and collared it behind the ears – and that was finished. Well, for my horse I had a bit of the rabbit and I had a bit of the inside of the stoat. I cut that up and dried it; made it into a powder and mixed it with other chemicals. And with this I could go home into the farmyard and they'd still be standing there nice and comfortable when I came back.

This on the surface is an apocryphal story but it was confirmed by two reliable witnesses who are both skilled horse-

*H.P. & M., p.147.

people, both skilled farriers. I shall include their testimony later, but I want now to quote the following before finishing with my account of Charles Rookyard.

Within the last few years I have been in touch with a former Helmingham resident, Ruth Butters (now Mrs Morrish), the daughter of a former Nonconformist minister in that village. She had added another dimension to my portrait of Charles Rookyard. My chief impression of him was of a real extrovert, a hail-fellow-well-met boon companion with few of the quieter social graces. This tallies with the village's estimate of him as being a 'boosting' (boasting) man. Ruth Morrish gave me an entirely different picture. She wrote:

> When we lived at Helmingham, behind the house was a large field. I walked the furrows there with Charles Rookyard. I must have been four at the time [1944], and I delighted in having my hand on the back flap of the horseman's jacket as we walked up and down. When it was bait-time we sat in the hedge and ate our bread and cheese. I was very much in awe of Mr Rookyard and remember him as very tall and dark; but I also recall that I walked myself to exhaustion just to be in the field as the horses pulled the plough and Mr Rookyard managed the horses.

While we were at Helmingham I also contacted a Welshman who farmed in Waveney Valley just on the Suffolk border. Through him I got to know Albert Love who once worked for him as a horseman in the village of Wortwell. Albert Love (born 1886) was the son of a farm worker who used to go up to Burton-on-Trent during the malting season. On the outbreak of the First World War he joined the Royal Flying Corps which was the precursor of the RAF. His trade in the RFC was a motor-driver and after the end of the war he was in Paris on duty at the Peace Conference. He met another Welshman there – Lloyd George who was then Prime Minister. He was once very angry with him because he failed to get him through the crowded streets of the French capital in time for an important conference he had to officiate at. Albert

Love had the countryman's horse-lore through his family who had been connected with horses for generations and he had been through the toad's bone ritual which he described graphically.* Referring to a skilled ploughman at a ploughing match he had watched he commented:

> He've been round 'the water and streams' – the toad's bone I'm alluding to, the walking-toad as we call it. Well, the toads that we use for this are actually in the Yarmouth area in and around Fritton. We get these toads alive and bring them home. They have a ring round their necks and are what they call *walking-toads*. We bring them home, kill them, and put them on a whitethorn bush. They are there for twenty-four hours till they dry. Then we bury the toad in an anthill; and it's there for a full month till the moon is at the full. Then you get it out; and it's only a skeleton. You take it down to a running stream when the moon is at full. You watch it carefully, particularly not to take your eyes off it. There's a certain bone, a little crotch bone it is, it leaves the rest of the skeleton and floats uphill against the stream. Well, you take that out of the stream, take it home, bake it, powder it, and put it in a box; and you use oils with it the same as you do with the milch (milt). While you are watching this bone in the water you must on no consideration take your eyes off it. Do [if you do] you will lose all the power. That's where you get the power from for messing about with the horses. But once you got the bone, you take it home, bake it and break into a powder. You can mix it in a bottle with the oil, so it's always handy in your pocket if you ever have occasion to use it. You put it on your finger, wipe the horse's tongue, his nostrils, chin and chest – and he's your servant. You can do what you like with him.

Albert Love went through the ritual on three occasions. He failed on the third attempt.

*D.T.W.H.S., pp.29–31.

Once you took your eyes off the bone you were helpless. That's what they always told me. And I did prove it in the end. The third time I went I could do nothing with it. Just down there in the water at the back here, going up to Alburgh. You'd think all these farm buildings right close were falling down. You see, that noise! Rattling – well all sorts of noises you hear; you nearly bound to take your eyes off. Of course, I turned round and looked up. It was never no use. It wouldn't work. It never would work! They always say that was all done, moonlight, midnight, full moon, *Chimes Hours*, and the Devil's work – the noises, the whole thing, toad's bone and everything. The first time I went to the stream I made up my mind I was going to do it; because I was horse-crazy I know.

Albert Love gave me many clues to understanding the farm horseman's involvement with the supposed magic. In addition to the above he also recorded for me his meeting with a former old horseman who had gone through the bone ritual.* He was living by himself and his body was covered with sores. Albert Love asked him:

However came them about? What are they? 'Ah,' he said. 'No doctor will ever cure them. I've been to the doctor's. I've been to hospital. They wouldn't be cured. They can't do nothing with them.'

This statement was analogous to the other instances of the old horseman who believed in and had gone through the ancient ritual. The explanation I believe, is that their minds had become a battling-ground for the confrontation of two religions: the old pre-Christian fertility religion that developed on a world scale and had grown out of man's contact with the earth and the seasons; and the comparatively modern Christian religion which the horseman had been brought up under.

A west Suffolk horseman from the Hargrave area, Harold

*D.T.W.H.S., p.32.

Smart (1889–1973), recalled that another fetish, instead of
the usual material with which the bone was linked, was used.
This was the spores of the bracken-fernseed which was tradi-
tionally supposed to have many magical properties.* Referring to the older horsemen he said:†

> They used to go down anywhere where there was
> bracken growing down to a brook or a bit of disused land
> or anything. There's some in the village. There's what is
> called an old *planten* [plantation] near a sort of river.
> They used to say they'd go down there and gather it.
> They had to go down there. They had to go at twelve
> o'clock at night and gather this bracken seed. They used
> to make out that thunder and lightning and rain came
> down. Well, they used to get this bracken seed and they
> brought that home. Then they'd find a toad, one of these
> *water toads* [probably a mishearing for *walking-toad*] and
> put it in an anthill, make a hole and bury it till the ants ate
> the flesh – which they will – and they used to get these
> bones and then go to a stream in the middle of the night
> and pick out the bone that would go upstream. And
> that's the bone they carried.

Roger and Cheryl Clark, who are well known in the heavy-
horse world, gave me additional information about the toad's
bone, and the practice of jading a horse.‡ Roger:

> I've heard an interesting piece about the frog's or toad's
> business. This was from another chap who'd been a
> horseman and his variation of the thing was this: You
> went through the business of the running stream and
> this, that and the other. But when you got the bone, you
> then boiled it and you got the power from a wild rose.
> The briar – that was as thick as your finger, and you cut
> that off and you dipped one end in the water or whatever
> you were boiling the frog's bone in. That was supposed to

*E. & M. A. Radford, *Encyclopaedia of Superstitions*, London, 1961.
†*H.P. & M.*, p.150.
‡*H.P. & M.*, p.146.

do the job. But the nearest I've got to the secret of the frog's bone – I believe – was what I got from a gamekeeper. A horseman, at Boxford Hall, when he was an apprentice gamekeeper, used to ask him for a stoat and a rabbit together, where the stoat had killed a rabbit – if he could shoot the two together.' Apparently he wanted the liver from them both.

This is a remarkable confirmation of Charles Rookyard's experience while ploughing, recorded earlier.

On this occasion I was recording husband and wife together, and Cheryl Clark confirmed the reaction of the horse to the jading substance that is implied here. She said:

This is a fact. Can you remember a horse I took up this lane and it suddenly stopped? It was absolutely terrified and I got off it. And there was a stoat killing a rabbit and I could not get that horse by! I'm sure that there is some substance in connection with the stoat and the rabbit, perhaps just as it's being killed, that is so offensive to a horse's sense of smell you can't get him past it.

I was first recommended to the next horseman by a friend, David Y. Evans, who came from near my home in south Wales, and whose family I knew. My friend came with his wife and family to live in Suffolk at the village of Redgrave, near the Norfolk border. For some time after writing my first horse book in the fifties, I had the impression that horse-lore, and a great deal of the tradition bound up with the pre-tractor farming and the life that went with it, was quickly vanishing, with the old horsemen I had recorded dying off one after another. I modified my opinion after being introduced by my friend to his neighbour, Mervyn Cater, who was born as late as 1936. Most of the men I had spoken to while writing *The Horse in the Furrow* had been born at the end of the last century and at first I had doubts that so young a man would be able to tell me anything fresh about the farm horse. I could not have been so astonishingly wrong. Mervyn Cater I found was a compendium of accurate information about the

Suffolk horse in spite of his limited though intensive experience.* But he was a very special and outstanding case. His father, Walter Cater, had chosen him as the son who was to inherit the tremendous fund of horse-lore that he and his ancestors had acquired during the centuries, as Mervyn afterwards told me. Mervyn Cater was dyslexic, and owing to this defect he never acquired the ability to read; and since his early schooling had started shortly after the outbreak of war, he became a wartime casualty. At school he spent most of his lessons working on the school garden, and owing to the difficulties of wartime evacuation and the disruption of normal working his tuition was minimal. His one real teacher was his father.

After talking with Mervyn Cater and recording him in two lengthy sessions I found that a surprising amount of the tradition had been absorbed by him under his father's tuition and from his own practical experience under his direction. And it alerted me to the possibility that a similar cache of the tradition was still fleshed in rare individuals like Mervyn Cater himself, vigorous but obviously attenuated by the lack of numbers of those possessing it. What his recordings did was not only to convince me of their worth but also to give me further confirmation of the authenticity and the historical wealth of information I had gathered in different areas of East Anglia from the preceding generation. Walter Cater, his father (1904–73), belonged to a later generation than the men I had recorded in the fifties. I found that the men who were approaching their maturity at the time of the First World War had not such a legacy of the tradition as those who were born in the last two decades of the century. The First World War was a definite watershed in the transmission of the traditional lore. For it saw the beginning of mechanization, and the erosion of the domination of the horse. Therefore although Walter Cater was certainly one of the 'inner ring' of horsemen, from what his son told me I doubt whether he had been left such a rich corpus as some of the older men.

*H.P. & M., pp.113–33.

He had less, I suspect, of the mythological material: he had not, as far as I know, been so involved as 'to go to the water and the streams' – to go through the bone ritual. And he is said to have spoken of 'black magic' disparagingly. Yet he was extremely expert in the lore, as one incident showed.* He was once taken ill with a thrombosis in the leg. The doctor told him he would have to be in bed for a month. The second horseman took over the horses and after a while Cater became anxious about them, for the second horseman had been trained in the army during the First World War, and was a bit unfeeling with the horses, working them too hard. Therefore he called his two sons Mervyn and his brother Kenny, to his bedside and told them: 'It's time those horses had a rest.' And he told Mervyn to get some soot out of the chimney and some linseed oil, and Kenny to bring some other substances to complete the concoction which they mixed in a hand-cup.† Then their mother diluted it with clean water. The two boys took a pail of the mixture down to the park where all the horses had been corralled during the night. They then painted the gateposts with the mixture. And the men could not get the horses off the meadow. They stayed there for five days. The men suspected who had caused them to be confined and kept saying: 'It's Walter!' In the end the farmer's shooting-brake pulled up outside the cottage and threatened Cater with the sack if the horses were not at work the next day. Since it was a tied-cottage he had no option. He told his two sons to take a bucket of the washing-up water and pour it on to the two gates. The next morning the horses came through and they were back at work.

Yet another incident‡ showed how Walter Cater was beaten by a much older man who was a horse dealer from a village near Redgrave where the farm was. He used to pass the farm every Friday to attend Diss market. The old man wore a top hat and old-fashioned clothes, and he drove a pony that was

*H.P. & M., pp.101–3.
†A galvanized iron bowl with a short handle.
‡H.P. & M., pp.105–7.

as strange as Rosinante. The farm men regularly used to take the rise out of him. This happened at the end of the Christmas holidays and Mervyn, who was nine or ten, saw the incident. The men were having their 'nineses', their mid-morning break; and there were six pairs of horses on the headlands alongside the highway. As usual they began ribbing the old man. This time he pulled up and said:

> Well, together, you've had your little laugh. Now I'm going to have mine. You won't do another stroke until I come this way again.

And he touched the reins and drove off to Diss. They finished their breakfast and just kept laughing and making a joke of it. They walked to their horses and not one of them would move. Walter Cater did everything he knew to release the horses. He went home and looked up his horse notebook and tried everything to release them.

They did not move until a quarter past four that evening when the old man returned. The farmer was there and the old horse-dealer told him that he had had enough of his men making a fool of him. Finally he said:

> You can goo now.

They just turned their horses; and the old man left. He had never got off the trap. Mervyn said that 'he must have been to the river'. But later I visited the exact spot with him, and after he had reconstructed the scene I was sure in my own mind that it was just another instance of the old man using a powerful jading substance, along with his careful choosing of the occasion, with the wind in the right direction – the east, as it usually is in this area at the beginning of the year.

Cater's knowledge of horse-lore – outside what he called *black magic* – was encyclopaedic. It is likely that *his* father had possessed the full traditional complex but had shed the oldest part of the lore, as already indicated, by the early years of this century, so that his generation became more sceptical of 'magic'. But what he had lost here was amply compensated for by his straight craftsmanship, and the breadth of his knowledge of horse-control. An instance of this happened during the war when the estate was not kept up to its pre-war standard. The fences were not seen to regularly and Walter Cater had trouble keeping his horses from wandering about the village. He asked permission of the farmer to graze a donkey in the field with the horses. He bought the donkey himself because he knew that a donkey is normally content to stay where he is; and horses always stay with a donkey. When Cater left taking the donkey with him, his successor had exactly the same trouble with fences.

One of the features that linked Walter Cater with the 'Whisperers' and James Sullivan, the eighteenth-century Irishman, who claimed he had been given the secret of horse-control by a soldier who bound him on oath never to reveal it, was his practice of talking to a horse in a locked stable. Mervyn recalled an occasion when he had the horse in a stable for twenty minutes. He waited outside and heard his father continually talking monotonously; but he could not hear what he was saying. He said that when he came out with the horse it was quivering all over, 'frightened to death'. His boss, the farmer, said that he would talk them to death once he took them into that stable. On the other hand, Mervyn had seen his father standing close up to a horse's head when they were on the road, apparently talking to it quietly, at the same time as he was giving it something from a little tin he had taken out of his pocket.

The foregoing, though not orthodox history, should be accepted unreservedly into the province of oral history for several reasons. But, it will be objected, there is no document to justify the claim that what these old horsemen were practising in their so-called magical rites was historical. That is true. Yet there is no need of documents. Their particular document is the whole world as travellers and anthropologists have demonstrated, during the last hundred or so years, by their researches among primitive peoples.

In the next chapter I propose to continue the evidence for the immense age of much of the horse material by describing what has been collected in Scotland through the oral tradition.

Sam Friend

4

Oral History on the Farm

After writing my first horse book I had a letter from a Scot who was a member of the secret Society of the Horseman's Word. Norman Halkett (1910–84) was a farmer's son from Aberdeenshire; and although he went into a bank as a young man he never lost his interest in the farm and country matters. When he was approaching adolescence there was a farming depression and it is probable that his father placed him in a bank because there was not much prospect of a farming career for his generation. Men in East Anglia of the same age, farmers' sons, who had to go into a bank or insurance regretted their loss of a country life for the rest of their lives. Here is Norman Halkett's letter. He wrote from the British Linen Bank, Thurso, Caithness. His letter is dated 2 April 1961:

I have read *The Horse in the Furrow* and greatly enjoyed it. Congratulations on the best bit of research yet done on the folk-lore side. I had read Thos. Davidson's article in *Gwerin* but did not think much of it because none of his 'sources' were new to me and he is inclined to draw wrong conclusions. I say this because I am a properly initiated member of the Horseman's Word – in fact I took part (an official part) in a meeting as recently as 16th March, 1961.

May I explain that although I am manager here of the British Linen Bank, I hail from Aberdeenshire, and until I left home to face the big wicked world in 1933, I lived and worked on the family farm. We never had a tractor until 1936 so I had plenty of horse experience. The H/Word was everywhere and the countryside resounded with tales of how a horseman who could work the word could bewitch a horse or a *woman* at will. It is true to say that in almost every case where a superior horseman could get fantastic results, he had almost certainly a way with women. This may have been due to superior intelligence, and doubtless some of those country women did not take much bewitching – but the tradition persists! A good horse has 10 parts of a good woman and only 2 of a man. *Ergo*, the Word works equally well on a woman.

I have been at many meetings in widely different parts of Scotland (from Orkney to Angus) but there was little difference in the ritual or in the lore. I saw little horse-play indeed; and what there is, is purely symbolic of a young colt being broken. The initiate(s) are led through various manoeuvres – 'by crooks and straits' – to the altar and this part of the ceremony symbolises the progress of the colt. You know how fractious they can be. If the colt is not restive enough, they supply the restiveness. That apart, there is no horse-play at all. Certainly, at certain parts of the ritual the initiate could get hurt (slightly) *if he does not do what he is told* but he is well warned; and this of course is to teach him in the same way as the colt is taught.

The actual initiation is extremely interesting and here I would make the point that 'Both in One' is not correct. This came from Macpherson's book. He obviously got some old Horseman to talk but what he got was in the way only the general meaning of the 'Word'. 'Both in One' does not give any idea or implication of the dominating part to be played by the Horseman. In some ways '3 in 1' might be a better application. The Word is clever indeed: you can search the whole dictionary and you'd have to admit it is the only word that will suit. It is a word which invokes and implies the maximum of applied psychology.

I do not agree that the part played by 'The Auld Chiel' is in any way debasing. This character is no more than some ancient agricultural deity who, probably because he was horned, became confused with 'The De'il' or was more likely dubbed 'the Deil' by the Christian Kirk in their efforts to stamp out witchcraft. The part played by the Auld Chiel is plainly a supplication for fertility and abundance.

The use of the oils and all that is still taught and much more that will help the young horseman to master his trade. I must stress that all are cautioned against using any of the secrets experimentally. An expert should always be present for further and final guidance. I have seen the brows of farmers darken at the very mention of the cult – they had doubtless had a good beast spoiled through the inferior attentions of some young blood anxious to try out his new found knowledge. There is quite a lot (which you do not mention) all to do with smell *and taste* that a horseman would do in facing a new horse, pair or team, for the first time.

An Orkney farmer told me that his father was always too poor to buy good horses, so as a young man this chap had constantly to wrestle with animals which had a fault. He says that the instruction and information handed out at H/W meetings helped him greatly, particularly in the 5 points of feeling. There are five points where a horse is most vulnerable and it is up to the horseman to find his weakness and take advantage. He says he never yet failed to find it. Another bone (besides the frog's bone) was used: it came from a much more Sinister Source: it was this chap who told me where to find it. The shape is much the same – the frog on the foot. We know the colt-milt as the foal's-pad but its use etc. is identical. A horseman of old never travelled without it.

In connection with the cult there is a tremendous amount of question and answer, all of which the initiate(s) must go through before he gets as far as the altar. At this stage the Chief Horseman (the man who in fact is conducting the meeting and imparting the lore) takes charge of him and tells him the secret answers. e.g.

How high is your stable door?
How were you made a Horseman?
Where . . . do . . .?
What are the chief points of Horsemanship?
What are the 3 'Cs'?
What are the 3 'Ps'?
How many links in a Horseman's Chain?
Name them.

And so on . . .

This is all very clever as the meanings of the secret answers become immediately clear to the initiate when he goes through the ritual. The Horseman's oath is taken in a certain way that one will never forget but if you do not do it right you can get slightly hurt or at least damned uncomfortable. The oath binds you to your fellow horsemen and the horse. You do not mention the 'toasts'. These are interesting. Every one present gives one – many of them handed down from generations afore gone. There are two which the initiate must memorise – one to his brother horsemen and one to the horse – these of course tie up with the Oath he has just taken. The toasts are drunk in raw whisky of which there is aye plenty. The entry fee varies slightly from one district to another, but basically it is the same – a bottle of whisky and a loaf or half loaf – the sacramental elements of a former day.

Realizing as I do that if this generation does not preserve the cult and all the lore attached – it will die forever – I have been at much pains for some years to keep the thing going. We lost the great part of the glamour of farm life when we parted with the horse, but I do not see why all the lore, etc. should die. Some two years ago I convened a meeting at a farm in my native parts, initiating no fewer than 6 old farming friends. Thirty years ago not one of us would have been allowed in – we were all farmers' sons. Recently we have had to change the Oath to cover 'horse-lovers' – there is practically no one left actively working horses – in fact most young farmers or farm servants of today could not even yoke a horse – a well trained one at that. This is the only meeting at which I actually presided although I usually take a minor part in the ritual, etc. of any meeting I attend. I may say that the 'impact' or success of any meeting depends almost entirely on the command, personality and knowledge of the Chief Horseman in charge. Forget me, but at every other meeting I have ever attended the 'High Priest' has always been a man of tremendous personality and prestige. I can see that where the opposite is the case the meeting could be anything – quite likely a drunken rabble.

Nowadays, in my humble opinion, the Cult has an added function which I consider important. You have probably heard of the famous 'corn kisters' or bothy ballads* of the North East, songs of the daily workaday life on the farms, etc. As a native of a part of Aberdeenshire particularly rich in song, I see the Horseman's meetings as the natural repository for all local lore. The initiation, etc, is always followed by a social evening and of course these meetings have meant the preservation of

Kist – chest. The farm men sat on the chest, and beat the time of the tune with their heels.

many songs and social lore. In fact, long ago many of
these songs were composed for Horseman's meetings –
there are sometimes veiled references in the songs. I
need not tell you about the function of the Cult as an
underground Trade Union (in addition to the Horsey
side): a favourite method of ridiculing a bad employer
was to compose a song about him and launch it in Horseman circles. Hence we get verses like this:

> For dinner we had mostly broth
> A splash o'neifs* an' bree.†
> We chased the barley roon' the plate
> But a' we coppt was three.

In continuing the meetings we are helping to preserve
the local lore that has always been part of the background.

I exchanged many letters with Norman Halkett and finally I
flew up to Thurso in February 1964. In the meantime I had
done a fair amount of broadcasting on the BBC, and they
commissioned a programme about farming, featuring the
farm horsemen who were key-men in the type of farming that
was quickly going out. I had projected a programme featuring these old horsemen, most of whom had retired when the
horses went off the land. They were all from East Anglia:
Suffolk, Norfolk and Cambridgeshire. After I had recorded a
dozen or so, I discussed Norman Halkett with David Thomson, the producer of the programme. He thought I should go
up to Thurso and record Halkett who could make a contribution by talking about the secret side of farm horsemanship. I
went to Thurso and recorded him on two or three tapes,
chiefly dealing with his own experiences on his father's farm
and his involvement with the Society of the Horseman's
Word. The resulting script *The Farm Horse and His Masters*
contained recordings from East Anglian horsemen and Halkett's experience of the Horseman's Society especially the

* – or neeps: turnip.
†barley-bree, a liquid.

oath the initiate swore on being admitted into it. The BBC gave the programme a good airing and helped me to a clearer conception of the whole horse-magic complex. The Scottish evidence was much fuller than the vestigial East Anglian contributions and explained some of the aspects I had failed to understand. For instance one East Anglian told me that when he'd gone down 'to the water and streams' to do the frog's bone ritual 'the Devil was looking over his shoulder'. It was clear after having a full account of the Scottish ritual that the Devil (or the De'il in *Lallans*)* was the Head Horseman, the leader of the group or coven, who was supervising the ceremony, and not the ecclesiastical Devil which was the popular interpretation. Other evidence from both areas, although the East Anglian was obviously fragmentary, made it clear that the ceremony described by the horsemen fitted in to the accounts of the classical descriptions of puberty initiations, or initiations into secret societies collected by travellers and anthropologists from overseas primitive sources. The fuller pattern of the Scottish initiation ceremony induced me to speculate: why was there such a difference in the two regions? Or put it another way: why have the practices of an historical survival and especially the organization, survived much more completely in north-east Scotland? The reason appears to be in the differing history of the two regions. In England by the end of the sixteenth century, the ancient craftsman's guilds or corporations had practically died, and many handicrafts became open to all who cared to practice them. In Scotland, however, these craftsman's guilds lasted until very much later and remained tight little societies bitterly opposed to the merchant guilds. This opposition continued until recent times in the Horseman's Society particularly; for no farmer was admitted to the Society, not even a farmer's son despite the fact that he might be working as a ploughman. But there are other crafts societies that have lasted to recent times in north-east Scotland: Millers, Sadlers and Hammermen. Remoteness, too, might have ensured

*Speech of Lowlands: Scots-speaking as opposed to Gaelic-speaking.

longer life for these guilds. Yet the persecution by the Church
must have had an effect on the nature of their practices.
Their form of initiation and their secret meetings caused
them, inevitably, to be identified with witches. The Kirk
appears to have been very vigilant in pursuit of the Horseman's Society but it is probable that it did not equal Matthew
Hopkins's* drive in East Anglia. The members of the Horseman's Society were always exposed but they were careful not
to take risks and offend the Kirk openly. When the danger of
being called witches receded the horsemen adapted their
Society into a kind of underground trade union, lampooning
an unpopular employer with scurrilous songs like the
example quoted in Halkett's letter. As he says, they became in
their meetings, especially, rehearsers and therefore preser-
vers of traditional lore.

The correspondence between the horseman groups and
individuals in both areas in the initiation ceremony and other
historical ceremonies in cults all over the world, show both
their authenticity and their age: the emphasis on secrecy; the
exclusion of women; the frequent use of symbolism: 'crooks
and straits' in the initiation ceremony to describe the analogy
of a young horse's progress; and the importance of the initiate's tutor who coaches him in preparation for the ceremony
and leads him, on the actual occasion, to the altar – an upturn-
ed bushel on top of a bag of corn. The toasts are also
important. The neophyte or initiate brings the necessary
articles for these: a bottle of whisky and half a loaf of bread.
There is also a certain element of an ordeal in the Scottish
ceremony as there is in many initiation rites. Halkett gives an
example of an initiate being ordered to go at dead of night to
a churchyard and to grope under a specific stone, identified
carefully by the instructions given to him; when he does this
he will find a whip that will give him for ever power over any
horse. In the meantime one of his fellow horsemen is
stationed under the stone, and when he reaches for the whip
he is immediately seized. He is very frightened, but this is the

---

*Seventeenth-century pursuer of English witches.

lesson of the ordeal: he is in the hands of a brother horseman although he does not know it; and, as the oath enjoins, he must have absolute faith in his brother.

Norman Halkett recalled an interesting incident when he had taken part in an initiation ceremony in Orkney. Part of the ceremony has the blindfolded initiate catching hold of the Auld Chiel's hand. After the ceremony the hut in which it was held was burnt down, and the police were going round questioning farmers to find out which of them had lost a stirk or steer – a young bullock. They had found in the ruined hut the remains of one of the properties used in the ceremony – the foot of a stirk.

One thing that is certain is that evidence of the age of the horsemen's beliefs and practices, both in East Anglia and Scotland, shows that it is a fit subject for the attention of the oral historian in a field that has hitherto been unsuspected and comparatively unexplored: the prehistory of our islands. Up to the present only the findings of the archaeologist have been accepted.

I was aware of another horse-myth from my early years in south Wales. Both my parents came from districts where the myth of the Mari Lwyd was very much alive. My father was born in the Blaenau, the foothills of Glamorgan, at Pentyrch a few miles from Cardiff. In his youth it was a Welsh-speaking rural village, long before it became a kind of dormitory for the city. It was then a pastoral community, including a few mine-pits, dug deeply into the core of the hill to extract iron ore. My father was born in 1866, long before the ancient, immemorial tradition had broken up and he had it in abundance. He had, more than once, told me of the ancient custom of the Mari Lwyd, which had survived in the Vale of Glamorgan, and of its annual celebration at Pentyrch at the New Year. A party of singers and reciters, led by the Mari Lwyd figure, processed around the houses. Mari was a man wearing a horse's skull which had been prepared by burying it in fresh lime. A pole about five feet in length was inserted into the horse's skull, and a white sheet was draped over his whole figure. Dark cloth cut to the shape of ears was sewn on the sheet and the whole was decorated with coloured ribbons, the skull particularly, and bottle-glass served for the eyes. The leader of the party knocked at the door of a house, and challenged those inside to an improvised contest of reciting and song. When the Mari Lwyd party were adjudged the winner – usually the result – the door was unlocked and they were welcomed inside. They were then treated to food and drink, and the evening's jollity began. This custom, depending on the party, was often extended over several days.

My mother was also born in a Mari Lwyd district, so that one could say it was part of my inheritance. Her home was Maesteg; and this town and especially the nearby village of Llangynwyd was a bright focus of the Mari Lwyd tradition. T. C. Evans, a well-known nineteenth-century local figure whose bardic name was 'Cadrawd', was a strong upholder of the ritual and, indeed, of all old traditions. Maesteg was also the birthplace of Vernon Watkins, the poet, who wrote the very fine poem, 'The Ballad of the Mari Lwyd'. With his poet's intuition he interpreted the contest as a dialogue between the living and the dead, and by so doing rescued a numinous legend from a bathetic descent into an occasion for seasonal amusement. Undoubtedly, as with many of the old rituals, Mari Lwyd was a part of a very ancient religion, probably connected with a totemic horse-cult, which was concerned with the eternal question of what happens to us when we die.

Some information, that has a bearing on this, comes from the same area of south Wales as the above and is provided by Susan Troughton whose home is Bryncethin. Her uncle, William John of that village, was a well-known adherent of Mari Lwyd, able to play at the contest 'for two hours without faltering'. So well known did he become locally for his prowess that he was commissioned by a publican in a neighbouring village. He led the defenders inside the pub against all comers, who vigorously strove to get inside with the promise of free beer if they succeeded. The only man, it appears, who was able to beat William John was his brother,

Lewis. But Lewis would not engage in this contest. He was very devout, and a deacon in a Nonconformist chapel. But though he would not 'play away' in a public contest, he would defend his own house with full vigour. So inspired did he become improvising metrical answers that the party inside the house eventually took pity on those outside and handed them chairs so that they could listen in comfort – the ultimate admission of defeat.

It is the John family of Bryncethin who have thrown valuable light on the origins of the Mari Lwyd custom that is of great interest to anthropologists. Susan Troughton revealed an important aspect of this custom:

> As a child I remember my grandmother who was married to Lewis John but also blood-kin to him.

She told me about the death of her own grandfather (back in the nineteenth century):

> As the old man lay dying it was thought fitting to have a horse brought close to the open window of the room where he lay. The reason for this is obscure but it does suggest an underlying but forgotten belief that the horse would serve as a mount for the dead man. My grandmother, when telling this particular story, did not seem to think it strange that this should be done.

It is clear that the horse was treated as a psychopomp, or a conductor of souls to the place of the dead. And it confirms the special relation of the horse to the living that was posited in Vernon Watkins's poem 'The Ballad of the Mari Lwyd'. The pattern is also similar to the Welsh and East Anglian legend that the origin of bees was in Paradise, echoing Virgil's ancient belief. This was a widespread belief in East Anglia. *Telling the Bees* used to be obligatory on the death of their owner. The old method of letting the bees know of their owner's death was for his widow or eldest son to strike the hives three times with an iron door-key and say: 'The master is dead.' If this was not done the bees would fly away or misfortune would follow. It was believed there was a strong bond of sympathy between the bees and their owner, exactly as was assumed in the Welsh custom. The bees in the old community were looked upon as psychopomps in East Anglia. This comes out in a passage of one of Osbert Sitwell's books and an interesting sequel it had. The Sitwell family had an East Anglian butler called Henry Moat; and he used to puzzle the Sitwell children by bringing to their attention the groups of cumulus clouds processing majestically across a blue sky, at the same time urging them 'to look at them great big Norwegian Bishops!' The Sitwell children looked dutifully but couldn't have been much the wiser. A short while after Osbert's autobiography was published, a correspondent wrote to him to say: 'The phrase that the children had misheard was "Norwegian bee-ships or bee-skips (bÿ skeps)" '. And the belief was once common that the souls of the dead are represented as bees and were thought to traverse the sky in what was termed as bee-ships or skeps. An old fashioned East Anglian straw-skep was a good analogue for a well-rounded cumulus cloud. There is, incidentally, a passage in Virgil's *Fourth Georgic* comparing a flight of bees to a cloud.

The Mari Lwyd survival shows again the outstanding continuity of these old myths. I am inclined to risk a guess that it is one of the oldest, and belongs to the palaeolithic era. The religious element in the myth appears to argue the case for its immense age.

A similar example from the Ancient World was brought to light in the early part of this century when John Cuthbert Lawson, a Cambridge classical scholar, wrote a book* after his two years' research in Greece and the Islands. His purpose had been to investigate the customs and superstitions of the Greek peasant and to test whether his findings might cast light on the religion of the ancient Greeks. He came to the conclusion that the Greek Orthodox Church, in the same way as the Catholic Church in the West, had not displaced or stifled the old pagan religion but had been opportunistic and

Modern Greek Folklore and Ancient Greek Religion, London, 1910. *W.B.W.A.*, pp.222–4.

had merely incorporated it into a more unified framework. Exactly the same development happened in western culture where religious customs had not been metamorphosed: the old ceremonies still persisted in an underground survival as folklore.

This is another demonstration of the truth that there is no backward limit in time to which it is not possible for oral tradition to refer.

Getting to know my neighbours when we first came into Suffolk, my interest was in arable farming. They told me the intricate details of the work and their careers on the farm and the field. They showed me the old hand-tools they had used in their work, tools whose design was very ancient such as the sheep-shears and the flail, but which had gone off the farm during their lifetime. They also described the farm operations like horse-ploughing, hand-sowing and threshing. I became interested first in the tools. This happened instinctively exactly as I had absorbed the use of the hand-tools by the miners: the mandril, the axe and the shovel. As one miner told me, he first had to learn the basic technique of using such a simple tool as a shovel:

> To move a heap of coal onto a tram or tub, you don't strain and go at it bull-headed. That way you'd soon wear yourself out. You just take the coal at the edge, the coal that falls onto the shovel; and then work gradually into the heap. You save a tremendous amount of energy that way.

In this way I valued the descriptive accounts of the farm workers and recorded them because, as with the miners, they were the bedrock of their skilled techniques. It was small undramatic discoveries such as this that persuaded me that recording the smallest detail from men who had spent their lives in the old hand-tool farming was a worthwhile pursuit. It was already, too, an historic activity, or would soon become so, for it gave the full picture of processes that were being quickly superseded after being used by man since he started tilling the soil. But one important fact came home to me as I studied the farming: a revolution was taking place and the tractor displacing the horse.

This made me reflect that the men who were going were much devalued, many of them written off as unskilled labourers after practising their varied skills that had taken them years to learn. A farm horseman, who was in Suffolk also a ploughman, was a real craftsman who had all the craftsman's pride in his work. I recorded an instance of how deep-seated was this pride, and how not to fall a fraction of an inch below his self-set standard was one of the horseman's main aims in his life. He would never forgive himself if he failed to keep it up. It was when Walter Cater was teaching his son, Mervyn, to use a horse-drill – a steerage-drill to drill or sow the corn.* This was an operation that demanded a high degree of skill, and care not to jeopardize one's reputation as a craftsman because any mistake made in the drilling would be visible to everybody once the crop came up. It was a Smythe drill and the father took him on some 'short work', a piece of land where no one could see it. The son was allowed to drive the drill up and down with the father walking beside him and behind him. He leaned on him and did everything to teach him the skill. One day he was having a lesson and his father was called away by the boss. There was a horse in the ditch and they had difficulty in getting it out. The son thought he was man enough now to carry on with drilling. It looked so easy just to follow the straight line that had been made already. He walked round to the back of the drill.

> I put the lever on and let the corn run; and I driv those horses across the field. When I looked back that was dreadful! That was inches out. When my father seen this he was hurt – not angry, he was hurt!

He was hurt because the reputation he prized, perhaps most of all, as an all-round expert on the farm had been dented.

Near the Norfolk–Suffolk border ploughmen used to walk

*H.P. & M., pp.116–17.

around on a Sunday morning in the spring to examine the ploughing on the various farms, admiring or criticizing each other's handiwork. James Seely of Bergh Apton*

> The old team-men would walk miles round the country-side to look at other people's work – well outside their own parish sometimes. At the time I'm speaking of, before 1914 when I was called up, the pubs were open all day during the week but on Sunday they were closed except during midday for a couple of hours; and then they'd open again in the evening. But if you'd travelled three miles out of the village you could have a drink in a pub at any time on a Sunday. So the team-men [or horsemen] used to walk their three miles to get a drink, looking at the ploughing as they went. Then when they'd had their drink, they'd walk round to another pub till they made their way back home. Some of them made a real outing of it, looking at the land and saying, perhaps: 'They've got a real good 'un here. Look at his work!'
>
> You take the ten-furrow work we had to do on the heavy land near Kirby Cane. That was tradesman's work. You'd take years to learn it. You had a nine-inch share to your plough and a stetch coming out at seven feet ten inches. You used an eight-foot Smythe drill and your work had to be right to the inch. But that weren't the only skill; there were half a dozen more: stacking – it's a rare skill today – thatching which we had to do on the farm, hedging, ditching, looking after half a dozen horses, and keeping them in good condition with little aid from the vet.

Suffolk farm horsemen also gave me a great deal of detailed information about their ploughing. I discovered that in their descriptions they were using dialect words I was recording for the first time. These words also showed the age of the processes. An example is a description of a *long summer-land* or long fallow that I have had from three or four

*W.B.W.A., p.65.

horsemen during the last twenty-five years. A fallow (some-times *falley* in the dialect) is an arable field that is temporarily uncultivated, allowed to rest and recover its fertility. It is also cleaned of weeds by repeated ploughings. The process is as old as the Romans. The *long summerland*, depending on the state of the land, was prepared every four or five years. After a corn crop had been harvested the land was left *naked* or bare. It was then ploughed straight after harvest before the winter frosts began so that the early frost would begin to break up the soil. To make a *summerland*, the land had to be ploughed five times. The horseman had a double-furrow plough – usually a Ransome Y.L. in Suffolk or a Cameron plough in the Bungay area. This was the *first earth*, ploughed up and down the field lengthways and left until Christmas. Then came the *two earth* ploughed in the same way. This was followed by the *three earth*. Here the ploughman drew his furrows across, at right angles to the ones he had already drawn, ploughing *overwart* [athwart] as he called it. This was a cross-ploughing. It is interesting that Peter Reynolds,* in his experimental Iron-Age farm at Butser in Hampshire, cross-ploughs in this way with his primitive ard, ensuring that the soil is well broken up and the seed-bed left in a friable state.

The *four earth* came next. This was the hardest ploughing of the year, usually in the summer in the month of June or July when the lumps of earth left by the previous winter ploughing were large and rock-hard making it very difficult for the horseman to follow the plough. It gave him terribly sore feet.

> They used to have several acres down to a *long summer-tilth* [summerland]. It wasn't easy a-walking while you were a-doing one of these. *Four earth* was hard work in the summer months, for men and for horses. It was all clods, big and hard clods. We used to have a Bungay plough for that job, an all-iron swing-plough, no wheel. We couldn't use a wheel on a *long summer-tilth*.

*Peter J. Reynolds, *Iron Age Farm*, British Museum, London, 1979.

James Seely* gave me this information sixteen years ago. He is now over ninety years of age and confirmed the difficulty of the summer ploughing. Charles Rogers† a Suffolk farmer from the Saints area of north Suffolk told me that:

> A man couldn't stand more than half an acre's ploughing in the summer. He couldn't stand it. [He'd been doing a full acre in the spring.] The horses couldn't stand it either; and it would have been the same with oxen in the Middle Ages. Even then he'd have to do the ploughing early in the morning before the heat of the day.

The last ploughing, the *five earth*, was for setting up a stetch or rig ready to take an eight-foot drill for planting the winter corn.

The Middle Ages was mentioned in the description of a *long summerland* but the process was much older than medieval times. I have written *earth* in my description of it for ease of orthography but its meaning is not our common one. Earth means *ploughing* and should be written in its Old English form *eorþe*, from *erian* the Old English word to plough. It is, in fact, one of the rare instances of an Old English word used in the dialect in this century after continuing for at least a thousand years in this area.

A few years ago I was involved in a film shot in East Anglia. It was called *Requiem for a Village* and made by David Gladwell. Many of the characters in the film were played by villagers. They were men and women who had lived close to the soil all their lifetime. They had direct contact with their natural environment. They reminded me of a farm worker I knew who was born at the beginning of the century. He was a good example in temper and achievement of the kind of people represented in the film.‡ I recorded him eight years ago. Jack Leeder:

*W.B.W.A., p.102
†Ibid., p.89.
‡Jack Leeder, Knapton, Norfolk. Transcribed from a tape-recording.

That's the job I liked best: breaking a horse in. That was one of the jobs I liked! If I was asked, as Wilfred Pickles [a BBC interviewer] used to ask: 'What would you do or see that gave you the biggest kick?' Well, there's three things: Seeing horses munch their food – have you heard horses munch their food? Seeing a youngster holding his father's hand. He don't care for hell or high water, do he? He's not afraid of anybody! And the other is: the spirit of a young horse – when he's right young. I never used to try and tear their spirit from them and destroy it. I used to do the very opposite to them. They [his mates] used to take the quietest and oldest horse out of the stable. I used to take the fastest horse. They are young. They want to run and kick and jump about; and I used to let them. Then they'd get used to you. They'd keep you so quiet; then suddenly there'd be a noise or a chain gets round their leg! Well, I used to wind a chain around their leg specially and they get used to it; and you don't have any trouble. I'd let them trot in a cart when they're young. They are like a child, they want action. The art of working with horses is common sense and patience. In the end I used to bend them to my will: I'd never let them get away. When I broke a horse in, I used to put a halter on him – what we call a *single halter* – tie him to the post and let him pull on it. Then let him be. Eventually, he'll try to get away, and the more he tries to get away the better I used to like him, because once he's learned that he could not break that rope, he'd never pull on it any more. He'd learned that lesson properly. And I used to have a short stick, about a foot or so long, and put it against his nose, because that's how a horse feels through his nose; and then I'd go round his head touching him with the stick and round his neck and all over him. And if he turned a bit nervous I used to let him rest a bit; and then go under his tail and between his legs. And I used to do that for a month when I was breaking them in.

He was, therefore, never afraid when you touched him. Afraid these horses are, because if someone touches them between the legs, for instance, they are not used to it. They won't kick when they are used to it. I'd put the trace around their legs. It's common sense, most of it. But some would put a vicious bit on a young horse; and he'd go across the field; and he couldn't move his head either to the right or left. But he'd generally turn out a kicker or something of that sort. As I've said before, you can cure one vice and make two more. The thing is if you like horses you take on: I don't think you'll ever make a team-man if you disliked horses. If you break one in – it's like a child. For ever after there's a bond between you. You can't explain it to other people – I suppose you think me an old fool talking like that!

I disagreed. He was talking the soundest sense in emphasizing this bond and the best way of attaining it. And I gave as an example the Society of the Horseman's Word. The Word is simply a symbol, enshrining this bond between the man and the horse he was using; and membership of the Society schooled the initiate and helped him to attain this bond by inculcating a discipline to put the Word into action. Membership, too, implied aid, assisting and giving advice to a young initiate to attain the message, this well-guarded, almost mystic Word.

Jack Leeder was the most unusual of the dozens of farm horsemen I have met. Like them all he was a practical man and was a first-class craftsman, both as a horseman and a ploughman, in the tradition of all good East Anglian ploughmen who worked a team of horses. As I recorded him I felt that he spoke with authority and absolute honesty. His interests were also wider than the average farm horseman and he had absolute independence of mind. His employer was a big farmer, for that time, who had between fifteen and twenty horses working on his land. Jack Leeder said he was a good farmer and a fair employer; but this did not prevent him from having an occasional argument with him. The farmer once remarked in a conversation he was having with him:

'Things have improved. You don't see children going about with holes in their boots like they used to.'

'Do you wish to see children going about with holes in their boots?'

'No, but it's a sign of better times. Besides, I see people getting a new bike, an expensive model too, with a three-speed on it and all.'

Leeder had himself bought a three-speed bicycle; and he came back with:

'You see some people too buying a new Sunbeam motor car, and he already had a motor bike and side-car, as well as three riding horses.'

'I can't talk to you.'

'But I can talk to you.'

I recorded Jack Leeder in his house. He was very critical of the development of modern farming as most old farm workers were and, allowing for the tendency in the old to disparage innovations, their bias was the right one, especially their criticism of the treatment of the soil. And he was surely right in his strictures about the pace of modern living.

Rushing about in cars and the speed of modern living, and we are no happier than we were years ago. It would take a week to get somewhere: today we take an hour; and we are no happier and no more forward; and I think that's the same with nearly everything at work. I used to get up in the morning, five o'clock to feed my horses. I'd whistle and they'd come; and I'd put the halter on them and they came; they'd go down to the farm. Now when you went across that field (I'm not a very good sort of bloke at all: I don't mean that at all), but if you couldn't believe there was a Higher Power than you when you used to see the trees bursting into bloom, your horses neighing to you when you came to them, the feeling that you had between you! I had a blind horse, and we had a bond between us: you talked to him; you loved him; he loved me, I'm sure he did. He relied on me – which way to turn and everything. It was a sad thing when he went away: he went for horsemeat to Belgium! I wouldn't have minded if they'd shot him on the place and had went off then. He was blind and I could see him being hit on the head: of course, he didn't know where to go. They didn't realize that horse had to work for them and had earned them pounds of money! That was altogether wrong. If I'd ha' known – well, I cried when he went: and I wouldn't be ashamed to say so. My wife used to tell me that I thought more about my horses than I did about her. I didn't really. But there's something people miss: I can't explain what it is. It was a bond. It wasn't any trouble for me to feed them and groom them. I'd give any amount of time to them. I think if people could get back some of those ways with the horse and the countryside, with the trees bursting out and the butterflies and the cattle we'd be much happier.

In my contact with innumerable men and women who were connected with farming and the land in East Anglia I have always tried to be objective as I could, only very rarely asking personal questions, keeping the conversation to ponderable things such as their work and the processes connected with it. That was, I believe, the material's first strength: it was matter of fact, objective and visual, even pedestrian; and its context had the perfect setting of the dialect – a direct and concrete language in which it was told. Occasionally, however, I met a man like Jack Leeder who was an exception. His language was down to earth, but he had great sensitivity and intelligence, and he was not ashamed to let that sensitivity appear when he talked about his work and his horses which he cared for devotedly. He was an artist in managing horses; but he did not boast about it. Yet one story he told me demonstrates his skill. He was taking his two horses to a field one morning. He was to spend the day ploughing with a double-furrow plough; but when he hitched up his horses he found that he had forgotten to bring the reins. Rather than go back to the stable to fetch them, he did his day's ploughing using word of mouth only: *cuppy-whey* (left) and *wheesh* (right). His work with his horses, though he drove a tractor towards the end of his career, was his life and the chief topic of his leisure when he retired.

mourne mountains

5

Ireland

I revert to our visit to Ireland to collect material for *The Leaping Hare*. My wife and I stayed with Jim and May Delaney at their home near Athlone. From there we visited some of his friends he had been visiting for years. The first was William Egan, a countryman aged seventy-three. He lived in a traditional two-roomed one-storey cottage on his own. The living-room had a half-hatch door, and an inquisitive hen kept hopping on to the lower half of the door and into the room until Jim swept it out with a broom. In the living room was a wide, open fireplace burning peat; and the sweeping arm of a crane dominated the fire. From the crane hung a hake to which a pot was attached and then swung over the fire. Before we left the cottage we met Darcy, William Egan's neighbour, a tall, younger man with jet-black hair.

Jim Delaney had arranged that Bill Egan should show us a holy well whose location was in danger of being forgotten. The well was near the River Shannon, not far from Clonmacnois, one of Ireland's earliest monastic settlements which included the ruins of many monastic buildings and a medieval university. We visited the well, a very ordinary looking spring, and more convincing therefore that Bill Egan's testimony was correct: it was the authentic holy well that had once been venerated. We later spent an hour or so in Clonmacnois before returning to Bill Egan's cottage. As soon as he got inside he looked around and saw the small bottle of whisky which Jim had brought him, still on the table. He said:

'I made a mistake: Darcy has been at the whiskey. I should have put it away.'

Darcy had been in and broached it; but there was no suggestion of blame. There was no further comment. And it was likely nothing more was said, as though it was recognized that the possessions of friends are rightly shared in common.

After recording Bill Egan for a short time and hearing some of his experiences with catching hares I recognized him as one of the true *seanchaithe*, the traditional story-tellers who had great status and respect in the Irish countryside before the old culture fell away and the story-tellers lost their audience. Seamus Delargy, who was the first Director of the Irish Folklore Commission, has described how they no longer gathered round the peat fire at night to listen to the tales. He recounted how the son of one of these old story-tellers, Sean O'Connell, in order to keep a grip on the lore he had taken a lifetime to memorize, used to repeat the tales aloud when he thought he was alone:

His son told me that he has seen his father telling his tales to an unresponsive stone wall while herding the cattle. And on another occasion on returning from market, as he walked slowly up the hills behind his grey mare, he could be heard declaiming his tales to the back of his cart.

Bill Egan was much younger than Sean O'Connell, and was too late to garner much of the tradition; but he was yet an accurate and worthy memorizer of anything noteworthy that had occurred during his span of memory. He knew, for instance, of how a man from his neighbourhood had been bitten by a mad dog and had been sent to Paris to be treated by Pasteur. I also had an example of his power of graphic description when I recorded his experience with hares:

> I seen a hare-hunt once, and they were coming from the place where we call *The Hill*. Well, we were watching this hunt coming in the bog. We had a right view and we were right up. So they came in the bog, two hounds after the hare. She turned straight to the bog-hole where we cut the turf out of. You know, that would be the height of that ceiling, into the water where the turf was cut away. She came; and she came to the edge of that. She wheeled short; went out of the bog. And in went the hounds, and into the bog-hole. Couldn't stop themselves! They throwed water up to the clouds out of the bog-hole. She was gone out of the bog; and there was neither tell nor count of the dogs. What was the use of following her then? She was beyond the other side of the Shannon before they knew where they were!

Another of Jim Delaney's friends I recorded on this visit was Patrick Johnston, a man of eighty-eight. He was a humorous old man who lived by himself in a remote stretch of the bog country, not far from Bill Egan. His wife had died and his family had left home. He gave me an example of the age of the oral material that was available in Ireland as recently as fifteen years ago: the catching of hares before the use of dogs. Patrick Johnston described getting a hare with a hunting-, or throwing-stick which was a primitive method of catching hares but still used up to fifteen or sixteen years ago. He cut me a hunting-stick which I still have. It is about thirty inches in length and a little heavier than a walking-stick. Blackthorn, hazel or *sally* (sallow) or willow were commonly used to make a stick. He preferred a hazel one which he chose very carefully: it had a slight bend about a third of the way down its length:

> And what you would want now to be accurate – get a bend in the stick so it would come out crooked that way,

with a hump in it. And whatever it does in there, it makes the stick carry accurate. I know that! I tested that. I tested that with a straight stick first, you know. And when it was *pegged* [aimed] it always took this side of the object. You see, I always peg a little out when I use the stick. But you should always, when a hare is passing you, peg a full yard in front because he'll be there agen the stick is there. How I used to do: I'd put my cap in the field practising to peg. And the straight stick would always bring it this side of the cap. And the other was accurate; used to cut the cap out of it. I never hunted hares without – I always carried two: two sticks with a different kind of bend in them, because if I did chance to miss with one, I hadn't to be looking for it. I had another chance in hand. Experience it is! You'll see your fault after a couple of turns; and if you're anyway smart, you'll pick up something; then you'll try some other game.

John Connaughton another user of the hunting-stick emphasized that you had to train yourself to use the stick:

Oh practise! They would practise. That was every Sunday when they came home from Mass. Put up anything for a target, anything at all; maybe a lump of stick, a kettle, a teapot, an old tin can, maybe a bottle sometimes. Well, when it was after a certain time, the rabbits get fit to hunt (they'd got to be about three-quarter size). Up to then they'd be fishing every Sunday when they came home from Mass. From that time till the springtime, they'd be off hunting somewhere or another.

In going round with Jim Delaney on this visit, collecting material about the hare, I learned a great deal about the technique of collecting oral information. His was a natural, unobtrusive approach which stemmed from his individual treatment of his respondent, not so much as a purveyor of information but as a long-standing acquaintance or friend, a man you were able to give actual sustenance and encouragement by your constantly visiting him. And you, for your part, receive co-operation and sustenance in return, as well as a reassuring conviction that you are engaged in a sociably acceptable activity; that you are adding a few bricks to an enduring structure of our past. For in spite of the modern documentary method of recording the past by committing its legacy to writing or print there is still a vigorous tendency, although much debilitated, to commit the essence of the past to a continuing communal memory, especially in the Celtic countries where the memory of this stage of their culture is still very active. This is true in Ireland and Wales and I suspect is equally true of Scotland: that there was a professional class of memorizers, bards or poets who toiled for years to discipline their memory to absorb a huge corpus of myth and tradition, and whose accuracy was checked by periodic scrutiny by their elders. This enabled them to recite and pass on their learning to the succeeding generations.

There is a new theory, recently put forward, that presupposes an intermediate stage of social development arising out of the primitive, and that it once obtained in many parts of the world. It is suggested that a highly organized and complex culture evolved without the use of the written word but which, nevertheless, reached a high standard of social development. This has been advanced by an American, Eli Sagan* who has posited an intermediate complex society arising out of the primitive stage and preceding the great archaic civilizations of Egypt, Mesopotamia, and the Aegean. As one of his examples he has put forward Buganda (now Uganda). When Speke, and later Stanley, the explorers, in their search for the source of the Nile, discovered Lake Victoria towards the end of the last century, they also found there, eight hundred miles inside 'darkest Africa' an extraordinary and fascinating society, that had evolved independently of more 'advanced' cultures into a complex, sophisticated kingdom. Lacking any written language, which for us has become the hallmark of civilization, Buganda had, nevertheless, developed an amazing variety of social and

*At *The Dawn of Tyranny*, London, Faber and Faber, 1986, p.xvi.

cultural institutions that we are accustomed to regard as compatible only with a culture capable of the written word. An authoritarian monarch, heading an aristocratic social structure of governors, sub-governors, and thousands of petty bureaucrats, ruled a million people. Politics was as sophisticated and as complex as that of any nineteenth-century English borough. The English explorers soon learned that in this sophisticated society they could no longer condescend to black Africans.

Studies of such cultures as these may well throw a new light on the 'dark period' of many peoples where it is assumed that, as there were no written records, ordered government was non-existent and the people had no history. Historians now are fortunate that the efforts of anthropologists, travellers, explorers, and colonial administrators over the past hundred or so years have amassed information, from all over the world, of peoples at varying stages of their development; doubly fortunate for not only have they been able to demonstrate from these findings the wonderful variety of social organization all over the world but they have also enabled us to possess a better appreciation of the beginnings of our own culture, and a near estimate of that phase of its early development when it was entirely oral and had no documentation.

Eli Sagan also identifies what he calls other advanced complex societies in the Southern hemisphere among the Polynesian peoples: the Hawaiian Islands, Tahiti in the Society Islands, and Tonga. These islands are associated with the period of Captain Cook's last voyage to the South Seas in 1778, and also with William Mariner, who survived a shipwreck and a massacre to return home and write *An Account of the Natives of the Tonga Islands*. The mutineers from Captain Bligh's *Bounty* were also at Hawaii and Tahiti but none wrote about his experiences. These islands were as richly fertile and provided as easy a living as Buganda, but as they were discovered during the last years of the eighteenth century they were quickly subjected to foreign influence and by the third decade of the next century the traditional Polynesian societies had ceased to exist. Therefore, compared with the discovery of Buganda eighty years later, little is known of the details of how these societies functioned.

We do not know what historians will make of the claim that an unlettered society like Buganda was run as efficiently as 'any nineteenth-century English borough'; yet it is an indication that the reliability of oral evidence tends to be underestimated rather than the reverse.

Certainly my visits to Ireland's rural areas gave me a deeper conception of the age and continuity of oral tradition, and why it should be considered as an integral part of the discipline of history, if only for the reason that the discovery and use of writing came a long time after the conscious harnessing of memory to carry a transmissible account of early society's experience. Moreover there developed in Ireland, as in Wales, a class of people, the bards who became the guardians of the communal memory, the virtual patrons of the careful noting and recording through memory of the most notable events in the community's history. My knowledge of southern Ireland has been acquired almost solely through James Delaney who has been steeped in its folklore and language all his life, and professionally for the last forty years. The material he has collected is on tape and transcribed on manuscript in the archives of the Irish Folklore Commission in University College, Dublin. It embraces most aspects of the oral material and a listing of the material objects related to the rural Ireland that existed at the beginning of this century. With his permission I am including a transcript of one of his recent discoveries.

Cutting the Worm's Knot

Griping pains in the abdomen, whether of man or
beast are very frequently attributed by the
uneducated peasantry to the irritating presence of
worms. A popular form of treatment, especially
indeed, in the case of quadrupeds, is to tie the
'worm-knot' on a piece of string over the body of
the affected animal (or human being) and then
loose the same knot by the instantaneous snap

which the peculiarity of the knot makes possible.
This operation is repeated three times, or in bad
cases three times three. Each operation is enforced
by a muttered blessing.*

The above is a description of a folk charm, or cure,
which was practised not later than forty years ago in
south-east County Longford. I first heard of this cure
from an old man named Padraig O Mainnin, who lived in
Ballyferriter West, in the Irish speaking district of West
Kerry, fifty years ago. He told me it was a cure for colic in
man or beast, and he showed me how the knot was made
and loosed over the patient in the name of the Father,
Son and Holy Ghost. The conversation was completely in
Irish and he gave the cure its Irish name *Snaidhm na
Peiste*, which means the *Worm's Knot*. Having once learnt
how to make the knot, I have never forgotten it. The
knot disappears as if by magic when the two ends of the
string are pulled apart.

I never heard about the Worm's Knot again until the
mid-sixties when I was collecting folklore from an old
man named Thomas Horan, of Ballyduff, in north-west
County Offaly, about twelve miles due south of the town
of Athlone. He was talking about his childhood and describing some of the local characters of that time, whose
words and deeds, still fresh in his memory after so many
years, he enjoyed relating in his own humorous way. He
began to talk about one old man locally known as Muckshee, who lived not far away from him down in the bog.
As he was talking about this old man he suddenly inter-
rupted the story to ask me did I never hear of 'cutting the
Worm's Knot?' I replied that not only had I heard of it,
but I knew how to make it. Then he told the following
story about old Muckshee and cutting the Worm's Knot.

Kieran, my brother, could cut the Worm's Knot.
And Kieran Muckshee came up one morning [to

*Wood & Martin, *Traces of the Elder Faiths of Ireland*, New York, 1979,
pp.192–3.

narrator's house] in a terrible state.

'Where's Kieran?' he says to my father. 'I hear he can cut the Worm's Knot. The jennet is below on the pasture rolling on the ground with pain.'

So Kieran went down and cut the Worm's Knot over the jennet and he got up and began to graze. Kieran came back real proud of himself and the jennet was all right. I did not see this but I heard it.

The third occasion on which I heard of cutting the Worm's Knot was in June 1975 from an old man named Peter Byrne, of Treel, Lenamore, County Longford. The following is a transcript of a recording I made of him on 13 June '75:

Well, th' aul' horse-quacks long 'go – that'd be about a hundred years ago – they all knew about the Worm's Knot. And I used to hear th' aul men talking about it, how they were curing horses that would have a knot in their guts.

And a man, a neighbour up here, had a good horse and he got very bad with a colic pain, and he had the vet out two days or three in succession. And the vet he said it was no use in he coming any more that he [the horse] would do no good. And I was above helping at hay the same evening, and when the owner of the horse came back to the reek [i.e. rick] of hay I asked him, says I:

'What does he say today?'

'Oh! He says he'll do no good.'

'Did ye ask him what was on him?'

'Oh! He says it's incurable.'

'Would there be a knot on his guts?'

'The very thing!' says he. He says there's no use trying any further; that there's no cure.

Says I: 'If ye got Johnny Cormack to cut the Worm's Knot over him, won't he cure him? He'll get all right!'

So he went on to Johnny Cormack and Johnny knew how to cut the Worm's Knot, but he never knew that it was a cure for a horse's guts. But I told Johnny the way I heard th' aul men talking, how to get on, carry on.

That night about eleven o' clock he went on and he cut the Worm's Knot over the horse in the name of the Father, Son and Holy Ghost. And in about half an hour the horse was up and he wasn't up the whole day before. And after about half an hour they brought him out, and he was as sound as a bell. And there was never a ha'porth on the horse after [i.e. anything the matter with him].

On 25 November '83 I again discussed the cure of the Worm's Knot with Peter Byrne, when he related the matter again almost word for word as in the above account, adding however, that the name of the veterinary surgeon, who had given up the horse as incurable, was Dolan and that he was still in practice in Longford, though an old man. Byrne also added that this charm could be used only for a knot in the gut and was useless for any other stomach ailment.

Byrne accompanied Cormack to the stable where the horse had been lying for two days to make sure that there would be no mistake in making the knot, so that it would unravel when the string was pulled at each end. If the string were not freed of knots, but became tangled the horse would die. Byrne was very particular to impress this on Cormack.

But Johnny made the knot all right and the horse came all right, and in a couple of days he was as good as ever.

Keogh, the owner of the horse sold it shortly afterwards and Byrne knew the dealing-man who bought it; used to meet him at fairs around the country, and the horse lived for years 'and lived to be as auld as the bog'.

(A note on 'cut' in the phrase. According to Partridge *cut* is an English dialect usage as in the phrase 'cutting a dash', *cut* – make, do, perform.)

'Cutting the Worm's Knot' could be listed under the common folklore belief in sympathetic magic; but it is the kind of practice that should be scrupulously recorded to allow a possibly better informed posterity to make its own judgement.

Abercynon colliery

6

Wales

It was in south Wales in the middle thirties that I first became
aware of the depth of interest – human and technical –
possessed by my neighbours, many of whom were coal-
miners. I listened to their accounts of their work and of the
changes in it that were impending at that time. From them I
got a fair idea of the working of the colliery; and I went down
pits on two occasions in order to get an accurate idea of the
actual working conditions. But much later, after the war
when I decided to write about my experiences in Abercynon
and Ynysybwl – the two mines I had descended – I discovered, much to my surprise, that my experience of coal-
mines was both very small and very one-sided. Dafydd Aub-
rey Thomas, an old college friend, had moved from the
Rhondda in the steam-coal area into a medical practice at
Onllwyn a few miles farther west in the Dulais valley. In the
sixties after I got a car I used to visit him and I got to know
some of his friends in this anthracite-coal area. I soon found
out from them that, far from knowing the south Wales

coalfield, I knew only half of it. For the anthracite area I was now visiting was basically different from the steam-coal district of my home: not only the actual coal but also the method of working it, and the rhythm of social life, were noticeably different.

Dafydd Thomas introduced me to his friends who also were his patients, and I was quickly able to correct my previous idea that I knew the south Wales coalfield. Talking to John Williams, a particular friend of his, gave me an excellent insight into the organization of an anthracite mine and the differences from the steam-coal area mines where I was born. I first met John Williams* on one of my early visits in the sixties, not long after he became manager of Banwen, the local mine. I visited him again in 1975 when I recorded him on tape: he had been retired for some years and was now living with his wife at Bryn Coch, near Neath:

I started in mining in January 1918, working then with my father as was customary at the time. Each boy when he was going to the colliery would be working with his father in stall-work. And there were so many of us – there was one disadvantage of working with your father: he was not giving you any pocket-money out of the pay. So we started scheming very young indeed: we schemed to go for a spell with somebody else's father – changing, you see. We might come off with about a threepenny bit pocket-money at the end of the week. But anyway, we started at 2s 7d a day; and we were having the 2s 7d and nothing more. But if you were working with a stranger – that had no children, especially – you'd be having ninepence or a shilling. This was in the anthracite district, in a colliery owned by D. W. Davies. He had three collieries, with a total of about 1,500 men. This was in the Swansea valley.

But as for my feelings when I started work: naturally, for months before starting, I used to go down and look at

*F.M.M., p.133, *et passim.*

this slant or drift – down this drift, not only me but other
boys due to start at this time; and we were looking forward to the day we would be coming down. And we'd be
wearing moleskin* trousers about a month before starting work – except for going to school, of course. And
there were things that, personally, surprised me. I was
disappointed in some things: I was pleased with others.
But it was the way of living – all Sunday school, chapel,
and the day-school, of course. And my father happened
to be a public man, a councillor, and secretary of the
chapel, and things like that. And in those days, men like
that used to do a lot of work for people. But I looked
forward to going down the mine. Yes; and that's what it
was: a badge of manhood; because you sensed *that* before
you went into the mine, because you were wearing the
moleskin trousers. It couldn't come quick enough! I
went, as I said, on 8 January 1918, me and two other
chaps (the two have gone now, passed on now), starting
the same day. *Having our lamps*, they used to call it.
'You're having your lamp on 8 January.' The old Davy
safety lamp. As I said, I was surprised with some things
and disappointed with others. People were working very
hard – harder than what I thought; and I wanted to learn
the way to negotiate a bit too soon to suit my father, you
see. He used to tell me:

'You mind your business. Do your work!'

I used to ask him:

'What are you having for this? And what are you
having for that?' And he gave me a copy of the price-list.

John Williams confirmed the need for great skill, learned
over a long apprenticeship, in working the *face* of the coal and
in the timbering to support the roof:

Oh yes! Oh, you were taught. In the timbering the craft
was; and working then on the face. The seam is layered
on a slope, with about ten to twelve inches between the

---

*Here, the cloth: a soft, but very strong, cotton fustian.

slips. Now you'd go into the corner now [of the stall] about five yards and work in, advance in. When you were working in that direction, digging under, you were putting in what they called a *sprag* [a short wooden support] to hold that while you were doing it. Then you knocked out all the sprags and the whole of the coal would fall. Now you had to be taught those things. A stranger coming in, however scientific he was, he'd have to be taught that, however intelligent he was. You were trained to understand the layering of the coal, to know where to look for it, and how to go at it when you find it. And another thing: you were encouraged to do it, to save explosives. Now you had to pay for explosives, at a shilling a pound. A shilling was a lot of money then, perhaps one-twelfth of your day's wage. So instead of paying for the powder, you worked a bit harder and more craftily in order to save paying for explosives. You'd often hear the term: 'Now I'll do it this way, save putting the powder in.' And it wasn't enough to have a pick and shovel; you had to know how to use them. Even in using a shovel, you got to learn. It's not simply just lifting it up. No! We as boys, you know, handling the *top*, bringing the *rippings* down, hard stone. Well now, if you didn't know how to shovel, you'd kill yourself in about five minutes. So you were taught now: 'You'd just take what's on the shovel until you work yourself right under.' It wasn't enough, as I have said, to have a pick and a shovel. People had to know how to use 'em. The same with lifting things in a small space. If you were chosen to work a *heading* – a heading is the main drive where the stalls are going off – you were a skilled man. Of course, you were the kingpin! You were chosen because you could keep the road straight – for which you were paid sixpence a yard – a big thing at that time – for keeping the road straight, sixpence a yard.

The tools that the miners used were few and simple. They changed very little in the period before the machines came in.

John Williams described first of all, an old implement that has been obsolete for half a century.

> When I started there was no machinery at all; and we had to haul the coal in the face by what we called *curling-boxes*, instead of shovels; so that you could see what you were putting in the dram, to see that you were putting no rubbish in. The curling-boxes went out just after the 1926 Strike. They weren't keen on them after that. I don't know why. But that's about the time they went out; because then price-lists were moving a bit: there were changes generally in price-lists throughout the south Wales coalfield.

It is likely that the curling-box was discarded owing to the speeding-up of production following the Strike. In shape it was very much like the flat cloth-caps that the majority of men wore after the First World War. The headmaster of the county school I attended in the twenties had noticed this similarity; and one morning, to some of the fifth- and sixth-form members who were getting sheepish about wearing their small school caps, he issued this injunction:

> Don't let me see any of you boys wearing those old curling-boxes in the town, or anywhere else for that matter. You have to set an example!

I have mentioned the difference between the anthracite and the steam-coal field: John Williams returned to this topic. The price-list and the bargaining over it appear to have been doubly important in the anthracite areas because here the collieries were labour-intensive rather than capital-intensive, to use the modern jargon. The anthracite mines were on the coal-outcrop, as John Williams explains; and a small entre-preneur with very little capital could start a colliery and begin to win coal almost immediately. He would then be able to pay his wage bill from the sale of his product almost in the first week of his operation. And later as he went further in, and *opened out* his colliery he would be able to accumulate capital. The owner of the colliery, therefore, was 'one of them', one of the community, in the sense that the miners could meet him face to face nearly every day. He was not remote, even though in a different sense his interests and theirs were polar opposites: he wanting to make as much profit as he could, and they seeking – indeed forced – to improve their working and living conditions. Farther south, in contrast, in mid-Glamorgan, tens of thousands, perhaps hundreds of thousands of pounds, had to be invested before the deep coal-seams could be reached. John Williams expands this in a note written after our conversation:

> The larger companies in the Rhondda and east Wales areas were directed mainly by people who were remote from the work-force. They could lay down stricter conditions of pay; and had the power to enforce them. To a large degree, they could dictate the terms on a 'Take-it-or-leave-it' basis. Again, geological conditions in those areas were more stable: they were freer of geological disturbances, without the sharp variations you find in the anthracite field. Moreover, in the anthracite area, colliery owners were part of the community; and you could sum it up by saying: Familiarity breeds contempt.

These facts were bound to have a tremendous effect on the *feel* of the two coalfields; first in the more obvious aspect – the conditions and methods of working, their scale, their tradition and so on – and then in the community itself. Briefly, it was the difference – at least at first – between small-scale capitalism and larger, more sophisticated undertakings. John Williams brings this out in the following account which also shows how oral evidence can reveal the nuances, the contrasts and complications that shelter underneath a generalization or simplification like the *south Wales coalfield*.

> But, do you know, the mine-owner – he was a very hard man, old Davies. Him and my father used to call each other by their Christian names. I'd heard him talk a lot about old Dafydd, the owner; and I thought Dafydd was a very kind man. But when I saw what was being done for

him, and what the men were having, I was rather disappointed; and my image of David – Dafydd – passed
away. I didn't like Dafydd any more.

But there was a sense of co-operation, and you'll find it
in the anthracite more than in other places. Because you
didn't need a lot of capital – I'm digressing now – you
didn't need a lot of capital to get an anthracite mine, a
drift-mine. You were into the coal, and you were getting
your capital out of the coal. And that is how old Davies
worked his colliery. So there was an intimate feeling
between the mine-owner and the worker. They despised
each other! The result was, the miner would cheat the
owner; and the owner would cheat the miner. But in
between you got the officials, manager, under-manager;
and they were working things quietly to make it easier for
the miner. For instance, if the standard thickness of your
seam was two feet six, you'd get 1s 8d a ton for working
the coal. But for every inch below that you might get a
ha'penny or a farthing for every inch – extra on the ton.
And when the officials were coming round every week
measuring [to see how much work had been done] the
method was: the fireman to go and measure in three
places along your stall and give the average. The manager and the under-manager would be sitting back on the
road with the collier. And he'd call out:

'What's the average?'

'Oh, two foot three.'

And the seam might be two foot eight average! Well, I
thought, here's a lot of liars; else they can't measure! I
didn't realize that it was a quiet understanding between
them to get a little bit more on the ton. So I asked my
father about it and he said:

'You want to know too much. You mind your business!'

But it came to this: after a few months I'd come to
know the terminology: what was this and what was that;
and the *cogs*. These were forms of timber you were laying
down to support the roof. My father told me:

'You must sit with me now,' [to train me to negotiate].

'You must sit with me now.' When the manager or under-manager came round:

'What have you got, Joseph?'

And the fireman would call out the average; and then: 'Four and a half cogs'. Damn it all! We hadn't put a cog in, mun! I couldn't understand it now; but I didn't say anything. And I went home and I told my mother my father was a liar. You know, the image of my father was broken. I said: 'He's a liar. He's saying lies!' So I explained to her; and do you know, she couldn't under-stand it. Oh, she couldn't understand it at all! But it was something – an understanding between the management and the men. Even the owner didn't know about it.

John Williams went on to explain how the chapel and religion were involved with the work. Undoubtedly, the influence of the chapel in the mining areas of south Wales has been underestimated. It was, at least in the first two decades of the century, a lively debating ground; and the Sunday school and men's clubs often nourished a criticism of religious dogma that became a springboard for social criticism and, later, direct confrontation with orthodox economic dogma. In fact, many of the miners' leaders, especially in the early period, were active chapel members, some of them even lay-preachers who turned their gift of oratory to a nearer and more visible target – the coal-owner instead of the Devil. Naturally, there was – as in every place and at every period – a degree of social 'policy' in much of the chapel-going, as one of the more realistic miners suggested:

When there was a religious manager who was going to a certain chapel, that chapel was full; and God help the poor bugger that was drinking. He'd have a place [underground], wouldn't he! He couldn't have half a shift off to go to his mother's funeral. But it was working the same way again, if the manager was a boozer: God help the ones that were pretending to be religious!

But, all in all, in its heyday the chapel was a positive and saving force in the mining valleys helping to soften some of the inevitable hardness and brutality that the conditions of work and the periodic and recurring poverty engendered. John Williams:

> Do you know, the chapel was a big thing at the time. And my father was chairman of the *Lodge* [The trade union branch. A Lodge of the union was attached to each colliery] as well as being secretary of the chapel. I remember him telling me, years after, that they went to meet Dafydd in his house – the owner, in his house. There was a ha'penny-a-ton dispute over the price-list. And prayer first. Asking the blessing of God now on the meeting. My father, two committee-men and the miners' agent; and old Dafydd and his manager, old Peter. And then they'd go on for hours, arguing about this ha'penny. But the ha'penny wasn't forthcoming. And, of course, when it came to a deadlock, they'd all stand up and pray again for God's guidance – or something like that. That was the fashion in those days, especially down there, anyway. But inside the colliery itself: 'We can't get the ha'penny . . .' because, the fact was, Davies the owner wouldn't be allowed to give it. He was guided by the coal-owners, his fellow coal-owners:
>
> 'Don't you give more than 1s 8d for that!'
>
> But, inside the colliery, there was a whisper now, the manager whispering to my father, and we soon saw what was going on. (That's why I emphasized: what are *cogs*? a form of timber support to the roof.) For in the case of that ha'penny some arrangement came about:
>
> 'We'll give you a long post for every twelve tons of coal!'
>
> Now I'm coming back to the system of cogs [which were made from a long post]: the price of a long post was sixpence:
>
> So for every twelve tons you fill you'll get sixpence. And we'll call it a long post!
>
> So they were having their ha'penny after all. Can you follow?

The intricacies of the price-list and the complications of the bargaining, the subterfuges and double standard of morality that were used by both sides to circumvent it, were among the chief reasons why the boys who entered the industry were kept in ignorance in their early months underground. They were not admitted to the 'long-house', the society of the men, until they had absorbed the skill of negotiating as well as the skill of the craft. They had to have sharp tools in both these skills, because in the period to which John Williams is referring there was a particularly bitter conflict between the miners and the coal-owners. For coal was then virtually the only source of power: therefore it was the base of most industries. The market price of coal dictated the price of any manufactured commodity as much as did the cost of wages. Accordingly, the demand for cheap coal was perpetual and insistent; as insistent as the demand for cheap food. (Incidentally, it may be remarked as a glaring contradiction in a society that claimed to be just and equitable, that the two 'primary' classes of pro-ducers – the coal-miners and the farm workers – were among the lowest, if not positively the lowest, paid.) But the miners were at the centre-point of tension in the industrial society of half a century ago. Negotiation, skill in bargaining, was thus vital to them in order to avoid the too-sharp edge of exploit-ation. They had had a long and hard training in this, and in countering the numerous kinds of manipulation that were used in an attempt to sell them an agreement that was not basically in their own interest. This is the reason why the miners have so often become a stumbling block to an unsym-pathetic Government. Through long experience at a tension point of industrial society they recognize that democratic government as we know it is largely the art of manipulation; and they have had practice enough in detecting the trend that goes counter to their own welfare however astutely dressed or concealed it is.

John Williams continues:

But we were kept – I and the other boys, were kept out of it for a few months until you came to learn to work *your own side*: your own side of the face; and your father would take the other side. It was then you were taught to *best* the owner and how to defend yourself against him. And that is why, that is why the anthracite was different from the big companies, P.D. [Powell Dyffryn] and the Cory's, and those companies. They paid no dispute money nor no allowances or anything like that. But in the anthracite, with this intimacy between the owners and the workmen, knowing each other in public life and things like that, there was ripe, all-round cheating. There was no question about it. So when *nationalization* came now, a lot of those things had to be explained. Why! for instance, in Tirbach where I was working then, and other collieries, they'd say: 'Why! Look here! You haven't put any cogs in!' Well, the old people didn't understand that [the cogs though mythical had become their prescriptive right]. So you were having these little disputes, you see. There was a dispute in Seven Sisters over a penny a ton, paid by some other means. But when the NCB auditors came along:

'Oh, we'll check this. Oh! they shouldn't have had a penny!'

That was the reason why there were so many disputes in the anthracite coalfield – there's no question about it – when nationalization came in. Or even before when big companies were taking collieries over. There were always disputes about prices.

But I did learn very early – as I said in that [BBC] programme, *The Big Hewer* – I learned to hit with the hammer of hate against the anvil of bitterness. I was feeling – I wouldn't say I was different from the other boys; but I was more interested. I became the leader of the boys in the St Aldwyn's Award.* The boys had to be kept

---

*Under the Coal Mines (Minimum Wage) Act, 1912, a Joint Board was set up, comprising representatives of the colliery owners of south Wales and Monmouthshire, and representatives of the workmen employed in the collieries. They met at Cardiff under the chairmanship of Lord St Aldwyn. The minimum wage agreed upon for boys under fifteen was 1s 6d a day, rising to 3s 0d for a boy over twenty and under twenty-one. These were raised to 2s 3d and 4s 6d respectively by 1915.

in their place in the beginning. You mustn't know it all. You must get developed, and tuned into the wavelength, now, in this cheating. As I told you, my first reaction, when I heard about the cogs, was: 'My father is a liar! He's saying lies. He's having money on false pretences.' I didn't use that term then, of course: 'He's a liar!'

Peculiar to some collieries, they put two boys working together on shares for a period of a year or two, just to test them out. Then you'd have a place of your own. You were king in your own stall then! Because all these fathers and uncles and whatever they were – colliers – they *were* kings of the stall. And it was a wonderful society! Each couple would go to their stalls. First, there'd be a little rest period, all together – sitting down together. Perhaps twelve couples: the boys over here, and the men over there – fifteen or twenty yards between them. And you'd go on then – the term was *mwcin* (it's a word that comes from smoking). We'd say in Welsh: '*Dere! Cawn ni mwcin bach*' [Come on, we'll have a little spell]. Of course, there was no smoking going on. Then on to the stall; call to food again, later, a break. And they'd all come together again, marking to one place and sit together: men together, colliers; and the boys together. And, of course, looking back what was interesting to me in those talks: you start the week, Mondays; talk would be nothing but chapel, you see: 'Who was preaching with you last night? What was his text?' And as you go through the week, things were going away from the chapel. Looking forward now to what the team was going to do on Saturday – the rugby team, in each place, you see. And there was that cycle every week. Monday, Tuesday it was nothing but chapel, what happened on Sunday. And I remember an old fellow – he was a member of a club, mun, a drinking club – walking about three miles every Sunday (Old Will Whatley his name was); well, he was a cast-off in the middle of them all! He was somebody from the planets or somewhere!

The expression the *face of coal* has, hitherto, presupposed stall-work where the face was worked from a small area. Each stall was fourteen yards in length. Hugh Hughes (born 1915), a collier from Onllwyn, described the working of a stall as he saw it when first working with a collier at the age of fourteen:

I went to the mines shortly after I left school. I had to wait about three months for the job. Things were full up, and no jobs going; and I went out on the side of the road there every day to talk to John Samuel – he was the under-manager. It took three months: January, February, March, '29. I remember the first day I was down. I was so small, you see, I couldn't hold my lamp – the Davy lamp – like that. It would hit the floor! The collier gave me a shovel straightaway; and I started throwing coal back; and I had to throw it back to the dram. On the first day I filled at least four tons of coal. No sentiment at all. You worked together on the face. In your stall you had fourteen yards. You had seven yards on the upper side, three yards on top of the road, and four yards on the lower side. You had seven yards on the upper side because most places were on a gradient and it was easier to throw down. You had to throw that coal; and it was hard work. It was working out about a ton of coal for about a cubic yard. And if you had fourteen yards of stall, it meant you had fourteen tons of coal; and then you'd have a yard of *rippings* [rock ripped down from above the seam of coal]; you'd have to bore and blow down this from the top to make your roadway, to get your road on.

Gradually stall-work was supplanted by machines. Instead of small stalls on which two colliers worked there was now a much larger length of face, worked by a mechanical coal-cutter and a conveyor-belt to take the coal away. The men, instead of working in pairs, operated in groups. Mechanization changed mining drastically, both the structure of mining and the work-organization. John Williams said:

But a lot of changes are for the good I expect, yet as far as contentment and trying conditions are concerned the miners were much happier on stall-work – the old system. There was a better atmosphere all round. When I became manager of the colliery that I had, in so far as part of the colliery was on stall-work and the other part was on mechanization. You could do something for one or two men that you couldn't do for a group. I don't want to quote this, but I remember a case when a man had trouble at the house. His wife had a nervous breakdown, and he had three children. Now I knew about him and he came to see me and he said he was in trouble, and I told him:

'Look now, if your partner can start on his own in the morning, you come in after you've sent the children to school. And everything will be all right. Don't worry about the pay.'

Now you couldn't do that with a man in a group: working in a stall you could do it. His partner could carry on; and the man had permission to come in at half-past ten in the morning. Those are the things that were going on between management and workmen. There was 'give' in the system. But in a group you can't do it. On the other hand when you are in group work, you've got a leader in a group. Tactics now! And if there's a dispute the leader would be showing off. He'd be speaking up for the other boys. Now if you looked straight into the leader's face and bang him with your trump card his standing was going down with the others. Well, in stall-work you can *bish bash* and it would finish there. But if you got a leader down in front of the others he is discredited and you win your case.

There are far greater stresses than the old days. In mechanization a man knows instinctively he's not the master of himself. The machine is the master. The machine has taken over. And to a large degree is the cause of absenteeism. A man is afraid to meet his master. Absenteeism in stall-work was very low. (And at first

mechanization was not as tense as it was later.) Afraid to
meet the master. Soldiers are men! Men working in drift-
mines, to give an example: this mine is closing and they
had to go down pits. Perhaps they'd been in a drift-mine
for thirty years. They were bags of nerves going down
the pit, even experienced miners. I've seen them. At
Abernant colliery [a few miles away in the steam-coal
basin]. There's a drop down there about two thousand
three hundred feet. I used to go there on week-end
drainage – consulting on week-end drainage – and I used
to meet a lot of the fellows who had finished on the
drift-mines [and had been transferred to the pits]. We
went down about fifty or sixty in a cage there. I knew a lot
of those fellows; and, do you know, they couldn't say a
word. The same with mechanization: a lot of them over-
working in fear, working in fear every hour of the day.
What can you say if a man doesn't feel well in the morning? Whether it was beer or whisky or over-playing,
doesn't feel well in the morning: I'm not going into that
mess!

And the humour, of course. The noise washes all that
out. People who couldn't read or write, but they could
think very deep. There were a lot of them in the early
twenties I knew. They hadn't taken – I'll put it like this –
they hadn't taken to education. But still they had some
intelligence; and although they hadn't the advantgage of
education they were good craftsmen. You think that a
man who hasn't been educated was dumb. But it is not so!
There was more union co-operation then [before mech-
anization]: and if you weren't present at a meeting you
were on the mat. Now in union meetings about three
hundred should be there but there are about fifty. A lot
of apathy. Do you know, I think a lot of influence has
moved from the individual to the mass. The mass can
more easily be manipulated.

The south Wales miners' position today [1975]: he has
two bosses. But the only boss he knows is the one he is
working for. He doesn't realize that the machine is the

boss as well. That's the performance goes on in the colliery today. That machine – the cost cutter – has got to
advance a certain yardage during the shift. And the
noise! Do you know, some men respond to a different
wavelength: the younger you are, of course, the higher
the frequency you enjoy and respond to. Take it now,
records and things like that: I want a record when there's
a good base tone to it. But my grandson comes along and
he says: 'Let's put a dance-band on!' There's a high pitch
and I can't bear it. And the older you are, with those
machines in the colliery. If the wavelength contradicts
your response there's a clash – a real physical clash.

In playing over my recording of John Williams, it struck me
that he was an ideal exponent of the time and place he lived in
– a rewarding subject for a collector of material for an oral
history. He was an all-round man, interested and a partici-
pant in a wide range of the community's activities. One of
them was, at first glance, alien to a mining community. This
was pony-riding. He was a District Commissioner of the pony-
club organization and his son was a keen member of Banwen
Pony Club. The villages of Banwen and Onllwyn at the top of
the Dulais valley are ideal for pony-riding and the young sons
and daughters of professional people and miners get a great
deal of sport riding across the commons on the hills. The first
time I met John Williams he had been to Wembley where the
Banwen Club had won the first prize in a competition. The
anthracite area of west Wales had largely escaped the mass
migration experienced by the steam-coal, further east, and it
was still Welsh-speaking. John Williams was fluent in Welsh
and English, and I remember a saying of his which sums up
his philosophy as a manager of men: *Dewch ac nid ewch [Come
now and not, a peremptory, Go!]* Many of his short sayings
were pithy and descriptive and therefore memorable. They
also showed his hard-headed humanity: 'Collective defence is
the chief principle and not self-interest' (as he summed up the
position of the collier under the old system); and, as he
characterized the self-sufficiency a collier felt under the old

system: 'A man is king in his own stall' – a phrase that illumines the trauma of mechanization as it was experienced by the older collier in a sudden shattering of his little kingdom.

During the early thirties I spent a great deal of time walking the hills, alone usually, as my former college-friends were settled in jobs in England. After a few months the inevitable period of apathy following long unemployment set in, but I shook myself out of it by the seemingly mad resolve to teach myself to write. Instead of waiting passively for something to turn up, I began to live actively in a mind that was stiffened by a secret purpose – secret, because I hadn't the effrontery to tell anyone what my intention was. About this time I met a man about my own age, a miner's son who had set up as a commercial artist at Pontypridd, a sizeable town a few miles from Cardiff. His name was Emlyn Morgan and his home was at Ynysybwl. I knew the village well as three of my fellow-students lived there when I was at college. It was just over the *mountain* from our house. (Everybody at that time talked about 'going up the mountain' although it scarcely was more than 800 feet high. This was not a conscious attempt to exaggerate its size but merely a colloquial rendering of the equivalent Welsh word for mountain which was close enough in sound to the English word.) I used to walk over the mountain to meet Emlyn Morgan and I eventually met his family.

This was fortunate for me in my new resolve to make writing my goal, for in meeting the Morgan family I got the stimulus I needed: a group of people that was alive to the need to cultivate the mind and the spirit. This was just at the time when I had found a definite objective, and my purpose was fostered and encouraged by discussions in the ring preserved by enlightened parents. We discussed politics (inevitable at that time), literature, local tales, and the story of the small parish of Llanwonno.

John E. Morgan, the father, and his wife had five children. The eldest, a girl, had already left home when I first met them, having married a Nonconformist minister. It was a time when tuberculosis was rife in the valleys, and Emlyn the eldest of the family died with it a little later after I had left for England. Megan, the second daughter, was stricken with the disease when she was quite young, but she was subdued neither in body or spirit and lived beyond her allotted span. The two youngest of the family were boys: Morien, the second son, joined the International Brigade and went to Spain. He was taken prisoner after numerous adventures but was repatriated at the end of the war. He qualified as a grammar schoolteacher and later married Elaine Morgan, the author and television dramatist. Glyn, the youngest, after qualifying as a schoolteacher left for Essex and has written books on the rural history of that county.

John E. or Johnny Morgan, as he was known locally, started underground as a collier's boy and eventually became a *check-weighman*. In the early days the colliers were paid by the actual amount of coal each had hewn out in his stall. They filled it in a tram or tub, marked in chalk to identify it. Each tram was weighed on top-pit by a check-weighman who was a representative of the men, a union position of great trust. John E. spent his whole life in the service of the community. He was a member of many committees associated with his work: ambulance, pit-head baths, chairman of the Lady Windsor Hall and Institute, and on a number of *ad hoc* committees that were set up during the long strikes of the twenties. When he retired he was able to give more time to his lifetime love of reading, also writing occasional articles and frequent letters to friends – both in Welsh and English. He also wrote a short history of the Lady Windsor Lodge of the South Wales Miners' Federation: *A Village Workers' Council*. When he was at the beginning of his life of public service, the wages for miners averaged well under £4 a week. At the same time an individual owning £1,000 in shares in the Ocean Colliery Company, which owned the pit, drew in annual dividends of more than the miner earned in a twelve-month. It was this inequity that Johnny Morgan spent his life battling against. He got a reward on 1 January 1946 when ownership of the mines was transferred to the State. At the ceremony to mark the event John E. as the oldest workman present, as well as the oldest Federation or union official, was given the privilege of hoisting the flag of the National Coal Board to signal the taking over of the colliery.

I lost touch with the family until after the last war; but in the middle fifties, when I had been doing a fair amount of radio work, the BBC (Wales) commissioned me to make a *Return Journey* to Wales and write a script which would go on the air under that title. I stayed in Abercynon with one of my brothers. Next day I walked 'over the mountain' as I had done many times before to call on John E. Morgan and his family. He had just recovered from a long illness, and Megan, his daughter, had just had an infected lung temporarily collapsed to allow it to recover. I called 'on the hop' as was the custom in south Wales: I was confident of getting a welcome. I spent a heartening couple of hours with them. Mrs Morgan was as remarkable as her husband, a real *Welsh mam*, understanding and enduring and with an acute sense of humour. She was telling me about the recent bout of illness she had nursed, with Megan and her father both sick. She said:

The doctor had given up the both of them. The trouble was: where they were to go when it was all over? John wanted to be buried in the cemetery up here in Ynysybwl. But Megan wanted to be cremated down in Glyntaf. What was I to do if they went off together? I'd be in a real fix. One wanted to go up the valley and the other down. But there you are! You see they are both still here!

Later I corresponded with John E. for some years and still have a file of his writings. One of the topics was his early years and his attitude to religion. He first began to think hard about the Deity, as he said, when he was a very small boy. He was allowed to sit in at Communion beside his parents. He was continually puzzled as he got older by the minister's emphasis on the Father, Son and Holy Ghost. How was the believer to distinguish between them? Then as the years went by, less and less seemed to be stressed regarding the third member of the Trinity. Later during the Evan Roberts Revival of 1904, when a wave of evangelism swept through south Wales, and boozers and backsliders became temporarily converted, the first member was left out altogether and all the emphasis was on Jesus. And studying the pulpit pronouncements he began to wonder how all those who had lived before Jesus were 'saved'. He went to a convention of Fundamentalists and owing to his defective hearing practically the only words he heard at all were: 'Jesus only'. He had some vague ideas about the Jewish patriarchs who had secured 'justification by faith', but he could not justify Christ's claim that only belief in him could secure eternal life. And as he had not come across anyone who had thought as he did, he had begun to think that he was a 'crank'.

He had also thought a great deal about redemption. He was a radical thinker, it was clear, and had thought hard about the gospel story: What great sacrifice did Christ make when he knew that he would be alive again in three days and soon afterwards enthroned in glory? Many secular martyrs, he argued, had died for a cause although they had no such consolation. He had the courage not only to think logically but also to put his beliefs into practice. During the Revival of 1904 although he was a comparatively young man, he remained seated when the minister made the revivalist appeal (in Welsh), to his congregation: 'Receive Jesus now. Stand on your feet!' It was not easy when most of the people, carried away by the occasion, stood up all around him.

He had thought deeply about these matters and his thoughts were confirmed by his wide reading. He was aware that many of the people thought it was presumption to remain seated and apart; but he knew that most of the 'saved' were infected by a mass emotion. After his retirement he had often thought about the Revival, and he decided to write an account of his memory of it and his own feelings towards it. The glamour of the movement soon disappeared as he thought it would. And the protagonist, Evan Roberts himself, subsided into obscurity; and there was a rather shamefaced reaction against the memory of the emotional transport that seemed to take hold of people and sweep them along in spite of themselves. Having written his paper he sent it to Dr Iorwerth Peate, at the Welsh Folk Museum at St Fagans. He recognized it for what it was: an important document by a contemporary who had given a well-balanced, factual account of a mass phenomenon that had blown through the industrial valleys of south Wales like a disturbing wind. It was as Iorwerth Peate claimed, a valuable historic document, and should be preserved in the National Archives.

John E.'s account applied close reasoning in a province which was widely considered immune to rational examination; and I admired his courage, which was considerable when we appreciate that these events happened three-quarters of a century ago. To me it reminds me of, and bears out, what a free-thinking miner, Jim Adlam from my own home just over the hill, told me in the thirties: 'Criticism of religion is the nurse of social criticism.' And it is, by the way, a pointer to the reason why many of the radicals of this period started as members of the nonconformist churches, often Sunday School teachers. John E.'s letters and papers also bring to mind the many south Wales miners I have met and read about, some of John E.'s generation and later ones, who have distinguished themselves in the public domain against all odds and expectations: men who have become Members of Parliament and leaders of valley communities, poets and singers, after the scantiest of formal education. They were stimulated by their determination to fight against the conditions they had found themselves in, and this gave them added strength and constantly renewed it. As John E. wrote in his book, quoting another author: 'Discontent is the sacred oil that feeds the lamp of progress.' The mining of coal was such a hard taskmaster, especially as it was done half a century ago, that it was bound to breed discontent and also men strong enough to rise to its challenge, determined to change the industry. In John E.'s time the divine discontent pricked many men to better themselves and others who stayed in the industry to equip themselves with up-to-date intellectual tools, through night-classes run by the education authority or the education department of the local co-operative, and the Workers' Educational Association. They saw also, as John E. did, that their lasting hope was to combine in a strong union. This doubled a man's strength and gave him added assurance that he could better his own position not only as an individual but as a member of a powerful class.

My visit to the valleys after so many years, especially my renewal of my acquaintance with John E. confirmed my rapidly forming conviction that writing about ordinary working people was the medium I should aim at. By now I had already started on my first East Anglian book and my experiences in Wales had already conditioned the form it should take: a writing about working people. Talking to John E. again and hearing him speak again about the environment I had known since my earliest youth gave me great satisfaction, and I often regret that I had not access to a tape-recorder on that occasion. Later, towards the end of my correspondence with him he was getting old and usually wrote in bed, but in a clear and perfectly legible hand. His mind was active as ever. After his retirement he wrote his book and his essay, which is in the Welsh Folk Museum at St Fagans, and countless letters. I recently reread the ones I have about religion in south Wales. He was essentially a *political* man but one who had thought deeply about religion.

Religion was an important subject and area of discussion in south Wales in the early years of this century, and should not be left out for the reason that many of its claims cannot now – eighty or so years later – be reasonably accepted. It has at least helped countless people to battle against, and get through, life's difficulties; and as religion is, in essence, entirely personal to the individual it cannot be used as a censor to inhibit a man or woman who is accustomed to thinking for himself. Therefore it should be included in the history of any community for no people has existed without religion or without one of its earliest forms which have now been down graded to myth or superstition. And it is likely that in future man will be constrained to live with the inexplicable in some form – that is, with a constant attempt to explain or to accept a surrogate.

We, therefore, can feel justified in projecting its history forward and in assuming that oral history, particularly, will be excused the responsibility of excluding myth and religion entirely from its area of concern.

In Ipswich I met another ex-miner from the Rhondda, Richard Lewis, whose family had moved up from Pembrokeshire to the opening coal-mines when he was young. He first worked in the mines in the Rhondda, and his particular discontent had spurred him on to the long path of improvement. He eventually gained the post of Education Officer for a progressive Co-operative Society at Ipswich. He did this with great enthusiasm and efficiency. I had experience of his work, for in the sixties I took a class for two or three years at Fore Street in Ipswich. It was sponsored by the Extra-Mural Board of Cambridge University and administered by him. The class members were all old-age pensioners, and it was one of the liveliest and most responsive adult education groups I have ever taken. Soon after I met them they persuaded me of the great educational potential that had been allowed to languish during their lifetimes and had never been reaped. Like John E. in his area, Dick Lewis became a tremendous asset to the town of Ipswich. He served on the Borough Council and its various committees for many years; and sponsored two or three successful choirs in his work as Education Officer. Later he became Mayor of Ipswich, serving in this office with distinction. He also contested the Woodbridge constituency for the Labour Party. His opponent who eventually gained the seat was John Hare, afterwards Lord Blakenham. He became the Minister of Agriculture in the Macmillan Government and acquired the unenviable reputation among East Anglian farmers as the Minister who held up for display a young pig by suspending it by its tail.

Dick Lewis retired in 1966 and soon afterwards he died. His widow wrote of him:

As he lay in Maida Vale Hospital he was mentally organizing his next moves: old people, comprehensive education, civic college, the co-operative and so on, all reflecting his thought and endeavour, at all times, for the other man. His high ideals, and the effort of his always reaching out to attain them, killed him. He could never stop.

St Margaret's, the big Ipswich church was full for his memorial service.

There are other reasons why religion should not be ostracized as a topic for consideration by oral history. Apart from a doctrinal adherence to a particular religion, it should be recognized as the current form of what are now classified as myths. And the development or evolution of various religions shows the incorporation of many of these earlier beliefs and practices into a later context. For that reason alone it is a fit subject for oral history. But it has also played a great part in the lives of the older generations now living, and in the past history of our people. That this is still relevant is shown by the present conflict in Northern Ireland when the phrase applied to the seventeenth-century dispute in Scotland, 'the killing time', when Covenanters (Presbyterians) were in conflict with Royalists and Episcopalians, is unfortunately an exact description of the present-day troubles, and the seventeenth-century catch-phrase is still appropriate. Religion is also important for the central part it has displayed down the ages in art. Painters, sculptors, poets, writers, musicians, singers, and actors could all be cited as witnesses to the unworldly, undefinable part of their existence and the part it has played in their inspiration.

7

A Port and the Sea

Until 1966 most of my work had been about the rural areas but, as I have mentioned, in that year I took an extra-mural course of retired people at the Co-operative Educational Centre in Ipswich. At that time I was working on BBC feature-programmes with David Thomson, and, having access to a lively and interesting class of Ipswich people, I suggested to him that we should do a feature about the town. We prepared an hour's programme and it went on the air in April 1966.

Ipswich was a town with a long history and strangely enough had been much praised by visitors down the ages. Thomas Tusser, the sixteenth-century writer on farming, moved to Ipswich from Essex where his wife had become ill:

> Then thought I best from toile to rest
> and Ipswich trie:
> A town of price, like paradise,

> For quiet then, and honest men;
> There was I glad, much friendship had,
> A time to lie [rest].

John Evelyn, one of the founders of the Royal Society during the seventeenth century, made two visits to the town and praised it highly:

> In a word 'tis for building cleanesse and good order one of the Sweetest Towns in England.

Daniel Defoe also thought highly of Ipswich; and William Cobbett, on one of his tours during the last century, remarked on the beauty of the town with its background of a frieze of windmills perched on the surrounding hills. But a few decades after Cobbett's visit Ipswich had lost much of its sweetness. By the years of this century it was christened – perhaps unfairly – as 'The Wigan of the South-East'. As one of the speakers in the programme remarked:

> There's nothing in the Town you can get hold of with pride.

The commercial interests got into the saddle and the town sadly lacked civic leadership and inspiration to counter the blatant commercial drive. The merchant princes had their head, and trampled all the 'ancient sweetness' out of the town. There appears to have been little of the opposition of enlightened and powerful families like the Frys and the Gurneys who helped to preserve the character of the City of Norwich, or a body like the University of Cambridge that was able to act as a brake to vigorous, yet brash and self-absorbed enterprise. Yet shortly after the First World War a start was made by a newly reconstituted Ipswich Borough Council to improve the town's facilities. I talked to some of the Ipswich people about the improvements, notably to Mrs Mary Whitmore who was socially minded and had a good conception of what was needed in the town. She was a member of the Ipswich Borough Council and had been Mayor in 1948. She had been a founder member of the Workers' Education Association

founded by the historian R. H. Tawney, an organization that
is still flourishing and doing a sterling job in adult education,
especially in the eastern counties, under the title the WEA.

My plan in making the programme was to record a fairly
representative cross-section of the people of the town: in fact
to get an oral history of Ipswich compiled through the
inhabitants. But it was not called that. As I have discussed the
term oral history in 1966 had not been much used to any
extent on this side of the Atlantic. It had just begun to be
heard and came awkwardly to the tongue. I began my
recording in Ipswich in the spring of that year; and one of the
first tapes I made was of Mary Whitmore. She immediately
confirmed the woeful lack of facilities in the town at the
beginning of the twenties:*

> I was on the Health Committee for the whole of the time
> that I was on the Council. There were wonderful changes
> although there was little done at the beginning. There
> was only one clinic in the middle of the town where
> mothers could take their children. I think it was perhaps
> largely as a result of women's suffrage that there came
> this endless change of emphasis where women and child-
> ren were important; and we began developing clinics.
> That was the most important thing we did while I was on
> the Council. We saw the infant death rate go down and
> down and down. To begin with we had a very bad infant-
> mortality record many years ago; we were one of the
> worst towns in the country – a very high death rate. It
> was through these slums where they had these refuse
> bins with flies collected round them. There was no
> proper sanitation. No sewage system. The result was it
> simply went to summer-diarrhoea. There was a death
> rate of a hundred and seventy-eight. I think that was the
> highest they had which was higher than the national
> average.

> The picture of the town as far as sanitation was concerned

*BBC script: *Change in the Town*, Third Programme, 8 April 1966.

had not changed since medieval times. I read some of the annual reports of the Medical Officer of Health for the early years of this century; and they make hair-raising reading: houses in the main street without proper sanitation, in one case with a cellar full of sewage. It wasn't until the early post-war years, the early twenties, that improvements came and some of the worst slums were cleared away.

I met and recorded two old brothers who had lived most of their lives in the town. Charles Chaplin, the elder (born 1883) was a town-horseman or carter. Town horses were, as one of the group I recorded described them, usually well kept, big, heavy horses loaded with brass on their harness, all polished up and tinkling as they walked, well groomed and their muscles moving under a shining coat. Charles Chaplin was an expert in well-groomed horses. In the early years there was a regiment of soldiers stationed in Ipswich, and he admired the horses that paraded through the streets.

> All those beautiful horses up at the barracks. See them come out there: eight horses on the gun. Blokes were sitting on them. There were eight: eight bays, eight blacks, eight greys we call them, but some people call them white. Eight horses on the gun. Blokes were sitting on them and there was a postilion riding aside on them. When they went away at ten o'clock, all the chains shined like silver and the horses' coat shined like silver. But you want to see them when they come home. The shine was all lathered. The horses were all of a sweat. They been all over the Heath. Practising shifting the guns to different places. It was lovely to see them!

Charles Chaplin also visited the jail regularly as part of his job; and he was one of the few people then living in the town who had seen the prisoners on the treadmill, turning a machine to saw up balks of timber.

> I carted wood in there for them to saw up, and I carted it out when it was sawed up. An old man by the name of

Martin Krans, he was the bloke what supplied them with
the balks of wood to cut up, and he took the wood away
when it was done. And I'll tell you another thing, there's
a lot of people never seen a treadmill, ever, when they
sawed the wood up. They were in jail then, you know.
But they're gentlemen in jail now. A man I knew did six
months in jail. When he came out, the first time he came
up the pub there they said: 'Aye, aye, sir, how do you
get on in jail?' Well, he said, 'I've had a bloody good six
months' holiday!' An that's a funny thing he hadn't been
out of jail long he was in there again, another six
months. Went to Woolworth's, started putting things
into pocket again. Six more he got.

Charles Chaplin's younger brother James's, contribution
reminded me that Ipswich was an ancient river-port. But he
did not start off as a seaman.*

I wanted to be a roamer. I went away to Yorkshire on a
farm when I was about fourteen and a half. Well, I
stuck that about two years. The money there the first
year was six pounds a year. The next was eight; and the
third, when I came away from it was twelve. I came
home here then to Ipswich. I'd enough of Yorkshire. I
worked in a dairy for three months. He wanted to sell
more milk than the cows give. I had to go out with a can
of milk. I don't know, I thought, I'll get out of this; so I
went to sea. I shipped in an old ketch, an iron thing
built at Falmouth; went to Plymouth with manure. And
we were seven to eight days from Deal to Plymouth: and
I wish I'd been on the farm, I might tell you. The wind
blew for seven days. When we got there it was all right. I
was going home: I reckoned I'd finished. But I didn't; I
stuck it.

I was on all sort of craft: ketches to brigantines.
Schooners, two-mast schooners, three-mast schooners.
All sailing ships, yes. Yes, I never went in steamship till

*BBC programme script. A fuller account in *D.T.W.H.S.*, pp.167–72.

about 1913, I suppose I was a man then, of course, a man, twenty-six,-seven year old.

As soon as steam came in the pace quickened up. Little steamers don't stop in port above a day or maybe one night. Might not – all depends if you was lucky. Oh yes, it took them no time to get the cargo out, you see. With steam head-winches – up she went. Fifty or sixty years ago you wouldn't see hardly a steamer in the docks. It would be all sailing ships and sailing barges. Of course, things are altogether harder, I suppose, if they get things to go faster. Still, I think I'd sooner have the old days when they went a bit slower, myself. It was hard work, but you used to get your enjoyment out of yourself. Oh, there's no enjoyment now much, is there? Wherever the pub is, whether it's in the docks or round the corner in the town: it doesn't make much difference.

I asked him whether there was enjoyment like singing on board ship. Sea shanties?

Ay, the big deep-water ships there were, yes. We never used to: we never had enough of us. There weren't no shanties. Hadn't got time for shanties. We never done much singing aboard, especially some of the boats. They had no bloody grub to sing on.

The latter part of James Chaplin's career was spent on the river at Ipswich. The docks at the port could not take large ships as there was not enough draught of water. Therefore the ships anchored in the Orwell Estuary at a point called Butterman's Bay, and from there they were lightered to the docks – the cargo conveyed in barges. The ships were moored on the Bay with stout ropes fixed to the bank. Chaplin mentioned the black rats that came in with the cargoes:*

They used to have things on the rope, bits of tin; pinned around the ropes so that the rats couldn't get ashore. It was the black rats what got ashore. In every port it was

*BBC script: *Change in the Town*, Third Programme, 8 April 1966.

the same. They were very strict on that business, the sanitary people. They'd come aboard and try and destroy all they could see, or get the crew to do it. They wouldn't do it, of course. And they'd have tins built around their ropes, their mooring ropes that went ashore. So that when they go to the tin they'd stop and they go back again then to the ship.

Another Ipswich man connected with the sea was Stanley Threadkell (born 1888).* His son was the captain of an ocean-going ship and naturally he was very proud of him and often spoke about him. His affection for Ipswich and the Orwell and his knowledge of the river's history were outstanding. There is plenty of evidence that the shipbuilding industry was flourishing in the latter half of the century. Suffolk oak was famous for its rot-resisting qualities and large quantities were transported to the royal dockyards. In the seventeenth century it was used for building many types of vessel, particularly colliers for carrying coal from Newcastle to London. As long as timber and sail were the materials of shipbuilding the construction continued but it never moved on to steam and iron. Stanley Threadkell recorded:

Ipswich at one time was known as the *London Shipyard* because most of the London merchants had their ships built at Ipswich, from the Suffolk forests which were mainly of oak. And the woods round were near and handy: the timber had not far to be hauled and it could be brought to the shipyards easily. I remember the remains of some of those old yards. There was one shed on the Wherstead Road: I remember as a child seeing this and I wondered whatever the shed was for. Eventually it was found out that it was a shed built over one of the launching ways.

After the sailing ships went out the barges came into their own – the coastal barges. There was quite a number of them built at Ipswich. Some went as far as Dublin;

*D.T.W.H.S., pp.172–4.

others went up the north. And these were wonderful ships because they were manned by just a man and a boy; and they carried a huge amount of sail in proportion to their size. We had all sorts of sailing ships in, boats from Valparaiso, Sebastopol, Melbourne; and on the jib boom, if you saw a shark's tail, you would know that the ship had come south of *the line* – been below the Equator. This was a sign among the sailors. On the way over they evidently caught a shark; and they could cut off the tail and nail it on the jib boom. There were another type of ship there which among the local people was called *Yonkers*. They were Norwegian, and they got the name from the pumps. Their pump was driven by a small windmill aft of the main mast; and, of course, the pumps were going yonk, yonk, yonk, and that originated the name of *Yonkers*. They came into Ipswich with either timber or ice. Before the people had refrigerators the blocks of ice were loaded there. I've seen tons of ice as large as tables, chopped out of the Norwegian fiords and brought over in these Norwegian ships.

There was a hospital ship, a ship used for smallpox cases, and the name was rather unusual. It was the *Bokanko*: it was a small barge, about 40 tons, with a deck and rail for an awning. And when there was a serious case of smallpox in the town, they were taken out and the *Bokanko* was towed about a mile down the river and anchored down there. It was an isolation ship left down the river. There was another unusual ship we had up here. We had the old convict ship, *Success*, which was a lot of interest to visitors. This convict ship was used to transport the criminals from England to Australia. It was, as far as I remember, a barque – three-masted and about 800 tons. The holds were in tiers. There were above five tiers; and it was a most awful ship to go aboard; and to go down and see the cells. The way these prisoners were being confined at that time of day! It was being taken round the country then as an exhibition ship.

James Chaplin had mentioned that the sanitary people were
very concerned about the black rats coming ashore from the
ships moored in Butterman's Bay. They had reason to be
alarmed for the rats were the carriers of fleas which transmit-
ted a disease to human beings with a mortality rate of 75 to 80
per cent. At this stage in my research for the programme I was
lucky enough to meet Dr David van Zwanenberg who was
researching these outbreaks and agreed to take part in the
programme. The disease with the alarmingly high mortality
rate was the bubonic plague, the disease that swept through
England in the fourteenth century, recurring at intervals
during later centuries. Dr van Zwanenberg:

> The last outbreak of plague that occurred in this country
> occurred along the shores of the river leading up to
> Ipswich and was traced back to rats coming ashore from
> these plague ships. In the years between 1906 and 1918
> there were about twenty cases of plague occurring near
> the river. Only five of those survived. In an intense inspec-
> tion in 1910 to 1911 many rats were found to be infected
> in twenty-seven different farms in the areas along the
> banks of the rivers Orwell and Deben. The plague is
> transmitted from rats to human beings through the fleas.
> The last case occurred near Shotley in 1918; and since
> then there's not been a true outbreak in England,
> although one case occurred accidently in a laboratory a
> few years ago.

To get the full picture Dr van Zwanenberg managed to trace
one or two survivors of the 1918 outbreak and was able to gain
marginal information to fill in details he obtained from the
documents: questions chiefly about living conditions at the
time; number in family, whether they lived in the old *two-up,
two-down* type of dwelling and where they got their drinking-
water from. They also had memories of the quarantine ship
with its yellow flag and place of anchor down the river.

The last excerpt of Ipswich oral history of twenty years ago
concerns an enterprising Scot who came south to Suffolk and

became a figure in the town. His grandson, Robert Pratt, tells the story. With his brother, Robert Pratt had a tailoring business which was well known among country people all over east Suffolk:

Well, I'm speaking now about my grandfather. He was very good at his trade of grocer and he saw an opportunity which existed at that time in the sale of tea. (This was towards the end of the last century.) Tea was a commodity rather confined to gentry because they had to take delivery by the chest, which meant that it was quite outside of the village and cottage dweller: they couldn't buy tea. The only chance they ever had of tasting a cup of tea was to get somebody on the staff of the big houses to surreptitiously take a little from a caddy. So my grandfather, seeing that the poorer classes could benefit by a cup of tea, decided that he would start blending his tea to suit the water, and carry the tea on his back. Remember, tea is very light: you can carry quite a quantity in a pack. And he became a packman and he travelled the villages here, round about Ipswich with this pack of tea on his back. He made it up into little packets and sold it to the country folk. Well now, he must have been very successful with this until the time came when the big concerns started selling packed-teas. This did affect his trade, but being a very go-ahead Scotsman he wasn't going to be put off by that. He had by that time bought himself a pony and trap; and – in a strange way I suppose – came to sell clothes. No doubt someone who he was selling his tea to said that they wanted something from the town in the way of a suit for their son, Jimmy: and he said:
    'Right. Well, I'll bring you one.'
No opportunity lost, you see! And from that he built up quite an extensive business in clothing. By virtue of his weekly or monthly calls, he could take the money for these clothes by instalments. That really is how the present business came to begin. I don't know how many ponies and traps he had but it was quite a considerable

number. And he did succeed to the extent of becoming a Town Councillor in Ipswich, where on the Council he earned himself the nickname of 'More Light Pratt'. The way that came about was this: Ipswich was poorly lit, as probably most towns of that period; and he felt that electricity being something new had great advantages to offer. He had to make his calls for his payments in some very dark alleys and courts where there was no light whatever. And he knew, perhaps better than most, what went on in those dark back roads.

Pratt, therefore, acted on his conviction that electricity was what Ipswich needed, and he decided to go back to Scotland to visit Glasgow, one of the first cities to install electricity. He studied the electrification of the city; and when he got back to Ipswich he sold his idea to the Council.

As a result of that Ipswich got its electrical undertaking and finally got its trams. And the elder Pratt got his undying nickname.

Going back to the sixties and to the transcript of the programme I recorded then, confirmed me in what I had first noticed in early Blaxhall recordings: the verve and the sinewy texture of the language of the men and women who were born in the eighties of the last century. They were nearly all brought up in contact with the land, and used language that was steeped in centuries of continuous usage, describing processes and situations and customs that had gone on uninterruptedly since farming began. It was as if their work, the work of their hands, had fashioned their tongue, and moulded their speech to economical and often memorable utterance.

James Chaplin is a good example. Like many of his fellows on the land he had wrestled with that other intractable verity – the sea; and this is probably what makes his language stand out from the other townspeople's. For reason of time, only a short excerpt from my field-recording was included in the final script. But I had saved the tape, and included it in much fuller form in one of my later books.*

In the last section I have touched on what has been a large and essential part of the life of many people who have lived in this part of Britain. This is the sea and the occupations connected with it. It is oral history in the double and authentic sense in that it is recording contemporaneous occupations, their recently displaced forms, as well as recording their long historical roots that are still visible. This is an aspect that is often omitted in oral history disquisitions: the emphasizing of the historical continuity that inheres in most of our exercises and the necessity to emphasize and point to the unbroken connection. I cite a Suffolk writer, David Butcher, who has done this and uses the oral history technique in his books about the sea. His last book was commissioned by the Fisheries Research Institute at Lowestoft and will be published later. In this he has recorded the accounts of about twenty people, giving the locations where they caught the different species of fish all around the British Isles. This book will be an invaluable record and will serve future fishermen, and also make an essential contribution to fishing research.

He has written four books: my preference is for the third where he records about twenty men and women, nearly all fishermen and *beatsters* (women who repair the nets) when fishing was at its peak. I have been encouraged by his developing independently, the same method that I had evolved in oral history of establishing a real friendship with the people who give the information, because it is a type of research that needs an entirely different approach: you are not consulting a document but asking questions of a person. The interview is a friendly talk.

My introduction to the seafaring life of the region was through the townspeople of Ipswich about twenty years ago. But since then I recorded at different times a few *joskins*, farm workers who went fishing for the home-season; a hay-merchant who was closely connected with the home-fishing season, through supplying the occasional hawkers with hay

*D.T.W.H.S., pp.167–72.

and often with horses; a fish-curer with a fair-sized business in Yarmouth; and, last of all, a three-generation fish-hawker. I had often to make a conscious choice in talking to these men: if Charles Hancy, the hay-dealer, digressed to talk about the fishing people, should I let him expound only on subjects that are directly concerned with hay? Experience has taught me to choose the first alternative and not to attempt to keep to one topic, hoping to return later to the side question. This is always a risky exercise. The informant will often be loth to go back to recount something which you hadn't given him room to include. He may even have *gone into the mole country* and you will never see him again, and possibly some rich material has been lost. My method in collecting material from old country people is to consider it, in the first instance, as a salvage operation. You attempt to get a full tape without rigidly excluding anything as long as the informant keeps roughly within the area of the material you want.

Charles Hancy is a remarkably good informant and he gave me a good deal of information about the fishing trade although it was not his line. He told me that a Scotsman, Barney Sutherland, came down from Scotland to both Yarmouth and Lowestoft bringing forty or fifty horses down which he hired out to the temporary fish-hawkers who toured the villages during the home-fishing season. Charles Hancy's father had also used him to get a few horses to hire out. He would meet him at a point nearby called Blindman's Gate on the road to Norwich:*

> We used to bait there or at *Carlton Crown*. They'd go and lay half-a-quid down so that there was beer.

Blindman's Gate at Barnaby was popular with the fish-hawkers:

> This gate hangs high and hinders none:
> Refresh and pay and travel on.

That's what they used to say. That's done away with now. I met some characters; and when I think of it now, you got

*D.T.W.H.S., p.142.

to be half a character yourself to get away with some of them. Yes, you met all classes o' people. There's no travellers on the road now, is there? There were gypsy chaps, good class of gypsy class; then there were those what we call *diddicoys*, like, hedge-crawlers. They were a rum little lot. Yeh! But there were some good chaps with the gypsies, good-dealing chaps. They were chaps – well, whenever they went once they could go again. There was a family round here, the Turners. Well, if you wanted a hackney, they'd bring you a hackney.

Horace White* was in the First World War. He was born in Kent of East Anglian parents, but when he was a young boy his mother moved back with him to north Suffolk. He was a natural for an oral historian, and I knew him for many years and recorded him many times. I first met him at a WEA class in the Saints area of Suffolk about 1960. And when we moved to Norfolk I used to see him quite often just over the border in north Suffolk. He worked latterly with the Norfolk and East Suffolk Catchment Board (the river authority). Later he became a Rural District Councillor, on the same Council as Adrian Bell (the Suffolk writer) with whom he was friendly. Horace White had an ultimate grasp of the disposition of power in the rural scene; and he was an unusual voice among the farmers, clergymen and retired military men. He spoke his mind without fear, but he got on well with most of the Council because they respected his sincerity.

He had many jobs after the First World War after being demobilized from the army. He worked first of all with an army unit, gathering hay from farms round the Saints (the area between Bungay and Halesworth, so called as the names of the villages were known by Saint: e.g. Ilketshall St Lawrence, or All Saints, St Elmham). They were clearing the last of the hay that had been commandeered and bought from the farms, and now they were selling it to Horace White:†

*D.T.W.H.S., *passim*.
†Ibid., p.102.

It was a decent job. You took two horses and a GS (General Service) wagon which was used by the army. It was used for anything. I'd used to carry corpses in France, I had. That was when they were dying with the flu. But it was a general-purpose wagon. Now it was carting hay. I walked miles behind it. It had a brake, and if you was brakesman you had to walk behind.

He then went herring fishing from Lowestoft:*

After I'd finished with the hay, work was very difficult to be got. It was not much, sitting at home playing cards. I'd got a brother come out of the army about the same time as me: he came out and there was nothing doing. We used to sit there in front of the fire: we could sit playing cards; and Mother would come to clean up; and when she'd finished we'd get back again! I thought: 'Well, it's time I got cracking and got away from here. I'll have to be doing something. This won't do!' So I went up to London, and I thought I'd get a *pier-head jump*; and I went down the docks, the East India Docks. You don't get this pier-head jump? Well, if a ship was a feller short, someone who hadn't turned up, they'd take anybody who was around and willing to go. The boat would be held up in the Port of London, perhaps in one of the locks. You'd get on the boat; and if they were short they'd sign you on, if not they'd clear you off pretty quick. I was staying in Lemon Street and Wells Street; and I was prepared to take anything that was going in the shipping line. I was offered a job in an eating house where I used to go and get some dinner. But that – I didn't fancy that game: I wanted to go to sea. Eventually, I got on a boat and went down to the locks; but it happened to be another chap who was lucky, and I didn't get away with it. But that evidently altered my life!

Anyhow, money began to get short, so I had to get cheaper lodgings. So I went into the Salvation Army hostel, Middlesex Street, Petticoat Lane – do you know it? But I finished up getting lousy there. So there was nothing more but to come home; clean myself up. I met a chap there, too, a great big chap I knew in France; as soon as I see him and the state he was in, I thought: 'This won't do either!' So I came home; cleaned myself up and went down to Lowestoft; and I went off Lowestoft on what they call *springing* at that time o' day: that was catching spring herren [herring] just a few herren used to be off there. I went a couple o' trips with that, just to get the hang of it. Then I went down to Lowestoft again, and I see a pal o' mine from the village, and I said:

'Have you got a crew yet?'

And he said: 'No, go and see the old man.' So I saw the skipper and he asked me: 'Have you been to sea afore?'

'Yeh, a bit,' I said. But he let me go: he wouldn't sign me on. But I hadn't gone along the dock very far afore a feller came running after me:

'Our old man want to have another word with you.'

I went back and he say:

'Look!' he said, 'you're fit enough, big enough. You can have a *three-quarter shareman's* berth. Come down here tomorrow morning looking something like a fisherman.'

I said: 'All right.'

Well, I went down and I bought the whole gear. That finished my army gratuity money off! Bought second-hand gear: jackboots – there wasn't many rubber boots about then, leather boots – *balm-skin** oily-long-smock; you got to have two or three *shiftenings*† and army kitbag, and a *go-ashore* suit.

Well, I done a bit of scraping [the hull] next day; and the owner he chucks a couple o' bottles of rum aboard. He was called H. W. Blanchflower; and the boat was the *Homeland* (LT – Lowestoft – 125). Well, they were a long

---

*Oil-skins, or *barm-s*. See *English Dialect Dictionary* (Joseph Wright, H. Froude, London, 1898).

†*Shiftening*, (East Anglian dialect) a change of linen.

time issuing out this rum: we'd been at this scraping several hours. I said: 'I don't know why they don't issue the rum out the old man brought aboard!' But no rum! They told me afterwards that they thought I'd be seasick! 'Blast,' I said: 'they put owd Nelson* in it after he was dead; and I'm sure I could manage it while I was alive. I'd ha' drunk that, seasick or not!'

Horace White went on two or three voyages, one to Fraserburgh, but he earned very little. His younger brother earned a sizeable sum on his voyages. Apart from this he did not enjoy his sea experiences, although he had the consolation of knowing that conditions were much worse fifty years before.†

I heard old Elshie Peck say that conditions were very bad when he went fishing. That was well back in the last century. They never had a ladder: they had a pole from the cabin. Some of these old skippers were very cruel to the boys, real cruel. I believe even to this day you got the toughest and roughest men here in the East Coast fishermen. But the conditions were very rough in these boats then, just after the 1914–18 War. You never had a toilet aboard them things. You never had anywhere to hang your oily-smock, and if you washed more than once a week, you was told they didn't bring water for you to wash with. You went down into the engine-room and had a damn good wash there on Saturday or Sunday. You never washed otherwise. When you had a wash you went ashore: put your *go-ashores* on.

Horace White was a very responsive long-standing friend. I often used to call on him at the village of Spexhall just off the main road through Halesworth to the coast. His second wife died, and he often called at our cottage on his way to Norwich. In a summer in the late seventies I had been away on a course at University College, Bangor in north Wales. Shortly after my return I heard of his death. He had died suddenly

*After Trafalgar, Nelson's body was brought home in a barrel of rum.
†*D.T.W.H.S.*, pp.184–5.

while I was away. I regretted not being present at his send-off. He was not a man you could easily forget. As well as being a very companionable exponent of oral history he was the sort of man you were always glad to meet.

Another aspect of sea-fishing was the curing and exporting, chiefly of herring. About twelve years ago I got in touch with Herbert J. Scarles (born 1906) of Yarmouth who was one of the last of the long-standing fish-curing firms:*

My grandfather was an exporter of cured herring to the Mediterranean and the Continent; and also my father up to the beginning of the First World War. A fish-house such as the one I was born in was a real working-unit, with its own stables, horses, carts, harness-room, box-making shed, a cooper's shop, where all the barrels used were made in the 'off-seasons', paper-stores, office, fore-man's house, workers' change-and-rest-rooms, salt-, dust-, and *shruff*† stores, smoke-houses; and of course stacks of oak-billet to be used strictly in date order, stacked up to and over twenty-five feet. But everything was as clean as a new pin, scrubbed and scoured – a place for everything and everything in its place. Our fish-house opened for full working on 1 September: the end of the herring-fishing season with us was the 30 November.

The first method of preserving herring was no doubt by salt, either by salting the fish as caught, or after removing the gut; *gyping*. For export trade the herring was always salted like this on the floor. Dry salt was mixed well in with the herring by *rousing*‡ them, turning them with a wooden spade, like the maltsters use, after the herring had been left in heaps or *cobs*; one or two men

*D.T.W.H.S., pp.190–205.
†Wood-shavings.
‡Cf. William Blake's 'The First Book of Urizen':
  He lay in a dreamless night,
  Till Los rouz'd his fires, affrighted
  At the formless, unmeasurable death.

throwing on the salt as two men roused, repeating once
or twice to get the herring and the salt thoroughly mixed.
The heap was then covered with a tarpaulin. But for local
shop-trade the herring was soaked two or three hours in
a salt solution or pickle and then smoked for four to eight
hours. You could make *reds*, the Yarmouth red herring
in a brine solution, left for forty-eight hours but turned
over and stirred after twenty-four; and then smoked
until they were a mahogany colour. These were sold in
the home-market. But for export they were always dry-
salted in *cobs* on the floor. The *Yarmouth red* or ham-cured
herring was processed by curing with salt, and then with
smoke in a way that is similar to the traditional curing of
ham by smoking it in a large open-hearth chimney.* The
Scotch cure is the process of preserving the herring after
it has been gyped.

The curing of herring is a complicated process and great
care has to be taken at the various stages, for instance, the
salting, the firing to smoke the fish, and supervising the
different forms of turning:

As I've said, the ham-cured Yarmouth *red* was salted on
the floor of the *barf-house*,† by rousing and then covering
until processing time. After being washed in the vats of
fresh water they went into troughs on each side of which
stood the women ryvers. A ryver would hold the *speet*
[spit], a rounded length of wood about four feet long and
tapered at one end. With the blunt end under her arm
she would ryve onto the sharp end as many herrings as
directed – about twenty-one herrings; this was the average – leaving a few inches clear at the sharp end of the
speet. You open the fish at the gills on one side, push the
stick in and out through the mouth; the herring then
hangs down on the stick so that it can't slip off. A ryver
would probably do five or six speets like this, supporting

*A.F.C.H., p.67.
†The shed or building where the first stage of curing takes place.

them across the trough, before *spacing*. To do this she balanced the pointed end of the speet on the trough, and drew the fish along to the blunt end, spacing them with her fingers at the same time. She left ten to twelve inches clear at the blunt end. She had now a speet with two clear ends for holding and hanging on the frames for smoking. By spacing with her fingers she not only equalled the distance between each fish, but straightened any fish that might have curled up, due to lying unevenly and then being stiffened by the salt. Fish so touching were called *clappers*; and after ryving they were dealt with by the *hangers*, the men who hung the fish in the smoke-house, so that the smoke could circulate between them. Filled speets were hung on a *horse* (wooden arms on a wooden upright) or on trestles, beams with short legs and heavy foot-pieces. In some cases the fish would be washed again, and then allowed to drip before going to the smoke-house. Herrings with damaged gills or heads (these were called *tenters* or *tanters*) were hung on *bourkes* or *baulks* – lengths of wood holding L-shaped nails.

The smoke-house is a lofty building; at the top – on the sides – are a series of *wickets*, wooden shutters controlled by ropes from the ground. These can be adjusted according to requirements, depending on the strength and direction of the wind, to help draw the smoke upwards or stop down draughts. The house is divided into *luvs* or *louvres*, frames extending from near the floor to the ceiling. On these the spits, full of herrings, are hung. The doors to the houses are like those in stables, in two halves [half-hatch] to assist control of the draughts in the smoking. The *hanging* of a full house of herrings calls for some experience.

But one thing I've omitted to tell you: about the *night-smoker*. He was on duty all night to replenish the fires as required, and *strike* [remove] any of the lower fish that had already been sufficiently cured.

The fires were built like camp-fires on the floor in between the *luvs*, a row of fires here and a row there.

Because there – we are talking of these herrings as being the long-cured fish for export, do you see, we are talking now about the red, exported herring. The amount of time needed to cure a red herring would be a matter of decision to the curer: to give them as much as they could take without wasting any; because they would gradually *pine* by the continual smoking.

Herbert Scarles gave some interesting notes on the different kinds of cured herring:

The bloater is a light-cured herring, lightly cured a silver colour. The process was discovered by a Yarmouth man named Bishop about 1835. One night he found a small quantity of herring that had been overlooked. So after salting them he ryved them and hung them in a *house* where a fire was already alight. Next morning he was delighted with their appearance, and later on their taste. So he began marketing them.

There was more of conscious design about the origin of the kipper:

It was a Newcastle man who originated the kipper in 1843: John Woodger of Newcastle. (I knew his grandson.) He cured them in one of those old country-house or cottage fireplaces, the sort you can sit in, stand in and look right up the chimney to the stars. It was known as the *Newcastle kipper*: and his first consignment went to London shortly afterwards. They became as famous as the Yarmouth bloater. John Woodger came to Yarmouth where he had a curing works, and started in a big way.

Here is a note about the history of the herring, showing that Yarmouth had been a port for hundreds of years before the herring industry fell away.

The close season was from the end of November. The Scotsmen went home; but the continental fleet used to fish, and so did some of ours, and land the herring on the Continent where they were processed and used for manure. But it was finished as far as we were concerned because there was no more quality. They'd spawned; they'd shot their roe and were *shotten*. *Shotten herring* as Shakespeare called them, a spent herring, unfit for human consumption, as far as we were concerned.

Counting the herring or *telling* cost an enormous amount in wages, an enormous amount for the telling of the fish. *The Statute of Herring* (1357) fixed the method of counting: there were to be four herrings to a warp (counted by picking up two fish in each hand: shotten herring meant a double count; two shotten herring counted as a full herring). There was six score to the *hundred*, a long hundred (120); and ten hundreds to the *cran* (1,200); and ten crans to the *last*.*

The fish-hawker or retailer was an important member of the fishing industry. To get an insight into this section of it I recorded Robert Thomas Spindler (born in 1890). He was living in Wenhaston, Suffolk when I met him ten years ago:

We have been in the fish trade for a lot of years, the Spindlers have, for a lot of years. The Spindlers have served the Bloises of Cockfield Hall for 132 years – Sir Gervase Blois who died a couple of years ago proved that from books that he found in his father's bureau which had been there for donkey's years. I served him, my father served him, my grandfather served him, and his grandfather served him. We always traded in fish, and I do now even at eighty-four. The Blois family had a monthly book, and somehow Sir Gervase was cleaning out and he read some of these. I think he burnt them all because they were no further use to him. I feel sure he did for there was a servant who worked for him said he had a clear-out: there was so much. It's a big house, Cockfield Hall. It was damaged badly during the war, and he had a huge amount of money war-damage; and

*About two tons in weight. *D.T.W.H.S.*, pp.206–13.

they spent every penny on that house. It's a beautiful
house. As a matter of fact I go there tomorrow delivering
fish.

When we were boys I and my brother next to me – I
was two year older than him: he's dead now – we would
work like men. My father was also a horse-dealer and
would go to these sales and buy horses; and we had a lot
of *laid down* meadows, we called them then; and we had
to go and ride a horse that had to be sold on a particular
week. We liked it but we didn't realize how hard we
worked because we were happy in what we were doing.
And we didn't have much money! I remember when we
went to Sunday school we had a treat once a year – which
was to go to Dunwich. The farmer used to lend a wagon
and a pair of horses to pull, and we used to sing our way
to Dunwich. There was a church on the edge of the cliff
there. I can remember that church well, but it's gone now
completely – into the sea.

I left school. The schoolmaster said to my father: 'Take
Bob away: I can't learn him any more.' So I left when I
was ten and a half, and when I was eleven I was driving a
pony and cart to the near villages round where we lived.
Then when I was thirteen or fourteen I used to go with
my father to Lowestoft buying fish. He used to buy, then
he learnt me to do it. Then I had to work hard packing
what he had bought, getting it away to London and
various places. That went on for some time. That would
be 1904. There were times when I had to go out with
carts intermediate between going to Lowestoft, and
sometimes I couldn't go because I was going on a round.
I've driven a horse and cart when I was twelve years old
from seven in the morning to seven at night selling fish,
day in day out. And you'd only got your overcoat in hail,
blow or snow. It was a helluver a life! But we had to do it.
You had to earn something when your father got nine of
you to keep. You got to earn some money, hadn't you?
You had to help. Well, what you did, you got your own
living. He didn't have to pay to keep you.

There's a place called Dennington Bell. Well, all the
fish carts used to pull up there. We used to meet there
and have some bread and cheese and beer. I've seen as
many as twelve, all doing the same job, selling the same
thing. Then you had to make haste and get out because
you had to take a certain amount of money which wasn't
much. You'd have a good day if you took a £1. And that
would be getting to where you went and doing the
round: it was almost twelve hours and you'd only taken a
£1. And all the cost of the fish got to come out of that.
But there it was, the life! Everybody was in the same boat.

But Bob Spindler couldn't escape experimenting with the
actual fishing. It was disastrous:

Are you interested in the actual fishing that used to go on
from Lowestoft? There used to be five men to go on a
boat. They were little sailing boats and they went all
round, down to Ireland and Cornwall at different times.
And at that time o' day they didn't get any wages. If they
earned anything, when they came back to Lowestoft they
had it. If they were in debt, which they were very often,
they hadn't a penny. And there was this parish here,
Wenhaston, and Westleton which is the next one, there
were about 150 men went to sea out of these two
parishes. I've heard them say if the owners gave them
their fare home from Lowestoft to Darsham, that's all
they had. And the wives had been living on credit to the
grocer in the village. There was one here and there was
one there; and they'd stand the food until they come
back. If they had a voyage they paid for it. If they didn't –
well, the grocer didn't do too good. One here – they said
he went bankrupt through it. But what happened at
Westleton I don't know. My father was born at
Westleton. I've heard him say how he went to sea and he
done two voyages. He got married just before he went to
sea, and he done two voyages and he didn't earn anything. And he was going again, but when he wanted his
clothes to go my mother had cut them up and burnt

them! So he had to go and get a job on the land, for ten shillings a week. I don't know how many of us were born then – three or four, I expect. (We were nine children in all: six boys and three girls.) But he had to keep us on that. But eventually he got a horse and cart, and he went into the fish trade.

Bob Spindler succumbed to the call of the sea about the same age as his father:

And these fellers used to go to sea like that; and in these boats they were gone ten and twelve weeks, and they slept in little bunks, and they never changed their clothes the whole time. I know that! I went once. I had to go for consumption. It cured me! One week, that's all I was there. They were afraid to take me any more. There was something the doctor couldn't move on my chest – what he thought was consumption. Didn't it move! It nearly took me off. I bled on the afterdeck so much I heard the skipper say to the mate:

'I shan't bring him any more when we get to Lowestoft.' I heard him and I thought to myself:

'I'm the best judge about that. You let me just put my foot on that shore, you'll never get me here again.'

I never went to sea any more. It cured me! Consumption I had, I'm told. That was my only seafaring experience. And when I came ashore – I'd been there a week – he gave me ten bob. It was kill or cure! Did I bleed! The afterdeck – of course those boats weren't so big as they are now – all where I laid, it was all over the deck. It frightened the life out of them. But I was then – well, I didn't care if I did die. It would be better to be dead. Yes, I went on that voyage as cook, and the beauty of it was the boat was called the *Happy Days*! But that cured me. After that I never had any illness. The only illness I ever had was twenty-five weeks in a hospital in Rouen with dysentery. I was four and a half years on the Western Front as a stretcher bearer and only one of the worst cases who had it and lived through it. I weighed eleven stone when I was in the Line: before I came out with that I weighed five stone ten. Then I came home to England on a stretcher. Apart from that I've never had a day's illness in my life; never been in bed a whole day. I might have been in bed with measles when I went to school, but nothing else.

The Spindlers used to cure their own fish, herrings which they brought in barrels from Lowestoft. Salting the fish on the concrete floor for twenty-four hours, and then hanging them. They burned oak that had been seasoned for three or four years. Only oak would do. If pine was used you could taste it in the herring:

Fish-curing was hard work: we had a rough time. I've seen my mother standing, what they call *speeting* herren, that is putting them on sticks to make bloaters, and when she finished she had to lay down. And they'd pull her dress off her, and it was frozen stiff. I had to cart water for her. They were hard days. There were no easy days, those days. We cured all our bloaters and our kippers, at one time. Of course, they've got out of all recognition today, but three a penny fresh herren were at that time. We had two big smoke-houses in the garden. We could put 10,000 fish in one. We used to put these herren up for red herren during the winter, and we'd probably put three lots or consignments. But we always put one par-ticular herren what we called the *October blue-nosed* her-ren because they never wasted when they were hung up. And they used to be like ham. They used to be sent to London and various places; and when we'd done all that we got four shillings a hundred for them. And in that one house we used to do 30,000 or more – we'll call it 30,000 – in three hangings.

Since history began, the sea has been the second great medium East Anglians have had to wrestle with; and during my work on the history of fishing I have been impressed by the number of irrational beliefs they have held connected with sea-fishing. I have collected a few of the more common superstitions because at one time many farm workers used to do a spell of fishing during the East Anglian fishing-season. A common one was the conviction of old fishermen that if they met a parson on the way to their boat they would have an unsuccessful voyage and it would be just as well to turn back. This is an extremely old belief which antedates Christianity and stems from a time when the form of society was matriarchal, and the prevailing belief was in a Mother Goddess (Ga Mater) in one of her many guises: Diana, Epona, or the White Goddess. Any representative of a Father God was therefore unacceptable, and parsons were shunned. (Apparently this belief has been breached at Lowestoft, and there is now a parson who has regular access to a Lowestoft fishing boat when it is in port.) Two of the common beliefs in ill omens which I have come across are a mention of the word pig, and the strict prohibition against whistling on board a fishing boat. They are both as old as the belief mentioned already. Each is taboo or prohibited, and undoubtedly they are remnants of a form of religion that has long ago been superseded. The pig, like the horse, was sacred to, and under the protection of, one of the pagan goddesses; and it was risky to be free with its name. There is a strong aversion to anyone whistling on board ship, in case through a kind of sym-pathetic magic, he whistles up an unfavourable wind. Fishing is an occupation where there is greater danger than is normally met, therefore there is added inducement to believe in 'good luck' as a strong counter to fear, irrational or otherwise. There is, too, the uncertainty of getting a worthwhile catch.

Another occupation which appears to breed a host of attendant apprehensions is the stage – or I suppose any form of play-acting. So much can happen in the staging of a play, especially when it is hoped to earn a lot of money by it, that many old beliefs get free play, and the players attempt to read the signs whether the play will succeed or whether they will soon be 'resting' again.

David Butcher has spent many years studying fishing and

recording fishermen, and he has collected dozens of old beliefs connected with the sea. It is likely that many of them are still held, though – as indicated – a new generation of fishermen seem to be following a more tolerant line.

8

Broadcasting

A great help to those writers who started oral history in Britain was given by well-disposed producers in the BBC. The invention of the Marconi L2 Midget portable recording-unit made it possible for a writer to go out and collect material almost anywhere. The Midget had its own battery-power, which was very important thirty years ago as mains electricity was far from being completely supplied in all the villages. Yet just as important for me as the recording apparatus that the BBC lent me was the opportunity it gave to get the recorded material on the air. As I have described I recorded a batch of five-inch tapes of my Blaxhall neighbours, and some have been transcribed at the beginning of this book. They were possibly the most important tapes I recorded, though not particulary for any outstanding technical quality they possess. At the time they were run-of-the-mill recordings, but looked at today they can be recognized from their content as already historic in that they demonstrated that the Blaxhall folk who talked with me then were some of the last representatives who were in direct line with the early farmers of Biblical times. Put like this it sounds dramatic and possibly pretentious. Although we were aware then that we were doing something novel in recording a tape outside a studio, what we did not realize was that in using the machine in this way we were at the beginning of a mass movement when the cassette-recorder and cheap tapes made it possible for sound-recording to be in the reach of everybody.

I had borrowed the tape-recorder from the BBC for a limited period as the Norwich station had started broadcasting and they wanted all their apparatus back. I did not transcribe any of the tapes I made at Blaxhall then and thought of them only in terms of material to be broadcast. It was only much later that I thought of the possibility of transcribing them and using them as historical records; and they remained in tape-only form for years. I recognized at length it was legitimate to translate the full flavour of the recordings to paper. By this time I had become familiar with the Suffolk dialect and had come to appreciate its special quality. I was soon listening to the speech of my friends in Blaxhall with the zest of someone who had discovered a treasure. It became my purpose to get not only fresh and lively descriptions of life on the land before the big changes but also to get as many examples as I could of the arresting language in which they communicated them. I took part in a number of short programmes from Norwich – called ironically (for me) *Through East Anglian Eyes* – arranged by David Bryson. Then in the summer of 1963 I met David Thomson at Broadcasting House and I arranged with him to do a programme about the farm horse; and he would produce it. It was the first long programme I had done. It had a Suffolk background, but it also had some exceptionally interesting material contributed by Norman Halkett from Scotland. It was well received. Later we worked on a number of features, chiefly on the Third Programme.

Then in a short while the whole pattern of sound-broadcasting changed drastically. The change followed a report by an American efficiency team. Its title was *Broadcasting for the Seventies*. It was a departure that effectively killed the old Third Programme and left radio the neglected sister of television. The report was composed to get across the message that the BBC was to be run as a commercial business. Cost-efficiency was the watchword that the American McKinsey team had blazoned on its banner. That was the beginning of the effective running down of sound-broadcasting, although a series of recordings collected mainly by historians and called *The Long March of Everyman* was launched shortly after the report. This proved the swan-song of a series of long features that had been broadcast since shortly after the last war, features by Louis MacNeice, David Jones, Dylan Thomas and Charles Parker, with his Radio Ballads. These writers had given us a number of radio classics which had now come to an end.

I recall vividly the atmosphere in Broadcasting House when *Broadcasting for the Seventies* was being compiled and the Americans were very active there. A few weeks before, I had been to Burton-upon-Trent with David Thomson. He was producing a programme I had already begun working on in Suffolk. It was to be an hour's programme on the Third about the annual exodus of young farm workers from East Anglia, just after the corn harvest, to the maltings of Burton to work in malting the barley they had recently harvested. The migration had been going on since the nineteenth century and finished about 1931. It was an extensive movement, and the seventy- and eighty-year-olds remembered their early days at Burton very clearly as I recorded them. It was quite an important movement while it lasted; but the documentary record of the migration was almost non-existent. Therefore it was an excellent example of oral history; and the bulk of the information was good propaganda for a new discipline in that it came from oral sources in two separate communities.

We got an interesting group of recordings* chiefly of descendants of Suffolk people who had settled in Burton permanently – from horsemen, particularly, who took jobs as carters. Shortly afterwards I went up to Broadcasting House to work with David Thomson on editing the field-tapes. When I got there I found he was in a sombre mood. He had met some of the efficiency team who were preparing the report and he very soon delivered his verdict on it. He told me succinctly: 'I smell decay!' It was clear the whole concept of sound broadcasting was in the melting-pot; and the prospect of unlimited support for oral history from sound-radio was quickly vanishing. In the bar of the pubs around Broadcasting House and in the Langham, the BBC club, opposite, there was a definite air of sober consideration. I had served for three or four years on the Radio Writers' committee of the Society of Authors, and I was aware of a feeling of consternation among writers on the committee who got their living from writing radio scripts. Television was now completely in the saddle and the Third Programme was effectively scrapped. Before long it would have only the occasional feature, and would be filled with music. The *word* was being demoted.

Another aspect influenced people at this period. The adoption of the American system of commercial television was in many respects the most disastrous blow that happened to British culture. It was got through by a selfishly inspired sleight-of-hand. Even many enlightened Conservatives were fully aware of the consequences of tying the spoken word and television to the market-place, wedding culture to *soap*, as the Americans themselves guyed it in their phrase *soap-opera*, ironically underlining television's complete dependence as an 'independent' organization on advertising and the market. By going over to a commercial system British television and sound broadcasting lost the undoubted cultural centrality and international reputation it once possessed. There was a marked falling away from the standard of excellence that once permeated the whole.

*W.B.W.A., Chap. 22.

It was proposed that features producers like David Thomson and Charles Parker should be moved to boring routine jobs in day-to-day production. The effect on my own writing was immediate. The original 'slot' of one hour planned for the Burton programme was cut to half an hour, and the truncated programme would go out on Radio 4. My reaction was a draining away of the expectant zest I had in working on a Third Programme feature with David Thomson. The project would now be a run-of-the-mill exercise, with no probability of a repeat broadcast, and with a less than full treatment. Moreover, it would be for only half the fee and therefore a poor return for the time and trouble that had gone into it. The money I had earned through doing these programmes made writing the oral history books much easier. And it meant now that a third of my income as a writer had dried up. Yet it was not as critical as it would have been earlier when our children were younger. Many sound producers were transferred to jobs that had no interest for them. David Thomson, rather than take a job he did not want, decided to retire early and switch to writing books.

But Charles Parker's whole life was in radio, and the change of policy affected him more than anybody. He was an enthusiast for radio and especially for the speech of the ordinary man. The BBC moguls did not dismiss Parker immediately. They temporized. He had made an international reputation with his series of Radio Ballads; and the prestigious Italia Prize was awarded to one of them, *Singing the Fishing*. They told him that his post as a chief producer 'had been eliminated' but there was no question of dismissal. Like other producers he knew what to expect. David Bryson who had set up the new area station at Norwich in 1956, and in a short time had given East Anglia a real identity on the BBC, was taken away from his East Anglian post and transferred to Birmingham to make educational programmes. Parker was passionately against the new system and refused to be shunted into a routine job of churning out non-creative programmes. He recorded a huge number of tapes for *The Long March of Everyman*, which was a good example of oral history as radio. I was in touch with him about the time he visited Cambridge, just before he went to China. He was having advice before his visit from Dr Joseph Needham, the Master of Gonville and Caius College. Dr Needham had spent some time during the war in teaching science in the university-in-the-caves in China when Mao Zedong was on the Long March. Parker was going to China with his tape-recorder. He left in 1972. The China visit was his last major project for the BBC. He recorded 110 hours of tape which he estimated would take him a year to sort out and make into usable programmes. Some time later that year I had a letter from him from the south Middlesex Hospital where he was a patient:

> I left for China on 1st April and distinguished myself on return by arriving at Heathrow in a state of collapse, and finishing up here with some sort of food poisoning contracted in that hell-hole Hong Kong! But I'm perfectly OK now, and simply waiting for the lab to confirm that I harbour no virulent Asiatic bug, so should be home by the middle of next week.

He had time to think, lying convalescing in a hospital bed:

> China was a total, regenerative experience: 800 million people who love one another and work together and draw you into their community. It has transformed me and makes the BBC business even more pusillanimous and unbearable. I'm sure you are quite right and I must get out of the BBC and confront the harsh world of freelance reality! I have in fact been offered a further eight month 'stay of execution' to be followed by an agreed four programmes a year for three years, but I'm not going on existing on this bloody hand-out from them. Your assessment is correct, I believe, they are corrupted and irredeemably philistine, and if I stay with them any longer I shall be corrupted – already have been in fact.

In the same letter he wrote his estimate of China under Mao Zedong in 1972:

The trouble is the China stuff is highly political! And the most startling thing is to find that the degree of openness and warmth and sheer translucent human love and fellowship impressed in the people we met, is in direct proportion to the degree of their political awareness and their capacity to articulate Maoist ideology. Very hard for us to take! But there is also a problem in what seems to be the Chinese mode of expression and attitude to experience. Even allowing for the difficulty in working through a translator, it is always extraordinarily difficult to pin people down to some particular and personal experience through which alone the social or economic or political event could be appreciated. I never cracked this one although I still got some marvellous stuff and was given carte blanche to record anywhere.

Eventually, in spite of a long fight and newspaper campaigns led by fellow producers, Charles Parker finished with the BBC. He wrote in November 1972:

The sickening process of my termination by the BBC proceeds amidst all this 50-year Birthday [of BBC's founding] jubilating! I alternate between despair and relief but find the prospect of earning a living like an honest (!) man, frightening at fifty-three! But I'm a bit like a rabbit transfixed by a stoat, at the moment, unable to move effectively. But it will pass.

During this period I got to know the Miners' Library in Swansea. This was a centre for coalfield studies which was the result of a coalfield research project at University College, Swansea. The Library is run in association with the University Department of Adult and Continuing Education, an extramural activity which made the Library a focus of instruction and culture.

As a result of the rapid shrinkage of the coal industry in the sixties, the old Miners' Institutes and their libraries became increasingly unused. Many of the books were bought up by entrepreneurs, notably a bookseller who set up at Hay-on-

Wye in Breconshire. The Institute Libraries reflected the miners' chief interests: politics, history and philosophy – in the main – but also a wider area where literature and music were represented. In addition to the books, the Miners' Library in Swansea houses the nucleus of tape-recordings of miners and is developing its own programme of video-recording. Within the past decade I have visited it about four times, taking part in conferences, and on each occasion I have been heartened by the experience. And I became more and more convinced that in tackling the main work of a community we identify the central historical topic. His work is the centre of a man's life: all, or most, of his physical and mental energy goes into it, and it is the medium – especially in mining – through which he gets support and comradeship through his Union. He becomes directly aware of the social pressures and experiences operating in their most characteristic form. The common phrase *working class* is at once an indicator of the main province of oral history and an actual pointer to one of the most fruitful areas of exercising the new technique. The working miner is politically conscious and he recognizes his work as his contribution to society; and in its turn he expects society to acknowledge his contribution with a just reward. This is a lesson I absorbed through my living among miners in the thirties.

On one of my visits to the Miners' Library in 1975 for a conference I met Charles Parker again. He had been given a Tin-Plate Fellowship for a year at the Miners' Library. He chaired a meeting I had to address. It was the last time I saw him. He later took a job as a part-time lecturer in Media Studies at the Central London Polytechnic. (A former BBC man, Anthony Schooling, lent me transcripts of the lectures Charles Parker gave there.) After returning home shortly after his last lecture, he succumbed to a massive stroke. He was aged sixty: this was in 1980.

Charles Parker was one of the most notable figures in the heyday of sound broadcasting. He spent his formative years during the war. He returned from six years' war service with the Royal Navy having been a successful submarine commander, gaining the Distinguished Service Cross. Shortly after demobilization he went to Queen's College, Cambridge; and after graduating he joined the BBC European Service. Later he went to the United States as a Visiting Producer and on his return he was appointed a Senior Features Producer in Birmingham in 1954. He did most of his longer productions from here. He recognized that the attack on sound radio in the BBC was inevitable after the Television Act of 1954:

> But what [he wrote] is so damnable is the hypocritical mask of public service broadcasting behind which it still operates.

He put up a tremendous fight for radio because he felt that it embodied both lasting and dependable values, and also the speech of the ordinary working man. It was on this conviction that most of his successful productions were built; the outstanding traditional language that the ordinary man had inherited and had used unself-consciously, was ideally fitted to radio. It was concise, colourful and pithy. During his long service with the BBC he recorded hundreds of ordinary people all over Britain and also, extensively, abroad. He drove himself very hard and eventually burnt himself out, leaving a legacy of public service that in its recorded form will be increasingly recognized in years to come. Historians of the post-war years will bless Charles Parker for the cultural gold he carefully stored up. He made a number of enemies during his career with the BBC, but what pioneer gets an undisturbed passage? He had a wide and absorbing vision which, by and large, embraced a celebration of the common man. He attempted to live up to it; and he had the courage to resist the downward trend that, in his view, had begun in sound-broadcasting. He had numerous rebuffs but he rode them all, confident that he was doing a socially valuable service not only to his coevals but also to men and women in the generations to come.

Some of the people who worked with Charles Parker were aware of the importance of his work. They joined with his widow to respect his wishes to found an educational trust. She transferred the ownership of all his material to a body of trustees, representing the family and friends. They originally formed The Charles Parker Archive Trust of 5,000 tapes and written material and his working files of correspondence, notes, transcription of lectures, production books, articles as well as a collection of pamphlets, his own library of at least a thousand books on the oral tradition, and music together with films and technical equipment. Recently (May 1985) the whole Archive has been given a permanent housing at Birmingham City Library.

I have written about Charles Parker at some length as he was a staunch supporter of the oral history movement, and followed its development with intense interest. His life work in radio is also important from the standpoint of oral history for the reason that he grasped the central contribution that this new discipline offers not only to history, which is its main aim and purpose, but also to literary scholarship. Language in its origin and development is necessarily *spoken* language and its strength is clearly seen in the way the common man uses it, particularly an old countryman who uses words and expressions that have survived the use of generations and the smoothing and polishing of thousands of tongues. His language and expressive diction, his concrete tactile imagery, arising mainly from his sharp powers of observation, have not been blunted by an attempt to handle imperfectly apprehended concepts. Fortunately, it is still alive and finds its echo in some of the best periods of English literature.

It is my view that Charles Parker was one of the casualties of the recently revived doctrine of 'private enterprise': the return to Victorian values recommended by some of our present rulers. 'Private enterprise' in its modern context has become a euphemism for one of the most deplorable of the medieval Seven Deadly Sins – Greed, which Charles Parker as a caring man, a champion of the working-class, spent all his energy in resisting.

9

Women and the Horse

From reading my various accounts of farm workers, people could easily get the impression that I was anti-feminist, writing about men almost solely. To deny a possible charge and to attempt to redress the balance I include this section on women involved with farm horses. If I was conversant with hunting or riding and show-jumping I could put up an even stronger case.

I heard that Jennie Caldwell had died and I felt surprise at the news for all the people I knew who had been linked with farm horses were usually in their eighties when they left their charges for the last time. Jennie Caldwell was in her early sixties. She was well known in East Anglia and, indeed, in most of the showgrounds of Britain as that rare being, a woman who could drive a six-horse, or even an eight-horse, team of heavy horses. I saw her a few years ago in charge of an eight-horse team of Suffolks at the Royal Norfolk Show. It was a remarkable sight: a slip of a woman handling a team of horses each weighing a ton or more, with apparently as much ease as if she were driving a pony and trap. I got to know her

151

quite well when I was writing my last East Anglian book about horses and their use in agriculture. She was quiet and unassuming, and to meet her casually for the first time one wouldn't have thought she sat on the driving seat before thousands of people, the master of six or eight huge horses, driving them around the show ring as though they were going for a quiet airing.

She had spent most of her life with horses, starting at the beginning of the last war. She joined the Women's Land Army at seventeen, and served on a Norfolk farm where she did all the farm jobs that needed horses: harrowing, rolling, hoeing, and carting: everything except ploughing. Her love for farm work was triggered off by a holiday in Anglesey before the war when she learned to cart water on a farm where they were still using horses. After spending some time in East Anglia she went down to Devon where she met the steep Devon hills. For carting corn they used a long two-wheeled cart; and on a hill that had a slope of one in seven she had to be very careful that it did not upset. It was probably a similar low-hung two-wheel cart, called a *gambo* that they used across the Channel in south Wales. She returned to East Anglia just after the war finished, and straightaway she got herself a job with a Suffolk farmer; at the same time 'getting wrong' with the Land Army authorities who thought that she should have got the job through them. But shortly afterwards they disbanded the Land Army and nothing more was said.

The Suffolk farmer, Charles Saunders, was a well-known horse breeder and trainer. He lived at Hoxne in the north of Suffolk in a modern house on an old estate where the big house has been demolished. But Oakley stables remain standing. They are a fort-like structure, a central space or yard bounded on four sides by stables and two impressive arches giving entrance on opposite sides. The first time I met Jennie Caldwell here she was in sole command of her little kingdom. It was almost a third of a mile from the main road; and she spent most of her time down here alone, looking after the horses she had in her charge, doing the jobs necessary to keep them in show condition; feeding, exercising, tending their harness, and seeing that they were properly shod. In addition she had to drive one of the huge vehicles that took the horses to the shows.

When she first went to Hoxne she did the usual farm jobs in this arable area; lifting sugar-beet, ploughing with three horses, and carting. Then about two years after she came there, the horseman left, and Charles Saunders suggested to her that she had better drive the team of horses that they showed. Unknown to him she was already having tuition in driving a team of heavy horses from Billy Potter who drove Mann the brewers' team. When she started to drive the Hoxne team, Charles Saunders found that her hands were so small that she could not handle the reins without some difficulty. So he had the width of the reins reduced from 1¼ inches to ¾ inch to fit her fingers more easily. When she was ready, away she went to the Cambridge Show. There were the usual competitors among the four-horse teams: Young's, the London brewers' team, had won the competition for several years before this. But Jennie Caldwell, on her first show, gave the Young horseman a close run with her Suffolks. So close was it that the judges called the referee to make the final decision. He gave it to Jennie Caldwell. Whereupon the Young horseman, Charlie Butler, chaffed Jennie by telling her: if she ever came to London he would take her by the hand and throw her into the Thames.

As time went on she competed in many shows and became a kind of horse psychologist, studying closely the character of each horse she had under her care. At one time she had thirty-two horses to see to; and she was down at Oakley Park most of the day. She started work at 4 a.m. and finished in the early evening: a seven-day-a-week job. She had to groom only the working horses, the ones that had to be showed, fortunately, not the ones that were out in the park. She was busy with one job or another throughout the day. She had a room in the stables, only going home to where she lived in the village to sleep.

Jennie Caldwell never married, and as far as I know had no attachments. She spent every day living with her horses. The horse were her sole life, and she gave them all her time and energy.

She studied the character of her horses most minutely, especially how they reacted in the show-ring. Out in the meadow they seemed listless and lazy-looking, and even on the showground itself. But once they got into the ring they seemed to sense the changed atmosphere and held up their heads, and their walk became brisker. She had one horse she called Jock who knew exactly when he got into the ring. He approached it lackadaisically, but once he was inside and felt the change in attention, he performed like a circus horse. Jock was a very good leader but he hated being behind. He always knew the way into the ring but, as soon as he got there and went round he would always try to get out again: therefore he had to be watched. Another horse, Emperor, knew when they had to stop in front of the grandstand after being round the ring once; and he also had to be watched very carefully in case he came round to stop before he should do. The horses have to stand in front of the grandstand with the other teams for the judges to examine them. The result is, that if you stop anywhere else the horses get excited, as much as to say: 'C'mon, why are we stopping here? This is a bad place to stop.'

Most of the careful work is done long before they get into the show-ring. Someone watched Jennie Caldwell harnessing up her team before going out, in recent years, into the ring. He was a knowledgeable bystander:

I stood there for an hour and a quarter while she harnessed up those eight horses to the wagon. She did it all herself. She may have had a little help to put the collars on, but all the rest she did herself. And when she had got those eight horses harnessed up, she went round slowly and examined everything, but especially the *billets* [the buckles fixing the reins to the horses' bits]. If there were three holes in the leather of the rein for fastening the billet, the identical one – say, the middle one – had to be used in every case. This is very important, as it means that as soon as the handler touches the reins and the horses get the signal, they all respond together, at the precise fraction of a second, and they then move off together as one horse. They all pull at once.

While all this checking and re-checking was going on the horses stood as quiet as mice, their heads down as though they were in contemplation. But as soon as she got up into the seat and took up the reins, up went their heads like a well-drilled squad of soldiers. And there they were, all alert and ready for action! Then she spoke to them in a small, quiet voice, and eight big horses moved off as one. It was pretty to see: no fuss, no hurry, like a mother who was in full control, quietly shepherding her bevy of children off to school.

Charles Saunders recently told me of the circumstances of Jennie's death. He said that the main trouble was she had a bad patch with her horses; something that was visited upon her and through no fault of her own. About eighteen months to two years ago three of her geldings died within three months, and a little later she lost a mare and a gelding. All this was in spite of the conscientious care and devotion she gave to all her horses. I was genuinely grieved when I heard the details of her bad luck and what happened afterwards, as told to me by Charles Saunders. He said that she took the loss of the horses very badly: 'Her mind and her memory seemed to go. She was no longer with us.' Another of her friends told me: 'In the end it got so bad she couldn't remember the right way to put a horse's collar on.'

Jennie Caldwell's life was dedicated to her horses; and I can imagine the shock to her innermost being that she suffered from the disastrous loss. The Suffolk Horse Society has already decided to set up a memorial fund for a trophy to be competed for annually. This will be a fitting reminder to countless people who saw her in the show-rings as she drove her horses with faultless precision and grace of gentle handling.

A few years ago I met a Suffolk woman whose husband was in charge of a big stable of horses on what was once an extensive estate. She was an example of a head horseman's wife who actively shared her husband's interest in his job: the care and treatment of farm horses and their breeding. It is worth recording the beginning of her active interest. Her husband was responsible for a large number of working horses, and on one occasion he had a mare that died on giving birth to her foal. The vet told him that to keep the foal alive he would have to feed it every four hours. It was while he was following the vet's instructions that Mrs Cater happened to go down to the stables to take her husband's lunch. At that time the mole-catcher was making one of his periodic visits to the farm. Seeing Walter Cater's constant journeys to the stables, he remarked to his wife: 'You could make it a lot easier for your husband, you know.' On going home she asked her husband, 'What's this about the foal?' He told her what had happened, and finally she volunteered to take the foal over. They brought it from the farm and housed it in a shed at the back of their cottage. She brought it up successfully and soon it returned to the farm. This was the beginning of a number of foals she brought up in the same way. They included one birth which demonstrated her husband's expertise and know-ledge of the arcane tradition of horse handling. She assisted her husband at a difficult birth. They delivered the foal only to find that the mare would not take it. She refused to let it suckle. Walter Cater waited for a few minutes and then he decided: 'Leave it for a while; we'll go and get the sheep-dog.' As soon as they brought the dog into the loose-box it raised the mother's natural instinct. It was as if she proposed to herself: 'That's not going to have my baby!' And she allowed the colt to suckle and they reared her successfully.

Cheryl Clark of Thorington Street, near Stoke-by-Nayland in Suffolk, is also well known in the heavy-horse world; and like Jennie Caldwell she has a marvellously relaxed and natural way of handling heavy horses. She and her husband Roger are both qualified farriers. Roger is a member of the City of London Guild of Farriers and is a City Freeman. He does most of the forge work now, and Cheryl looks after the horse they own: until recently a first-class Suffolk stallion, and a couple of lighter horses. The latter often have companions in the stables, left with Cheryl Clark to break in and train as riding horses. Only occasionally does she return to smithing when an emergency arises. Their farmhouse and the fields they own are appropriately called Weyland's, and it is a pleasant coincidence that with its evocative, traditional name it should now house two skilled, working farriers. The Clarks had a champion Suffolk stallion until recent years. He was called The Count. (The stud-book name was Rowhedge Count the Second.) He took prizes in most of the big shows in the country and was much in demand serving the mares. Cheryl travelled widely with the horse, placing him in the box with his gear and driving the vehicle herself. When she started, some of the mare-owners were embarrassed at finding a woman travelling a stallion. One said after she had got the horse out of the lorry:

'You are not going to use him, are you?'

'Course I am! There's nobody else with me, is there?'

She preferred, though, to let the mares be brought to Weyland's. For one reason they have a neat, secluded place, and again they have a 'trying' or 'teasing-bar' which makes 'standing at stud' a more satisfactory method. The trying-bar is a specially made structure. It is constructed of five railway-sleepers laid edgeways on top of one another and clamped by two massive steel girders at either end. The whole is sunk securely into the ground to form a strut-fence or partition about five feet in height. The mare is led to one side of this partition and the stallion is held on the other. He then teases the mare by playfully 'biting' her neck or rubbing his head against hers. If the mare is not ready, not *on song* as the horsemen say, she will not take the stallion. Cheryl Clark has seen mares smash the trying-bar when they are not ready to be served. That is one of the main reasons she prefers to stand at stud:

When you've got a stallion worth a couple of thousand pounds or more, that's the sort of exercise that doesn't pay. He could easily get damaged.

The Clarks had some very bad luck with their champion stallion, The Count. He was out grazing in the field near the farmhouse when he was struck by lightning. One of his hind legs was injured badly and in spite of expert care by an excellent vet, it never recovered, and the horse had to be put down. He was much lamented. The Americans wanted to buy him but the Clarks were loth to part with him. There was some attempt to get some of The Count's semen sent over to the States.

> Freezing is all right. It's exactly the same as a bull. But it's the unfreezing that doesn't work. Apparently the Newmarket experts over here are willing to attempt it, but it would be very expensive.

In view of what has happened, it is a disaster that it was not attempted.

The Count became famous in some unusual places. I used to go to the University of Sheffield on many occasions to talk to a keen, extra-mural group in Professor John Widdowson's department. My subject was rural culture which fitted in with a particular group of students who made a practice of coming bi-annually into East Anglia. Sometimes they stayed in Norwich, but on two occasions I met them at Flatford Mill Field-Study Centre. On one occasion I took the group over to Weyland's, and they saw, and were very impressed with The Count. Later, on their second visit to Weyland's, which happened after The Count's demise, Bruce Sutherland, the veterinary surgeon who looked after the Clarks' horses, took us as a party to an adjoining meadow where there were a half-dozen Suffolks grazing. It was a spring afternoon and the geldings and mares, with their bright chestnut coats, contrasting with the deep green of the meadow, made it a memorable sight. Some of the party remembered The Count as he was when they last saw him on their first visit. He stood in the farmyard, a huge noble-looking animal, of a massive build of seventeen hands, like one of the big war-horses in a Renaissance painting: with a sculptural quality, a fine intelligent head and a crest (the back of the neck) curved like a rainbow, big well-rounded haunches – 'like a cook's', as one farm-horseman said – a solid looking, indomitable creature that was the epitome of strength. He had a shining predominance over most of the heavy horses he met. I was back in Sheffield last December and one of the tutors at the university referred again to The Count as a horse that stayed in his memory. He was in good company. Sir Kenneth Clark, later Lord Clark, Curator of the National Gallery and compiler of memorable television programmes on Art, once said:

I think that the Suffolk Punches provide my earliest recollections of sculptural form.

We should not be surprised by the increasing involvement of women and young girls with the horse. This is in line with what we know of their quieter handling of horses, and the more frequent patting and caressing which they give them. Horses become sensible to the different treatment from men who are liable to use the whip-and-spur method. The response womenfolk get from horses is also mirrored by the regard women were held among those people who are historically identified with horses. The Arabs trusted their women to bring up their colts, and the Bedouin left their horses for the first three years of their lives in their sole care. Gypsy women were also skilled in the rearing of young horses and they had an important hand, as I found out from examples in East Anglia, in keeping their horses fit for the travelling which was essential to their way of life.

Mervyn Cater recalls his father's account of a gypsy woman who had a local reputation for her horse-skills. It illustrates particularly the undoubted empathy some women possess in their handling of horses.*

There was an old gypsy woman called Mrs Silver, and she always told the age of a horse from its behind! Always used to, never its teeth. Father said she was more accurate than those horsemen who looked at the horses' teeth.

H.P. & M., pp.74–5.

She often bought horses and ponies from him, and of
course he knew exactly when these were born. He said she
was very accurate with the age she put on them, a lot more
accurate than the men who gave the year of birth: this old
girl would give the month of birth – she was that accurate.

I remember him telling us one night that she used to
come to a public house in the village: they used to buy and
sell ponies at this particular pub; and this is something
he'd seen her do several times. My mother also mentioned
her several times. She was the same lady that my mother
and father moved near to when they went out Hoxne way,
(he was horseman out there for a time). She was very
clever, and the gypsies lived at Denham at that time. Now
one of their boys was taken ill and he'd got to be in
Norwich Hospital as fast as possible. And she rung – or
one of her boys rung some gypsies that were relations.
They were on Mousehold Heath; (near the Norwich Hospital) and within a few hours one of them had come down
with a trap and a mare. This mare had had a foal a short
time before; and when they turned her round she went
back to this old Heath flat out all the way. There's a lot of
psychology there, isn't there? She knew which horse to
pick: she told them which horse to send with this light
trap. They had to force the mare to come away from the
foal; but once they laid that boy in the back, left the
doctor's care here, the shortest period of time possible was
between the doctor's care here and Norwich Hospital. She
was running back to her foal, and she was flat out all the
way to Norwich. Luckily, my father said, the gypsy knew
too much about a horse to let him kill her. The mare could
easily have killed herself going back if she was allowed to.
And the gypsy said afterwards he had to hold her back all
the way to Norwich. I remember my father saying that this
gypsy woman knew more about horses than most of the
horsemen in this area.

It was John Cossey, the blacksmith in the village of Brooke in
Norfolk, who first drew my attention to the success of women

in handling horses. He found that, on the whole, young girls are much better with horses than men. The men are usually rougher: the old type used to break a horse's spirit rather than try to get around it. They got worse results that way:

But the girls sometimes make it difficult for the men. There's a stud of Arabs not far from here, and there's not a man on the place. They are mostly young girls looking after the horses; and I and the vet are the only men who go near there. And we don't get a very good reception. Those horses don't like the smell of men. I've tried everything to make my job easier when I go there – even to sprinkling some of my wife's talcum powder over my clothes. But even that doesn't seem to answer.

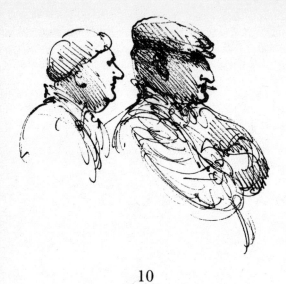

10

The Importance of Language

One of the reasons that I have recorded ordinary working
people is that I found so many of them tell what they have to
tell in language that gives their account an added interest –
sometimes even displacing my intentness on their description
or story to the actual manner of its telling. I am always on the
alert for an arresting phrase or an apt expression and I
memorize it for writing down later. The big advantage of
tape-recording is that you have the actual words and context
that you can file away and savour at leisure. Sometimes, you
have no machine with you and you hear gems in casual
conversation, such as a young boy's phrase, undoubtedly
heard from his grandfather when he was describing a heavy
snowfall: 'It snew a masterpiece.'

Like Charles Parker, Professor Seamus Delargy, who was
Director of the Irish Folklore Commission, was a great
admirer and advocate of the language spoken by old

countryman or working man who unconsciously held the millennial oral tradition. He spent a long time studying the language of the Irish speakers in the Blasket Islands where the mode of life had been unchanged for centuries, and where speech was still related to things and the community and its rhythm of life. As well as being a vehicle for daily converse the use of language was a leisure-time activity. It was a real re-creation, a story enjoyed in spite of the fact that it had been told many times before. Seamus Delargy once lectured in Dublin to a group of post-graduate students on The Defence of Illiteracy. I have sympathy with his choosing of this subject, for I myself found among Suffolk people I recorded thirty years ago an identical quality of speech; and sometimes the speakers were sought out to tell their story time and time again to people who had heard it many times before. This happened in my experience with the old horseman from the Saints area of Suffolk. His name was Jack Page, and after playing a recording of his describing how a cow got between the shafts of a tumbril and galloped about, I was many times asked to play the tape when I went into the Saints:*

Have you got Shiner Page and the cow in the tumbril?

This is a tradition as old as the ancient Greeks where a good story-teller was highly prized in any community. Jack Page told me he used to listen to his father telling tales at night with the only light the light of the fire. This particular story is a humorous one, and it evoked an interesting comment when I played it recently in the Saints:

> We seem to have lost the habit of real laughter, the kind we've just heard in these recordings – spontaneous and unforced.

Rereading some of my tape transcripts and listening to a few of the actual recordings, it has struck me forcibly how much changing work-patterns, and consequently changing social

*D.T.W.H.S., pp.116–18.

conditions, affect the language. In my recordings I have chiefly been interested with two generations: the people mainly born after 1875 and those born around 1900. Both these generations witnessed massive changes in work-techniques but the older generation had the much more interesting language. This was impressed upon me when I listened recently to James Chaplin, the Ipswich seaman who had his early seafaring experience under sail. The voyage under sail was more onerous while they were afloat, yet when they got to port their stay there was longer and more leisurely. On balance, they preferred the slower sail-boat rhythm. As James Chaplin said: 'they got more enjoyment out of themselves'. Now, as in most forms of mechanization, there was an increase in speed, and the worker had to adapt to it. Steam winches quickened up the loading and unloading, and the ship spent much less time in port. The life around the docks became gradually less communal. Many pubs in the dock area closed when iron and steam replaced wood and sail. Consequently, the rhythm of life quickened considerably both on board and in the port. James Chaplin, who was born in 1886, saw the revolution in his work when he was a com-paratively young man. His older brother, Charles, was a town-horseman or carter and his work did not change appreciably. Yet even if he had worked as a farm-horseman his work would not have been affected unduly. Steam was in fact used on the land over a century ago, but owing to the unsuitability of the shape and size of the fields and the weight and general unwieldiness of the steam-tackle it did not prove a popular method of land-cultivation. The land had to wait until a generation later before farming was revolutionized. Since the last war the farm worker on many farms has no one to talk to all day but himself. The days are far distant when he could stop for a break at the headlands and have a brief chat with men ploughing on the same field or, during the winter, in the cosiness of the stable during bad weather. The present day farm worker, with his portable radio, is not likely to be in the same predicament as the old Irishman known to Seamus Delargy. He was a teller of tales but owing to the changes in the community his fireside audiences had slipped away.

The countryman's language is often the major part of his life, a prized social bond, an accomplishment which enables him to fit himself comfortably into his community. In a sense, it is his spiritual breath with his fellows. It fosters, too, the assurance that the dialect on his tongue is keeping alive a worthy and valuable tradition: it is an old and tried language and if someone disagrees and speaks up for Received Pronunciation, RP, two language authorities can be cited in support of the dialect-speaker, one established, Max Muller,* and one recent, Robert McCrum.† Max Muller wrote in the latter half of the last century:

> It is a mistake to imagine that dialects are everywhere corruptions of the literary language. Even in England, the local patois have many forms that are more primitive than the language of Shakespeare, and the richness of their vocabulary surpasses, on many points, that of the classical writers of any period. Dialects have always been the feeders rather than the channels of a literary language; anyhow they are parallel streams which existed long before the time when one of them was raised to that temporary eminence which is the result of literary cultivation.

Robert McCrum writes:

> ... rather than talk about *accents* and *dialects* of English, we talk of varieties. Again and again we found that the line between *accent*, *dialect* and language is not a sure or steady one and is often disputed by specialists ... Using *variety*, we avoid the pejorative overtones of dialect.

Amidst this lively discussion among the experts Received Pronunciation appears to be moribund: RIP.

But the attitude to the dialects of some of our best-known writers has been, in my opinion, the most reliable one. Sir

*The Science of Language, Longmans, 1875, Vol.1. p.55.
†The Story of English, Faber and Faber and BBC Publications, 1986, p.13.

Walter Scott and George Eliot, for example, were great advocates of ordinary speech; and this side of their work, where they quote common speech, stands out from their sometimes mannered prose. George Moore states his preference for the speech of the common man rather than the educated one in very definite terms. He is reporting a conversation with an American:

> Society is always being *shaken to the roots*, and it would be interesting and instructive to keep an account of all the solecisms, pleonasms and French words that have crept into the language, overlaying and poisoning our homely English speech and its very spring-head in the market-places, villages and fields.
>
> I wish I had told Mr Husband how one day while partridge-shooting in the north of England I began to forget my shooting, and on my friend asking me for the reason for my inattention I answered:
>
> 'I am thinking of the beautiful English your game-keeper speaks.'
>
> 'But is not your aim in writing [he asked] to write the language of good society?'
>
> I cried out like a dog whose tail had been trodden on and told him:
>
> 'Not at all! My object is to separate myself as far as possible from the language spoken in good society.'
>
> And to explain what I meant I searched among the money in my pocket for an old coin, and finding one almost defaced, I said:
>
> 'This sixpence represents the language spoken in good society.' And, my friend, being a man of taste was converted to the beautiful idiomatic English spoken by the game-keeper; and in the evening after dinner he told me of many beautiful locutions he had heard in the fields; and words he had laughed at, thinking them vulgar, but knowing at the bottom of his heart that he was not thinking the truth.

Some of our best prose writers of the last century have

concentrated on vernacular speech recognizing its virtues: its sharp imagery and its preference for the concrete, particular instance. Both Dickens and Scott were two of the pioneers. Scott used the Scottish tongue to wonderful effect. And it is this aspect of his writing that has worn best over the years. Some of the narrative passages both in Scott and Dickens now date a little, but the dialect comes off the page as fresh as ever. Take Baillie Jarvie in *Rob Roy* as an illustration, how he describes the way a woman gave him the cold shoulder:

> Her reception of me this blessed day was muckle on the north side of friendly.

Or Rob Roy himself:

> What ails thee, man? All's well that ends well. The world will last our day. Come, take a cup o' brandy.

Sam Friend, the Suffolk farm worker, is a good example of the quality these old writers recognized. He and his wife lived in the village of Cretingham, not far from Framlingham. He was the finest speaker of the dialect I have come across in my recording in East Anglia. They had brought up a family most of whom had left home but their youngest son, Dick, was still with them when we lived in the area. When I began collecting material, one of the Blaxhall people offered me an open invitation: 'Drop in at any time if you want to know anything. If I haven't got the time I'll make time. *Made time* is the best time, so they tell me.' Sam Friend could well have said that a few years later. I lived near him at Helmingham and if ever I wanted confirmation of an aspect of the old farming or the meaning of a dialect word that was new to me I had only to call on the Friends to be sure that I would get accurate information. And it was always given in the purest dialect, in phrases that were often pure poetry.

One day, however, he told me a surprising piece of news while talking about the village of Cretingham: 'You know this village was once famous. It was the place where the curate cut the parson's throat. That was some bit back; but it happened.' When my face showed my disbelief, he said: 'You ask my

wife.' Then they showed me an old newspaper-cutting from
the local paper which gave details of the trial. The outcome
was that the curate was found guilty and 'ordered to be
detained at Her Majesty's pleasure'. It seems that Mrs Friend,
who was then a young girl, was working on a farm not far
from where she lived then, and she saw the curate leaning
over a gate with his head in his hands. He had just come out
after it happened, and had stopped at the gate, beside himself
and not knowing what to do.

Usually, however, the information they gave me was much
less spectacular, and more concerned with the everyday
events of their lives before the big changes that had happened
in farming and the village. Yet it was not so much what Sam
Friend told me that I was interested in, but the manner and
the language of his telling. He had a sharp wit and a memorable way of turning a phrase to spice a story. He was also a
good singer of old songs, which he sang in village pubs. One
of his sayings – I believe of his own invention – was told
against himself: Ringers and singers are no home-bringers.
That is, they spent a lot of their money in the pub when they
should have been adding it to the family budget. Sam Friend
used to visit The Ship at Blaxhall, a famous singing-pub
which had the reputation of being a very contentious place.
He told me:

> If you want to get on in that place, you got to put your
> foot down where they take theirs up!

Mrs Friend was an invalid in her later years and he did most
of the work, treating her with rough humour. She sat in a
corner near the fire unable to do much except pass a sly
comment or laugh at his jokes which were often pointed
good-humouredly at her, as when he said:

> I married her when she was in her fair bloom, and I got
> to stick with her now she's an owd stalk!

His talk was a wonderful example of the vigour and arresting
imagery of the pure speech of the countryman. When I went
to visit him after moving from his district he was talking about

his younger days when he had a family to support. After working all day in the stable and the field he would have to toil in the evening growing vegetables for the family, working in his own allotment or *yard*. He told me:

> It would sometimes be 10 o'clock before I came home at night. I'd have to dig a quarter of an acre. And it was uphill work coming home afterwards; and if I'd ha' hit a cobweb I'd ha' fallen back'uds. I was like a dead lamb's tail.

His stories about the temper of life in Suffolk before the First World War were innumerable. The barn-owl was an example. It was a common custom to leave an aperture in the gable of a corn-barn so that an owl could come and go as it pleased, thus helping to keep down the vermin in the barn. In some areas an unofficial initiation ceremony connected with the barn-owl involved a form of christening. When a boy first entered the stables he was told to hold a sieve below the trapdoor entrance to the loft. Standing on a ladder he dutifully held it up: they were going to catch the barn-owl which one of the men would drive down through the loft entrance. The boy stood expectantly looking upwards, the sieve above his head. But instead of the bird, he received a bucket of cold water. Many of these tales had been told Sam by his father, and it is likely that this one comes from outside the area as we do not get the picture of a classic East Anglian barn which, on the larger farms at least, has no loft but was open to the roof like the nave of a church.

He told me one tale of his father that has the authentic mark of the area at the latter half of the last century. His father was a horseman on the farm where Sam Friend himself spent most of his career. Friend senior looked after an outstanding Suffolk stallion they called Nelson. The stallion did a great deal of work on the plough as well as serving the mares during the season. In those days, especially on the stiff, heavy land, farmers aimed to get most of their ploughing done before Christmas, before bad weather made ploughing impossible. One Christmas, as soon as the holiday was over, the farmer came to Friend's father and told him, as the horses had been idle for a few days, to take Nelson out and exercise him. Friend disagreed: the horse did not want exercise. An argument arose and finally the farmer said: 'Well, it's my horse, and I want you to let him out in the field for a run.' Friend took the horse out into the meadow; and the farmer went with him. Like any horse that is let loose after being some time in the stable, it capered about wildly. It ran and reared up and finally put its feet on the gate near where they were standing in a kind of challenge. It then tore round the field making a noise like thunder. Suddenly it slipped. Its legs slid from under it and it lay on its back and was still. 'Now,' said Friend, 'dew you send for the knacker. The horse is finished.' The local vet came, and the farmer wanted Friend to blindfold the horse while they shot him. He refused.

> It was a great loss [Sam commented]. He was a wunnerful horse, the apple of the owd boy's eye. He was a horse like in an oil-painting, with his crest like a rainbow.

I had noticed before Sam Friend's ability to select an arresting simile to evoke a telling image. He was once describing a field of wheat that had been laid by a high wind and rain. He summoned up a natural and appropriate figure to describe it: 'It dew look like the parting on a bull's forehead.' It reminded me at the time of Adrian Bell's chronicling of a Suffolk farm worker's speech:

> About this time when I just started as a farm-apprentice, I had to go out horse-hoeing, taking a horse carefully between the rows of tender young plants; and this is how one of the farm-men instructed me:
> You lead that mare as slowly as ever foot can fall.

He went on to identify the phrase 'as softly as ever foot can fall' – an almost identical expression in Shakespeare's *As You Like It*. I have a similar experience with one of Sam Friend's most striking phrases. Talking about a high wind he said:

> It were a whoolly fierce wind. It took nine tailors to hold the needle up.

170

I recorded the sentence, writing it down as soon as I got home. I am still wondering about its provenance. Knowing Shakespeare's fondness for making tailors figures of fun, as in *Henry IV: Part 2*, I suspect it may have a like origin to the phrase Adrian Bell quoted, not in an actual Shakespearian text, but in a language that was common in Shakespeare's day, and has continued current in country speech until this century as long as everyday objects and processes remained identical with those of earlier times, and the words and phrases to describe them naturally remained appropriate. It would have been straining credulity too far to imagine that Adrian Bell's horseman and Sam Friend had any knowledge of Shakespeare's text. They were both of an age when, as horsemen and therefore above average intelligence, they would have left school at twelve and not at fourteen, and would be unlikely to be familiar with much work of Shakespeare's except perhaps one or two of the songs or a patriotic passage from the historical plays, learned by heart for recitation.

Sam Friend was like Tolstoy's philosopher in *War and Peace*, the soldier-peasant he met after the burning of Moscow – Platon Karataev – who spoke like a book (perhaps that is why Tolstoy chose the name Platon). He had memorable phrases, such as Sam Friend's 'What can't speak can't lie', 'I was so mad you could boil a kittle on my hid', 'If things don't get any better I may spreed my wings and goo to Canada'; 'Dew we git older we git wiser'.

Arthur Chaplin, a head-horseman at Stowupland in Suffolk, was a well-known ploughman who set himself the highest of standards in his craft. He confessed to me: 'I used to lie abed and do it.' He once harrowed a field that had a tree growing in the middle of it. He did it so carefully that the passer-by would have the illusion that the harrow had passed exactly through the tree. The harrow marks corresponded with those at the other side.

Over the years I have collected a number of other phrases which illustrate the range and vigour of the countryman's language:

171

He'll dig a hole for anyone [of a captious man].
Two hids are better than one even if they're only sheep's
hids.
It's raining over Will's mother. [I have not been able to
discover who Will's mother was: she may have been a
venerable village matron, or else a witch or a fairy.]

An old gypsy woman wanted to tell Nellie, a Suffolk woman,
her fortune.

But Nellie said she 'knowed it already: she were married'.

The highest testimonial in an East Anglian village:

A very nice man is Mr P., quiet and never interferes with
anybody.

On old age: He's the old man now. He's got no ink left in his
pen; or:

His arches have dropped. He's spent all the pennies in
his purse.

A bus conductor's comment on an old man:

A nice owd boy. But he's going hoom fast. I didn't know
him when he got on the bus. I'd not seen him for six
months. Another couple of clean shirts and he'll be gone.

You ought to have a pain in your tongue not your leg,
then you might not use it so much.
She allus had pork in the pot and beer in the cask. And at
harvest she'd be out raking corn behind the wagons till
ten o'clock at night.
That is a real jubilant job [a job well done].
If you can't do what you would, do what you can.
They used to take an interest in the way they made
corn-stacks in the old days. To make it harder for vermin
to get into 'em they used to draw a wagon alongside a
stack, and stand on the wagon with a scythe and then
trim the stack. They moved it round the stack. Those
stacks looked as if they been turned out of a tin.

The reader may recognize Sam Friend's comparison in the above and in the next ones:

> [Children today] got the frame. Well, if you live tidily that make the marrow; and the marrow make the boon and the boon make the frame.
> 'Striplins!' We were not very wide across the shoulder at that time of day.
> I was a bit staggery. But I'm a king to what I was.
> If Christmas Day fell on a weekday you got paid. But if it fell on a Sunday you didn't get paid for it. On Christmas Eve we worked up to six o'clock.
> When I was a prisoner of war in Germany I didn't know a Sunday from a weekday.
> A young girl in her fair prime and pollen.
> But the old days have gone. Money and Two Big Wars have killed 'em.
> That bike had a 28-inch frame. It was much too mighty for me.
> She were a big stroppolin' mawther [girl].
> You'll never miss the water till the well runs dry.
> A tramp is a traveller or a turnpike sailor.
> The black ox has trodden on his foot. [He has met with misfortune.]
> He was put in with the bread and took out with the cakes. [A brick-oven image: a bit underdone or, 'not quite twenty carats'.]

The following is evidently a malapropism but is in use in the dialect, and seems an apt misuse in this instance, a rather stronger word for a species of liar.

> He's such a fornicator! He tells you one thing to your face and another behind your back.
> Will-gill [or he-she] an alternative name for a *morphadate* [hermaphrodite] a cart or vehicle which is an amalgam of a wagon and a tumbril.

The following exchange took place at a Suffolk doctor's. It did not involve the particular horseman who invariably referred to the doctor's waiting-room as *The Doctor's trav'us*, the annexe to a smith's forge which formerly housed the trave, a wooden or metal frame, a contraption used to shoe a recalcitrant horse or bullock. It was possibly one of his friends who went to see the doctor about his foot: he had no feeling in it.

> *Horseman:* Artheritus it is, I reckon.
> *Doctor:* (after examining the foot) Don't worry. It will get better when the cuckoo comes back.
> *Horseman:* The cuckoo! The cuckoo ha' now flown back hoom! What am I a-goin' to do till the lil' owd basket come back agin?

I can name the person in the next vignette. He was Percy Wilson who was a wheelwright at Witnesham, Suffolk for many years.* He lived until he was well over eighty but when he was forty-five he had an operation for gallstones. They removed his gall-bladder. He was insured and after he had come out of hospital the insurance agent turned up to pay out a sum that was in the region of £20. After they had settled the business the agent said:

> I've got some good news for you, Mr Wilson! We can insure you again if you agree to leave out your liver! What! leave out my liver. Why I've never heard such a thing. You can't insult my liver just like that.

All the time I was attempting to record the people and the language of the old community in East Anglia, I also kept acquiring stories and titbits which I thought were worth preserving but which were difficult to include in the context of the books I was then writing. Therefore I am appending them here. This story comes from Aldeburgh from Connie Winn, an old inhabitant. She was once in the dining room of her home and there was a terrible noise coming up from the kitchen: saucepans appeared to be clattering unduly and there was an occasional crash of broken crockery: 'I made to

*W.B.W.A., pp.28–35.

go down the stairs to see what was happening. When I got halfway I heard the angry voice of the French maid saying very aggressively:

"You got nobody like Napoleon!"

'Then came the calm, decided voice of the Suffolk cook:

"And don't want! We got Oliver Cromwell and all sorts."'

At one period I came across the expression: *This side of the balk*. I was puzzled by it and eventually tracked it down in north Suffolk. The balk is the *tie-beam* in a timbered house or barn; and I first heard it used by an old friend of mine, Horace White whom I mentioned in Chapter 7. After coming out of the army at the end of the First World War he was glad to be alive. He was young and unmarried and free to enjoy himself. He spent a great deal of his leisure time in the pubs and inns. At that period, he recalled, they were not merely drinking places but somewhere where there was entertainment, singing and dancing and good fellowship. He said, 'We used to sing these songs and we'd say: "Look! Altogether, this side of the balk." The room in these old pubs was usually divided by a beam in the ceiling, somewhere near the centre. If you sat on one side of it you were "on this side of the balk" and there would be a contest with the men on the other side, to see which side would give the best rendering of a song or recitation.'

The same custom was alive in Norfolk, especially on occasions like a harvest *frolic* or *horkey*, or other special evenings. Michael Riviere of Dilham Grange quotes examples, from his own family, of singing on each side of the balk. This happened in the Paston Barn built by the famous Paston family in the sixteenth century. It is one of the most massive barns in East Anglia. Harvest frolics were held regularly here. This was the pattern when Michael Riviere's great-grandfather, Hugh Paston Mack was alive. A long table was arranged lengthways down the centre of the barn. It was dominated by the big central beam which divided the party into two groups. When they got towards the end of the meal and the speaking had been completed the company remained seated, and someone – probably after repeated badgering by his neighbours – would get up to sing, breaking the silence. As soon as the song was over the cry went up: 'Well done, our side of the balk!' This phrase, it appears, is still used in north Norfolk as a kind of friendly challenge in similar informal contests, and is equivalent to saying: 'Do better if you can.'

Michael Riviere recounts a family memory about a specific occasion in the great Paston Barn at the time of John Paston Mack. He recalls a Paston man who rode in the Charge of the Light Brigade at Balaclava:

> He came safe home and was given a celebratory dinner in the Barn. Towards the end, and no doubt full of beef and beer, they got him onto his feet; but despite encouraging shouts he was speechless. My great-grandfather, trying to help said:
>
> 'Come on, Jack! When the Charge sounded and you all began to ride forward, what was the first thing you did?'
>
> He came round a bit and said firmly:
>
> 'I hulled away my swad.'
>
> There was rather a stunned silence while everyone wondered why, so old John Mack said:
>
> 'Hurled away your sword! What did you do that for?'
>
> 'So I could have both hands to hold on with.'
>
> Roars of sympathetic laughter from his Paston friends. And that was all he would say. I think he wasn't much of a horseman, perhaps hadn't been in the regiment very long; and the great achievement in his eyes was that he had managed to do that long and difficult gallop without falling off. Unless he rode over one, he certainly did no harm to the Russians.

I have collected these examples chiefly of the dialect or every-day country speech to draw attention again to the virtues of its concrete imagery. This type of language is the mark of some of our best writers. An example comes from George Eliot's *Adam Bede*. George Eliot was brought up in the country and her childhood was steeped in country speech. She writes of a rather self-important gardener:

who is like a crowing cock who thinks the sun rises of a morning just to greet him alone.

In the same book there is an interesting figure of speech applied to a person in danger of getting above himself:

He stirred up the young woman to preach last night, and he'll be bringing other folks over to Tredleston if his comb isn't cut a bit.

The figure here is again a cockerel that is doing a bit too much crowing. But the word *comb* has an entirely different resonance in East Anglia although it is used figuratively in connection with the same type of forward person as the above in mind. A comb is a measure of corn equivalent to four bushels. It was a word used in the sixteenth century and found in Thomas Tusser, a near contemporary of Shakespeare. Under the old system in this mainly arable area it used to be estimated at the end of the last century that a farm worker's weekly wage was equivalent to the market price of a comb of wheat. So to cut someone *down* a comb implied a very sharp correction indeed.

11

Migratory Labour

In the late sixties I discovered a fruitful province where oral history could operate with advantage – migrating labour. There had been this kind of travelling about the country in the building trade since the Middle Ages. Stonemasons travelled all over Britain building the cathedrals and bigger churches, and they left to work elsewhere when the job finished. The *stonies*,* as they were called, ceased to migrate here, in any extent, in this century when concrete elbowed out many of their numbers, and many fewer stonemasons now move about the country and ponder on their life, seeing the buildings that have stood for them as visual biographies of their career. During the last century, and up to the present, there were large numbers of Irishmen crossing over to work in the mines and the factories and steel foundries of south Wales and England.† Many also crossed from Ireland in this century to help with the corn-harvest in East Anglia; and I

---

*Seamus Murphy, *Stone Mad*, Routledge & Kegan Paul, 1966.
†*W.B.W.A*, p.237.

178

met a number of Irishmen from Northern Ireland, harvesting potatoes in Ayrshire during the last war.

It was also during the nineteenth century that the malting industry expanded in various areas, chiefly in the barley-growing areas; but in the case of Burton-on-Trent the quality of the water was said to be responsible for the malting industry being sited there. The young farm workers started their seasonal migration to Burton as early as 1870 and it went on until the early 1930s when unemployment in Burton halted it. I spent a year or so in the sixties researching this migration from East Anglia.* The chief focus of my work was Burton itself, where I got the help of a Burton historian, Colin Owen. In order to get a full picture of the movement I interviewed a number of Burtonians, who were originally East Anglians who had come up to work during the malting season and had then settled in the area and raised families. I recorded at least three of these. After preparing a broadcast programme, I recorded a man who worked in the maltings near Bungay, a few miles from where I live. He was Charles Edward Fisher (born 1888) of Wainford near Bungay. He left school at thirteen, and went to work on a farm kept by a Mr Holmes. He looked after sheep and cows to start with and got half a crown a week. When he was about fifteen he started to plough – on ten-furrow work. In 1910 he left and went to work in Bury St Edmunds at a maltings, and he stayed there until 1911 when he came home for a holiday. He met Mr Mann, the manager of the Wainford Maltings, who told him:

> You don't need to go to Bury to work. There's always a job for you here.

He took the job and spent his working life there, eventually becoming foreman at Wainford Maltings:

> They were bringing the barley in from the farms at that time with horses and wagons. There'd be rows of them working during the mornings all up the road here. Some

*Ibid., Part Four

179

had thirty or thirty-five combs of barley and some had less, depending on how many horses they had. Some had two; some had as many as four. Four black horses used to come from Brooke way, all out at length. The horseman had a rein on the front horse: he could drive them, I think, anyhow. They were lovely things. He'd probably worked half the night on 'em. They looked so well: brasses all cleaned up and shining. Their coats shined, and they had ribbons on their manes and plaiting in their tails. The horsemen were pleased because they had journey-money – a shilling – six pints of beer!

We carried the comb [four bushels] sacks, sometimes up two flights of stairs – each sack sixteen stone and four pounds for the sack. You stuck that all day. That was a heavy job, and you didn't want rocking to sleep at bed-time. We got seventeen and a tanner a week when we started on that, just before the First World War. And the latter end of September they started in the malting and I went into the maltings. There wasn't so much carrying, and we got £1 a week then: a seventy-two-hour week of seven days. It went on from the second week of September till June. Then during the summer we used to do the painting and cleaning up the place. Then when I was sixteen, I went into the army. I came out in 1919; spent all the time in France.

I came back to the same maltings. When we carried the barley in then we used to put sixty comb on the malting floor and get that dry and put another sixty on at night. A man came in at night and opened the windows or closed them according to the weather. As it came in the barley had to be dried. After we finished barley-carrying the wherries came up with thirty tons of coal in each; and we had to unload that in skeps, each carrying ten stone. We had a pad on the shoulder when we carried the skep. It was some business lifting them onto your shoulder. All the time they were malting they were still drying the barley.

It was put in these here bins, and as you wanted it you

transferred it to another floor on top of the *steeps*, the wetting boxes; some of the barley was in the water for sixty hours, some for seventy-two. Then it went from the *steeps* onto the floors. It was on the floors in cold weather for twelve or thirteen days, growing and sprouting all the time. We had to turn it two or three times a day, turning it with wooden shovels and forks till you get it ready for the kilns. We carried it on the kiln; everything was done by hand – no machinery at all. The green malt was on the kiln about a foot thick. We had to fork it morning and night during the three days it was a-drying. The temperature – he would never let it go above 105 the first day. Then they let it get gradually hotter – ten or twenty degrees; 140 the third day. Till the fourth day they give-off about 205 or 210; depending on what colour you want it. Pale malt was about 210. (We made a special malt once. It was over 300 on the kiln.) After this malt came off the floor it had to be screened. This meant separating the growth on the green barley from the kernel itself. They had two big contraptions or screens.

The Burton-on-Trent maltsters told me:*

The malt came off the floor and it would go into a garner, then it had to be screened. They did this on two big screens they called *Joe and Charlie* – two big screens – in Burton. You'd get your good barley and the muck [the shoots, etc.] would go behind the screens. You had to throw the malted barley up against the screen. It was done by a fan as well. It was hot: it would nearly kill you. We had to have masks for this because of the dust ... When you came out of there you were drunk from the dust of the malt – without having nawthen to drink! No, you didn't want anything to drink when you come out of there; you were absolutely drunk! Then if you lied down for a few minutes, have a few minutes' sleep, you were right again.

*W.B.W.A., pp.259–60.

Charles Fisher continued, about the colour of the malt:

Pale ale went 3½ colour. Dark ale went 7–8 colour. You need to take a grain of malt and split it open to look at the colour. If you weren't sure, you would take a sample across to the office. Then take a few grains and grind them into a powder on a little grinder they had there. Then you got this malt meal you got from grinding and you lay it on a flat black board. Then you could see the colour better. We used to send samples up to London for the colour to be analysed, as a kind of check-up.

We made about three kinds of amber malt between the two wars. It was cruel stuff to make. The temperature on the kilns was over 300 and we had to get 30–40 colour on the grain. When you went in the kiln you had to pick your feet up right quick or else you'd get burned. [In Burton they used to supply boots with leather bottoms and canvas tops.] We made *oatmeal* malt for oatmeal stout. *Wheat* malt went to the distilleries in Scotland. We also got a lot of barley from abroad: Californian barley and Ooshak. I don't know where Ooshak comes from I'm sure. It was all black and white. The foreign barley used to be landed by ships at Lowestoft. It was brought here on the river in wherries. They put the barley in sacks to come in the big ships, and put the sacks in wherries to come here. That was never dried. It came from a dry country. It was stored in big heaps and we used to screen it from these heaps. They made pale ale. That's all they done for years. They never done no English barley for years and years. It was all this Californian and Ooshak stuff. The wherries eventually finished and Mr Walker had a steamboat: it used to tow the barges up. There's only one wherry left now: the *Albion*. It carried forty ton of coal or a load of barley.

This was in 1969. The *Albion* is, I believe, still sailing. Its skipper, at the time Charles Fisher describes, was Jack Powley, father of Happy Sturgeon* of Bungay:

*F.M.M., pp.71–85

When we used to cart up the malt to the railway station we had to cross the water to the other side of the river to get the malt stowed on the wherry. We had a platform in the middle and *deals* [boards] across the water. We had one man there if the wind was wrong, so that there was a ripple in the water, he dursn't go over. He went over one morning and he got halfway across and he see a ripple and away he went malt and all, into the river. He'd just look at the water, and couldn't do it. We got him out safely, and the malt too; and there was little harm done because the malt could be dried on the kiln.

I was foreman for twenty years. I used to like the old floor-houses best. It seemed like interesting work. You could see everything that was happening. It was hard work because it was all hand-work. Now it's all machinery, and it was more money than the present: just work eight-hour shifts. You used to have a fixed malting season of six months because of the weather. Now they go right through the year, sometimes.

Yes, I remember Rider Haggard. He lived at the top of Ditchingham. He was a magistrate they tell me, if you went up in front of him you got stung a bit. He used to come down here nearly every Sunday. Mr Mann lived here and he used to have tea with Rider Haggard and his wife. Mr Mann was the owner of the maltings at first; but got broke when they built that place in 1891. Then Barclay and Perkins took it over. He became manager for them. (John Courage owned it and now Crisp.) We knew Rider Haggard's daughter, too, Lilas. When we went to school we had to salute them: the girls had to curtsey. Later times were better than the times we had then. He was the Squire.

We rarely went out of the village. I have often made my boys laugh when I'd tell them of going into Bungay on a Saturday night to have a haircut. And this is what I spent: haircut, a penny; shave, a penny; pint of beer, tuppence; and half an ounce of tobacco, three-ha'pence. And a ha'penny change out of a tanner [sixpence]. When you went out as a young man into Bungay, and you had a half-crown [two shillings and sixpence] you were Roths-child. There were no pictures, no dances then. The pubs were the only places to go. There was singing there sometimes – and step-dancing. There used to be plays chance times. They had them in a tent behind where the Co-op now is. A concert-party used to come – Raikes's Theatre. I remember one of their plays was *Play-mates in a Bar-room*. They stayed here for several weeks. Sixpence to go in.

While recording older men such as Charles Fisher I have been impressed by the number of them who have an ambivalent attitude towards their young days. For example, in spite of more pay and shorter hours, many older miners during the change to mechanized mining, with coal-cutter and conveyor-belt, were much happier in the old pick-and-shovel method, with nothing but hand-tools. It was harder physical work but the noise and clatter of the machines in a constricted place made the accustomed talking–companionship impossible, along with the humour that made work more bearable. Under mechanized conditions the noise also prevented them hearing the small tell-tale warning sounds that preceded a movement of the roof. They were compelled to be – it seemed to the older men – dumb appendages to the machines. Most farm workers definitely did not ache for the old days, and they envied the shorter hours of their successors; but they did not envy them being in the field all day with the only company a machine. Before, they at least had the companionship of their horses.

I sometimes wonder whether a rosy view of the past is due to the tempering of former hardships whose memory is glossed over by the remembered vigour of youth, or, as the more cynical would say: When age is in, wit is out. Yet I am sure that the social climate which many farm workers experienced, helped to contribute to their distaste for the 'old days' when some of their former employers took upon themselves the role of squires and treated their workmen as medieval serfs. I have recorded elsewhere an example of this.* It is one of those long anecdotes full of contributory details that are nevertheless well worth recording, for the wealth of detail they include is a mark of a man who knows his environment intimately and can embellish the story with an authentic note that most of the listeners can recognize and unconsciously approve. In this anecdote, for instance, a blacksmith's rasp is mentioned. This is a rough file made of very hard steel for trimming and cleaning up a horse's hoof before fitting a new shoe. An old rasp often developed a secondary use and was fashioned out of the straight file into a hook with a sharp edge which was a useful tool in a garden.

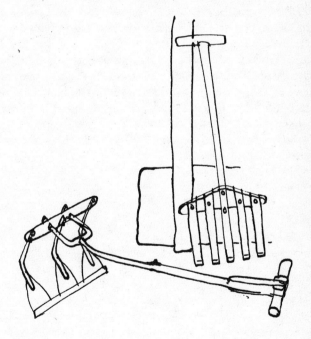

*H.P.M., pp.172–6.

Some of my best insights into the life of the old rural community have been gained from remarks or observations made in the course of atmosphere induced by an anecdote. Many of my informants have launched jeremiads against the use of artificial fertilizers, and the modern emphasis on maximum production without any regard for the long-term effect on the land itself – the country's most important capital. Yet they could not have predicted the one situation which is causing present-day farmers to reconsider their livelihood. This is the production of too much corn, a process likely to compel them to change not only their technique of farming but also to force them to grow an alternative product. At one time the old farm workers and farmers – as older men in their industries – were often sought out by their successors for advice on problems they have met in their work. Now we are not only in a different age but in a different environment in the corn-growing areas where farming practices and the new 'prairie' farms are irrational according to the accepted wisdom of a few years ago. This wisdom was acquired by a millenial tradition and through the farmers' and workers' own lifetime experience on the land. Today the land is farmed differently, and the paid-for wisdom is negated and is no longer transmissible.

Huntingfield

12

Recording a Centenarian

Rose Luke, who was unmarried, dug up her potatoes on 21 June 1982, her hundredth birthday:

Yes, I was hundred on that day. I had been doing that on my birthday, planting and digging up my potatoes ever since 1919. I had 150 cards, twelve bouquets, four telegrams – including one from the Queen. But I valued the one I had most, the one I had from one of my Sunday-School boys. I valued that more than the Queen's, I was really touched by that boy. He now lives at Cambridge. He's done well: the whole family did. He's about sixty now. He's head of an insurance business. I did appreciate that boy when I heard from him. They were all like children to me. I was born at Green Farm, Cookley,

Suffolk. Father was under Lord Huntingfield for thirty-eight years. It was hard work on the farm: butter-making, cheese-making, and dressing the fowls, and the chickens, the ducks and the turkeys. We were only six-pennorth of coppers' knocked down, as you might say. They knew me well in Halesworth, the nearest town. I used to stroll round the edge. I didn't go to just anyone: the doctors, the vicar, the auctioneer – all the top ones.

For breadmaking we had a brick-oven shaped like a dome, almost like a horseshoe. It took about an hour to heat that oven. Lot of people used to use bushes, but we had a lot of wood. We never used bushes. We raked the ashes to the side. The meat used to go near to that, and the bread all the way round; the cakes and pies and all that in the centre. The bricks used to turn white when they were heated. Once a week we used the brick-oven – the end of the week. If we wanted a joint during the week we used to use the wall-oven. It was in the wall and had a fire underneath and a flue went across to the open fireplace.

I had four brothers. They're all gone now. Poor little Cinderella is left.

'Four brothers to look after you.'

No! It was the other way about!

I did some work on the farm. I have milked and I used to warm the milk from the farm for the calves. They couldn't drink it cold. Father used to have hoggets [year-ling sheep] to feed off the turnips. We only kept a few hoggets. My main job was to go by pony and trap to Halesworth every week with fowls, butter, and cheese. We also went to the Maltings for malt. (The village malt-ings have all gone now.) We brewed our own beer twice a year: half a comb of malt in the spring and half a comb in the autumn. There was always a barrel down in the cellar – always. The *small beer* we used for drinking every day. When the malt was first wetted it was left – I forget the exact time it stood – and then it was taken off, and it made nine gallons of ale. Then there was a large tub –

well, it stood about my height and as big round as a table. I could just see into it as I stood up. Then it was filled up again with some boiled water to stand until the next day [the second wort] and that was called the *small beer* for the dinner-table. There was a beer we kept apart [*the first wort*] so that anyone who came specially to see us, we'd serve them that.

That's one thing I did once: cut up a whole pig. It was during the First World War. A neighbour and a friend killed it. He could do it beautifully! So my father said:

'We'll have one done, and we'll have it in the house.'
Before the rationing got bad during the war, you see. That would be on a Saturday. So I thought to myself: I know what's going to happen: I would be in a mess all Sunday. I don't know, I might have been in my twenties. The pig hung up on hooks in the kitchen on a great beam. I thought to myself if I could do that and get that done! I got up about five o'clock on Saturday morning – so I thought to myself I'll do it! Because it looked big to me. So I pushed the table underneath the pig and loosened the hooks on it, and it gradually came down and laid on the table. And I got the carving knife and I got to work on it. And Father came home later in the morning and said:

'Where's the pig?'
'In the dairy.' (Calm as you please.)
We used the butter-*keeler** for putting the joints in. The pig was hanging from the beam, cut down the centre all in one piece with a *bucker*† to keep the halves apart; and we also had the steel-yards to weigh it. But I didn't want to weigh the pig as long as I got it down. Father said:

'She made a good hand of that ham.'
You got to cut the hams up, trim them and make a nice shape. I could do things then: I get so annoyed with myself now: I could do things then. I can do it in my

---

*A shallow wooden tub.
†A curved piece of wood with a nick cut at each end.

mind but I haven't got the strength. We had what we called the pluck. We used to give some to our neighbours. The meat used to go to Halesworth to be smoked. Cook Kent made wooden barrels and things and had all this sawdust. We had what they used to call a *smokey-house* – a brick shed with a roof and door and no windows.

The meat was hung up on hooks in the shed, and sawdust and wood chippings were laid on the floor at the base of the walls. The sawdust and wood was lighted; and the door was closed. The meat was truly smoked after a day or so. This method of smoking meat was described by Thomas Tusser in the sixteenth century. When we lived in Blaxhall I described a 'smokey-house' to a group in Bentwaters, the American air-base, and I was interested to know that some of the American airmen and their wives recognized the old method and one of them from Texas knew the term, 'smokey-house'.

Miss Luke again:

I did smoke a ham once in our own fireplace. It was a large place a great open fireplace – with a great open fire and a copper. There were huge chains hung from the chimney; and they were left there when we came away. And there was this big hook hanging from the chain. I thought to myself: Well, I don't know whether I should do that; and I put the ham in a hessian bag. So that it didn't get scorched when the oven was going I took the ham down and hung it up again afterwards. It did well.

We did bake a ham once in a wheatmeal crust in a brick-oven. That was lovely. The ham tasted well, and the bread crust was fed to the pigs. The ham baked uniformly. My brother came to stay with us once and brought his five children. We took twenty-two loaves of bread out of that oven. We used to use five stone of flour at a time; it was in a sack. We also baked French loaves – long loaves. We called them *sticks*.

I called on Ruth Luke just as she was about to prepare her lunch. She lived by herself and saw to most of her needs. We

talked for about three quarters of an hour when I recorded
one side of a five-inch tape; and, not wishing to tire her, I
switched off. Yet she carried on talking; and not knowing
whether or not I had finished recording her, she switched to
talking about her early days with the family and the tensions
within the family. One fact became clear immediately: she did
not get on well with her mother; and I became aware that her
resentment against her was very deep as showed from its
lasting nearly nine decades. I suspected some such tension
from a remark she made when I recorded her. To my
remark: 'Four brothers to look after you,' she replied tartly:
'It was the other way about.' What had happened was that
Ruth, as the only girl, was literally the Cinderella as soon as
she reached thirteen or fourteen. Until then her mother
employed a housemaid, but as soon as Ruth was able to take
her place she was dispensed with. Soon with the coming of the
war she became an essential part of the household; and when
her mother died she became tied to the kitchen for the rest of
her life on the farm. This left an undercurrent of bitterness;
and I was struck by the spirited way she described her reaction, and the deep feeling that was behind it. It is possible she
would not have revealed her feelings with such frankness if I
had recorded her. In any event, the ethical question whether
or not to reveal them now does not arise because Ruth Luke
died a year or so after our conversation; and she herself came
out of the long family impasse without the slightest tinge of
blame.

E. H. Carr one of our outstanding modern historians, who
died a few years ago, wrote:

> It may make perfectly good sense to say, for example,
> that we are nearer today to the Middle Ages than were
> our grandfathers a century ago.

Historians had laboriously worked the whole field of
medieval history during the nineteenth century yet there is a
revival and a popularization of medieval studies which have
been particularly noticeable since the last war. Recently, I

wanted to consult some old records and I visited the Record Office in the nearest city, Norwich. I entered a fairly large room which was completely full of researchers. No seat at the tables was empty, and three or four places had been fitted up in the corridor outside. It was suggested that I return within an hour when it would be likely that a chair would be vacant. I did this and got ready attention. But I was a little surprised at the popularity of historical studies during holiday time in the middle of August. This, however, may be partly accounted for by the new facilities that are now available to researchers: mechanical aids, for example, that enable them to consult a series of photographed documents in a short half-hour whereas previously they might spend the best part of a morning searching through the originals. It is probable that only a small proportion of the researchers on this particular morning were concerned with medieval history. Yet the general desire to research farther back in our history has undoubtedly arisen from the feeling that we have in recent years seen the effective end of the Middle Ages. To give one small example: most of Ruth Luke's activities in her long life in the kitchen and on the farm were being followed in exactly the same way in the fourteenth and fifteenth centuries: the milking of the cows, the harvesting of the corn, the baking of bread in a brick oven, and the brewing of beer.

The growth of local history societies and the popularity of record offices attached to libraries have greatly increased medieval studies; and the introduction of classes where students can learn to read the cursive Gothic scripts has increased the interest in pre-modern history. Periods of rapid change induce a consciousness of the actual process. This leads to a consciousness of the process itself and an awareness of similar periods that have occurred in the past. The beginning of the nineteenth century was such a time when industrialization began and mechanical industries proliferated. This saw an accompanying founding and flourishing of learned societies, and a general quickening of interest in the immediate past; just as we are experiencing today: the setting up of organizations to preserve old things: engines, cars, photographs, tools, and antiques – a kind of compensating attitude to knit ourselves to a quickly disappearing past. In this century the providing of local facilities for studying the past such as the university extra-mural classes and the Workers' Educational Association groups has changed the position. Many people have been introduced to a wider conception of the past than they had hitherto been initiated into. Yet I believe a contributory reason for the renewed interest in medieval studies is the manifest examples of the end of processes, tools and customs – the whole apparatus of a material culture that is coming to an end almost before our eyes. This is most dramatic in the countryside where the mechanization of agriculture has caused a revolution in production and has effectively brought an end to animal traction; especially the horse that has been in farming since the twelfth century in Suffolk. Methods of cultivation, and technical terms that were part of the vocabulary of farming and of country life have now gone into limbo or have been left marginally alive in local word-lists. It is as if, unconsciously, we have a not wholly welcoming feeling towards this new world which is evolving, and we attempt, therefore, not finally to cut ourselves off from an irrevocable past.

There may, however, be an added or deeper reason for our interest in history at the present time; and one writer has commented on this and put forward a reason for its occurring. He is Mircea Eliade, a professor of comparative religion who is well known in Europe and the USA. In one of his books* there is a chapter on Western man's abnormal interest – one could say his passion – for historical writings and the resulting paramount importance which Western philosophers ascribe to history. He states that the new interest in history dates from the second half of the nineteenth century. It is true that from the time of Herodotus the Greeks and the Romans developed the writing of history, but this history had a different purpose from our present-day discipline. Historians then, and even those of later periods, wrote history to

Myths, Dreams and Mysteries, Fontana Library, Collins, 1968, Chap. ix.

preserve examples and pass on models for later imitation. But during the past century, Eliade maintains, history has altered its purpose, whether consciously or otherwise, and aims at an accurate chronicling of the adventures of mankind: 'an endeavour to reconstitute the entire past of the species and make us conscious of it'. He concludes that this type of history is only written in the West. Non-European cultures are without the same historic consciousness. The writing of history, for example, in China and the countries under the Islamic culture still has as its main purpose the holding up of exemplary models.

Eliade then goes on to examine this intense passion for history in our own culture in order to find out why we are so preoccupied with it. He brings forward a reason that is widespread in many religions, and also in the folklore of European people. This is the belief that at the point of death a man remembers his past life in minute detail. On the analogy of this belief our preoccupation with history and modern culture would portend its imminent passing away. He believes that for modern man death is no part of life: it is emptied of its traditional meaning. For Western man death is followed by nothing; and before nothingness man is paralysed. This is in direct contrast to the state of traditional man, the so called primitive, who was led by a careful initiation to a gradual experience of the trauma of death which effectively innoculates him against the anxiety of his actual death that he experiences, usually much later. This experience is part of the rites of puberty as soon as he reaches that age. In many primitive tribes there was a hut reserved for initiation. It was situated apart in the bush or the wilderness where the candidates for initiation or entry into the tribe underwent the ordeals of their initiation, and their instruction in the secret traditions of the tribe. The cabin symbolizes the maternal womb, and he lives the start of his life symbolically, and progresses by instruction by the tribe's elders, until he reaches the state of pre-manhood. He is led by them into the wilds where he is purposefully terrified, haunted by demons uttering strange noises. (These noises are simulated by the bull-roarer, a whirling piece of wood on a string that gives out a moaning, frightening noise.) He learns at his time in isolation the names of the gods whose voices the bull-roarer purports to be and the ritual knives whose purpose was to increase his fear. In short he is introduced to a minor death to strengthen him, enabling him to reach the next stage of development – his manhood.

The primitive is, therefore, prepared for his death and has none of the anxiety of modern man when his thoughts dwell upon it. He is confident that it is only another stage or progression on his journey, another door to a different continuing mode of life. Modern man's anxiety in the face of death is rendered more acute in this nuclear age when a real fear of the end of the world makes its reappearance. This has surfaced repeatedly down the ages and yet man still has the confidence, as his ancestors had, to believe that life will continue.

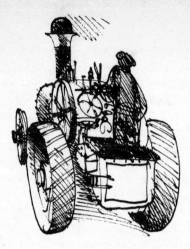

13

Threshing

One man has given me tremendous help in writing my later East Anglian books. He is Aston Gaze who lives in the next village of Howe. He comes of a family of auctioneers and farmers who for generations have taken an active interest in the land. I have recorded him many times and he was particularly helpful when I was researching the use of the commons and small pieces of common-land. He was born at Scole in 1902 and brought up at Diss, and he has had an eventful life. Enlisting at Christmas 1939 he was six years in the army.

His unit, Recovery Section, the Army Field Workshop, sailed for France in April 1940. From the neighbourhood of Brussels he was in the retreat to Dunkirk. When failing to embark with his unit, he took some wounded men in his ambulance to the British Hospital. He was then asked to take the ambulance to the quays. He was in this work for nearly the whole of the evacuation. He noticed that the Germans sent their bombers to bomb the quays every twenty minutes and he timed his forays to get the wounded to the quays as soon as they headed back. He was at the hospital when the Germans came in. He was taken prisoner and finally landed up in Strasburg; and he was employed driving lorries. Eventually he got over the wall, and walked for a fortnight through occupied France, swimming the river Looe to the unoccupied zone. He was finally interned at Marseilles. After three unsuccessful attempts, he crossed the Spanish frontier and walked for seven days to Barcelona. He went to the British Consulate who forwarded him to the British Embassy at Madrid where the Ambassador, Sir Samuel Hoare, who had a Norfolk estate, took considerable interest in his story and his knowledge of Norfolk. He was sent by train to Gibraltar, and was soon on his way back to Britain.

He was glad to be home but back in the army he soon heard that escaped prisoners would not be sent abroad again. However – possibly with a kindly word from the Ambassador, who was then on leave – he was soon on the boat for the Far East. Here he was transferred as a Sergeant to the XX Indian Division. He was with the Division through the advance to Rangoon. The atom bomb was dropped and the war was over. He got home about May 1946.

Back in the seventies he reminded me that in my books I had not yet written directly about the threshing-gangs that were a prominent feature of the farming scene in East Anglia, until the coming of the combine-harvester had made them redundant. He told me of one of the last threshing-gangs in the district. It was linked with the Magpie pub in Fersfield, a village near Diss. The landlord, Reginald Hoskins, the former owner of the local engine and threshing-drum, had a son and a grandson who were both members of the gang. It was at a time when the Magpie was about to close. During that period many pubs were closing owing to a change in the character of the road traffic: with the passing of the horse and a quickening in the development of the motor car after the war, many roadside pubs were closed and became private houses. The carters and the travellers to the towns no longer stopped to bait their horses, and the pubs had outlived their original

purpose of resting places for horse traffic. Aston Gaze heard
about the Magpie's closing and suggested that I should record
the threshing-gang as it would probably be the last time they
would get together. I agreed with the suggestion, and he
organized the remnant of another gang from the Suffolk
border and they joined the group. This included Frank
Stevens who had inherited the threshing business from his
father and James Thrower, the oldest man present and once
employed by Frank Stevens's father. He was eighty-nine
when I first met him at the Magpie; and he was the star of the
evening. James (Jimfer to the rest of the gang) was the
'feeder' the man who fed the corn into the actual threshing-
drum. The engine-driver and the feeder were the two most
important jobs in the threshing.

I have written elsewhere about recording in a pub; and
the whole experience confirmed my reluctance to try and
conduct a group-recording. There was no question of custo-
mers coming into the pub to be served as the place was
effectively closed. We all sat around in a half-circle, and I
recorded one member of the team at a time But they were,
for some reason, strangely inhibited. Their responses were
stilted and hesitant; and I came to the conclusion that they
were averse to exposing themselves before other experts. But
the exercise was saved by Jimfer Thrower who was older than
any of the others by nearly a generation. He was direct and
unselfconscious and gave an account of the threshing experience from the age of eleven, with the total recall of a man
describing his young days. I have noticed before that men of
his generation, born about 1880, were the best performers
before the microphone. They spoke positively and naturally,
possibly because they had not had much experience at school
where they learned a different language from the dialect, and
where they were urged to speak 'good English' and the dialect
was frowned upon. The brighter ones, too, at that period got
away from school early, at twelve years of age, as Jimfer seems
to have done. Yet Aston Gaze was right in emphasizing the
importance of the threshing-gang, in spite of the lack of

complete success of the experiment. For threshing the corn was the farmer's real harvest, the culmination, as he would not get paid until the corn was in the sack after threshing. And there was a feeling of achievement at the close of a successful threshing, the real climax of a year for a farmer in the corn area.

I have transcribed Jimfer Thrower's account of his threshing experience, starting in 1893:

> I was born in Scool* in 1882, and I was with the late Mr Edgar Stevens [a threshing contractor], and afterwards with his son, Mr Frank Stevens. I was thrashing for most of my life. I can recollect the time before I went to school: I can recollect that! The doctor told my father that he wouldn't bring me up, for some cause or other. I don't know why: I was never vaccinated nor nothing. But they did bring me up! I don't think I was really eleven when I left school; but you used to go at half-time – at any time – that time o' day. The first day's threshing I done was for a man by the name of Rogers, Harry Rogers. I got ninepence for that. A man got one and eightpence, and threepence allowed for beer. My first job was pulling away *colder*,† and carting chaff. After a little while I went on to the drum with Mr Stevens' brother, Sid; and then I got a full man's money, one and eightpence, a lot o' money to take home then. I was somewhere about fourteen. We used to thrash in the winter-time; and then, of course, we had to do something else in the summer. That didn't go on all the year. We started in August and went on until the job was finished. Of course, we only got one thrashing set at that time o' day, you see; and we'd finish in March or the fore-part of April time.

---

*I have transcribed the word as he said it. It is probably the authentic name of the place.
†The refuse of threshed corn: light ears, bits of straw, etc., rubbish piled up behind the drum. The chaff, like the husks of corn, was saved in bags.

I remember the old *portable** engines very well. The first one I recollect, I was about five years old; and there was a man by the name of Gooderich had one at Scool, an old portable. How long he had that before then, I don't know. I became a *feeder*, feeding the corn into the thrashing-drum. It was a bit of a risky job. I got a fork stuck through my hand more than once: I got several tips off here and little stabs and one thing and another. But I didn't pay much regard to that: that were all in the day's work. There was a man I worked with – I done seven seasons along with him: and there wasn't so much as an angry word or *dammit* passed between us. Of course, we had to walk to work at that time o' day. We walked 108 miles one week, and we earned eightpence each for the week! (I got an owd cutting from the paper of when he died and that: I meant to put that little piece in my pocket; but I come away and forgot it. I got it lay at hoom.) That was about 1907 or '8. We walked from Little Thornham to Stearns of Shimpling; and we walked there for a week. We went there with a new cloth on the drum, as near as could be; and when we come away there wasn't a piece of it no bigger than your hand. Wind! Wet! I got wet and then I got dry! and we couldn't do this job because of the weather. And there were oak trees stood up there; and it snapped three of 'em off just like snapping a match. That was a rum wind!

But, of course, you wouldn't recollect the heavy wind. That's about seventy-five years ago. Well, that was a lovely Saturday. On the Sunday morning that started – the wind started blowing. And that was a funny, funny wind that was! That blow scores of trees down: cattle, horses on the meadow, some on 'em. It just took 'em up like that, and took 'em across: some were lying in the

---

*The precursor of the traction engine. The portable had to be pulled from farm to farm by horses. Horses, too, transported the necessary threshing-gear: the tumbril of coal, the elevator and so on, as well as the threshing-drum.

ditch, some in the hedge. And I've been wanting to ask if they got a record o' that at Pulham St Mary. The parson there, the chapel parson, he went there; and it just lifted the roof off the chapel like that and killed him in the pulpit, blew in the wall. As dead as a doornail! That was in 1856.*

It took all the stacks up – tons and tons – and simply took 'em up like that off the ground and scattered them over the fields. I know a man, Mr Pymar, Spencer Pymar who lives at Diss. His father sent him after an owd man somewhere to come hoom; and he had an owd pony. And the wind took him up pony and all, and plumped him up against the hedge. He was telling me about that not long ago.

To come back to the thrashing: I can recollect one little incident. We were working on a farm, and I had a little dawg; and another chap with me he had a little dawg. And I think, if I remember right, they killed around about 170 rats while we were thrashing; and they had no netting round the stacks then. Anyhow, we finished; and when we were gathering the things together, these little dawgs they got a rabbit. And the farmer came arter us in what you'd call a hurry. He would have prosecuted us if it hadn't been for Mr Stevens – just because the dawgs got that rabbit! He would have prosecuted us. Yeh! And he told Mr Edgar Stevens:

'Never bring them men on my place no more!'

Yeh, yeh. We happened on some good 'uns, and we happened on some sort of funny ones when we goo round. There were some good uns, good old fellers. But there were a lot o' poor farmers at that time o' day. They was poor men but they were good 'uns. But there was some of 'em, they wasn't any too good. There was a lot of 'em; and I told 'em about the thrashing:

*Sunday 24 March 1895. George Dearle of Diss, a Baptist minister, was struck in the pulpit by falling masonry. His skull was fractured, and he died the next day after 'the operation of trepanning was carried out' in Norwich hospital. The *Norfolk Chronicle and Norwich Gazette*, 30 March 1895.

'When it comes to the last quarter of an hour, you want to have that last a long while!'

They was always in a hurry, but they didn't do anything properly. And there was a rare lot of them. They didn't make owd bones. They didn't make owd bones! It was no good. When you go arter a job like that, if you're doing as fast as what the machine will take it to do it properly, you can't force it. I very often wonder how they do as they do today. When we went thrashing we had to set our things level to do our work. Now they can take a combine, they go uphill, downhill, side-hill – any owd way, and away they goo! We must have been fules, you see, to have took all that trouble to level our things up!

I used to steer the owd engine when it went on the road. And I steered that, I may say – hundreds of miles is a lot, I know, but I could bring that into hundreds. When it has been properly dark, there used to be one man walking the road in the wheel-track, carrying an owd lantern, a horn-lantern with a candle in it. You had to steer by that. Did I have an accident? No, I never had no accident. They used to fly at me sometimes because I used to give a fairish amount of room to these things [other traffic]. But if we'd had an accident they'd allus have been on our track, wouldn't they? So we . . . *prevention is better'n cure*; that's what I told a lot of 'em.

In the period of unemployment on the land during the twenties and thirties, young men would travel for miles, usually during the winter, just to get a temporary job of threshing, and they would present themselves at the gate of the farmer's threshing yard on the morning after the engine appeared. It was embarrassing for the farmer who had many more applicants than he needed. He usually solved the problem by calling out the married men and sending the single ones away. A grandson of one of the Suffolk family, the Goddards of Kettleburgh, told me a story of his grandfather who faced a similar dilemma at the beginning of the century. Many Irishmen came over at that time to help with the harvest. He kept them out of the yard, behind a locked gate until he was ready to let them in. It was his way of demonstrating who was the boss. The Goddard family specialized also in the production of hay; and one of the family, an old lady, Evelina Goddard* a niece of John Goddard of Tunstall, was an authority on the making and marketing of hay which has been called the *petrol* of the working-horse epoch.

Aldeburgh

14

Archaeology and Old Beliefs

After my studying of the old prior community both in Wales
and East Anglia, and elsewhere, I was recently encouraged to
find a chapter from a book by Colin Renfrew, Professor of
Archaeology (of St John's College, Cambridge), one of Dr
Glyn Daniel's former students: it draws attention to the help
the old communities can give to archaeologists; and it is a
vindication of the method of scrupulously recording the men,
the tools, and the techniques used in the old hand-tool communities. Professor Renfrew, in his book *Before Civilization*,
stresses the need for new evidence in the discipline: 'Artefacts
alone are not enough. To study population, intensive surveys
of whole regions and the careful consideration of land-use
become necessary.' A few years ago I saw a television film of
one of his 'digs' on the Greek Island of Aphrodite (Crete). In
it we saw a recent procession in honour of the Virgin Mary.
The form of the procession with the vases of flowers lining
the route was similar in shape and design to a procession for

Aphrodite depicted on ancient vases; and the receptacles holding the flowers were identical with some of the vases excavated in the Island. In my work in East Anglia and elsewhere, I have found similar examples of belief that have survived from very ancient times and have been grafted on to a newer religion. For a long time I was puzzled by the crowded churches in East Anglian villages to celebrate the harvest. Invariably the church was well decorated and instead of having a sprinkling of worshippers as it had for most of the year, it was crowded; and there was a far bigger proportion of men among the congregation. It was clear that the old pre-Christian impulse to hold a ceremony at harvest had still been sustained. The farm workers were easily picked out: their faces shining and weather-beaten, and their hair, often uncharacteristically disciplined with the help of oil or pomade and flattened on their scalps, both emphasized that it was about the only occasion in the year when they had been to church. And looking at them one would find it hard to be certain that any specifically Christian doctrine in the ceremonial had percolated through. They were, rather, obeying an ancient impulse to thank and placate whatever Power there is for, yet again, granting another harvest to bolster them over the coming winter, calming an ancient fear that still persisted in spite of the state's partial concern in keeping hunger and the effects of bad weather at bay.

While we lived a Blaxhall, I came across confirmation of my feeling about the persistence of the ancient pattern from another observer. I was talking to my near neighbours, Robert and Priscilla Savage, and while discussing the village as they remembered it earlier, Priscilla showed me a booklet written by Lady Graham, the wife of Lord Alistair Graham, who owned one of the farms in the village. They were both active members of the Church of England and Lady Graham had written the booklet for use in the Church. She stated that there were many pagan beliefs that had still not been eradicated from people's minds. Accommodation with the former religion started very early in the foundation of Christianity in Britain. There is an extant letter of Pope Gregory giving suggestions to St Augustine, one of the first Christian missionaries, that pagan temples and shrines should not be destroyed but after being ritually cleansed should be used for Christian worship. Therefore, there must have been some initial ambivalence in the minds of the early Christians as to the nature of the new God they were worshipping; and doctrinal subtleties were not likely to be scrutinized too carefully. This is understandable, as up to the beginning of the present century most of the tools of farming and many of the articles of everyday living in the rural areas, the furniture of existence, were very similar to those used in the period before Christianity first came to these islands. The context of living, as Professor Renfrew observed, was very similar in the non-industrial societies; and this is the kind of society he had in mind when he advised archaeologists to find an approximate context against which to examine artefacts they have discovered. At first glance they would naturally look at those people who have not progressed very far from the primitive conditions of a prior culture. Yet evidence can sometimes be gained about the identity of an artefact from a contemporary rural community. A wooden object was once discovered on a site and archaeologists attempted to interpret its use. The interpretations were various: a musical instrument, a machine for making peat-bricks, a model of a boat, and a device for catching pike. A Scandinavian, Holger Rasmussen, recognized its true use: it was a wooden object still used in Eastern and Central Europe for entrapping the foot of wild animals.

In addition to helping archaeologists place the artefacts they unearth in a recognizable setting, a close examination of a rural area in Britain may still have a great deal to tell them about the organization and the processes at work in a small self-contained community, and how it was likely to function in the time they are seeking to reconstruct.

I have referred to anthropology in connection with oral history and I suggested that the pursuit of oral history has many links with that discipline. Anthropology is primarily concerned with the basic social universals, mental processes of which cultural institutions are actual expressions. Is it that these universals are more likely to be apprehended by the oral historian also for he, like the anthropologist, records directly from people? If this is so the emphasis on the oral tradition and the field-work that this entails is more likely to induce the student occasionally to forsake the narrow ground of his own speciality and to become aware of a wider horizon and to ask himself: are the old people I am meeting and talking with so very different after all from their grandchildren? Is it true they are not and yet in many respects, they are as distant in years by as much as half a millennium, probably more. And yet they were not strange to us although this new world of technological revolution was strange to them. Their upbringing in an essentially different society has made them different, but their identity with us in human feelings and preferences argued that semblances far outweigh their differences. This being so, the student of the oral tradition should find it easier to apprehend that people living a few thousand miles away in a different culture may, under their surface differences, belong to the same human ground-plan, be moved by the same universal laws, whether or not these laws are peculiar to humanity or yet partake of the same structure as the physical or inanimate universe. By the same argument, he should not think it bizarre that he could consider that people who lived in the same area and followed in a similar occupation and ploughed the same soil, although by different means, in an identical context, hundreds of years before could come, at least substantially, alive to him.

It is not difficult to list beliefs and practices that show in some areas of the old people's thinking they were not so very different from their remote ancestors. I once heard a Suffolk villager refer to a man born out of wedlock as a *self-sown man*. The expression has a chthonic ring about it, linked with the phrase *Mother Earth* and the belief that the earth is the inexhaustible source of all creation. Again David Butcher in his researches into East Coast fishing has found that some skippers in the fishing boats in the twenties and thirties, when they first carried wireless receiving sets, would switch off when they heard livestock market prices broadcast in case

207

they should hear the names of some of the animals that were taboo words on board ship – pig or hare, for example.

A few years ago I was taking an extra-mural course at the Moot Hall in Aldeburgh. When talking one night, after the discussion had ended, a member of the group told me a story which I suspect she refrained from mentioning during the discussion for fear of being accused of 'drawing the long bow'. Her father had been, earlier in this century, the rector of a remote village in mid-Suffolk where there is a large and reputedly deep pond. One day he was passing it and saw some people on the edge of the pond, and in the water a man struggling, obviously in difficulties. Yet in spite of this, the bystanders made no attempt to rescue him. He rated them, and between them they got the drowning man to the bank. Later, on questioning them, he found that they believed that if they rescued him, the pond would demand a surrogate, someone to drown instead of the intended victim. I could hardly credit the story when I heard it, not because the lady who told me it was not reporting a true happening, but because the only place I had heard of a similar belief was in China.* There, boatmen were very unwilling to rescue any-one falling into the Yangtze river. A charitable institution had been compelled to offer a high reward for rescue work:

> Moreover, it was necessary to double the reward if the victim was drawn out living, for the boat people were more inclined to allow the river god to have his sacrifice and then rescue the corpse for burial.

Here is another incident taken from one of the survivors of this last generation who had in their keeping the very ancient traditions. He was Anthony W. Lankester of Helmingham in Suffolk. The great-grandfather of one of the Lankesters, and grandfather later, had been in charge of a stud of Suffolk horses belonging to the Duke of Grafton and later the Duke of Montrose at Easton in Suffolk. Anthony Lankester was a farm horseman all his life. He had tried the frog's bone ritual

*C.P. Fitzgerald, *A Short Cultural History*, London, 1942.

but apparently was not successful; therefore he was not among 'the inner ring'. He told me:

> Most of the owd horsemen used to keep the *know* to themselves. They said: why should I tell you? I'll take it into the ground with me.

Although he was not in the inner-ring fraternity he appeared to have the cast of mind that could well have qualified him to belong. He told me once of an experience he had of *casting a spell*, as he called it, on his next-door neighbours at Helmingham where there were a number of *double-dwellers*, pairs of semi-detached dwellings, each on a half-acre of land:

> I shouldn't tell you this – but we once had very bad neighbours, and it went on and on. And I said to my wife one day: 'We'll have to do suthen about it!' So I got some hairs out of the *nap* of my neck – have you ever heard of this before? – Well, I took these hairs and put them in a saucepan and covered them with *aqua vitae*. Then that night we closed all the doors in the room where we were going to do it. We sealed up the room. [Probably it meant placing gummed paper along all the joins in the doors and windows.] Then at the stroke of midnight I put the saucepan on the fire. I said to my wife as we watched it:
>
> 'Keep to it! I'm with you. There's nothing to be afraid of.'
>
> As soon as it boiled there were voices in the chimney there, as plain as if they were in this room. Then there was some shrieking and howling. Well, they weren't there long after that. The buggers were out of that house in three months.
>
> There's a way of doing harm to people even if you're nowhere within six hundred miles of them. But you can't get the stuff – herbs and things – now.

He once went to Manchester and stayed with his brother-in-law, and he said to himself:

> This is the place where a lot of foreign ships come in. I'll get the horse recipe made up here in Manchester.

There was an old chemist but he retired before he could get it. So he gave the recipe to his brother-in-law. (It appeared to be a drawing-oil: oil of rhodium, burdock and, possibly, oil of aniseed – he couldn't remember the third.) He told his brother-in-law to say it was for rats. The chemist said:

'This is not for rats, this is for a horse!' The chemist, however, agreed to supply the recipe; but when he learned the cost, the brother-in-law wrote to Lankester telling him the cost would be £8. Lankester refused to go any further with the transaction:

'It wouldn't be worth all that to me at my time of life.'
He was forced to continue with his old method which was experience and common sense:

> You've got to be quick in mind and action with all horses. And with the young cowts [colts], the same as all horses; you got to watch their ears. If their ears go down, you know you go to do suthen quick. And if they fall down, get into a knot, get tangled with the reins, like the time I'll tell you about, get your clasp knife and cut the harness quick to liberate him. I had a mare once who got the rein tangled in his shaft-hook; and she were frightened and kept a-backing. The boss's car was just behind the tumbril, and I had to do suthen quick. I cut the rein with my knife. The farmer was a bit angry; but I told him if I had waited to unloose the rein the tumbril would have been into his car. Besides, it wasn't difficult to splice the rein afterwards.

He also told me about taking *the know* out of a difficult horse in a sandpit on a moonlight night – a horse that was being very difficult. As far as I could gather this was simply using the post method, used by Charles Rookyard with the cords:

> You had to use anything to get the master of a horse, or he'd be the master of you. You had to be cruel to be kind: you had to do it. About the sandpit on a moonlight night, there's something about the doing of it then. That's where you get the ghost side of your business. The frog's

bone was the same thing. You got the black owd toad out of the garden.

Although he had failed in his toad's bone episode, he described the ritual as recorded elsewhere; but he kept stressing that it had to be at the dead of night, midnight on a moonlight night.

One could equate little of his recording with the farm workers I have recorded, but I am fairly certain that such beliefs were not uncommon among the remote villages in East Anglia.

15

Influences

I sometimes wonder why my writing has taken the direction it has during these later years. Starting with verse and short fiction, with a concentration for some years on writing for radio, I changed to an almost complete concentration on writing about the work of ordinary people, many of whom found that their traditional skills, acquired during a long lifetime, were made redundant by the big modern changes. Some writers have characterized these changes as heralding the Second Industrial Revolution. This term is used comprehensively to include modern farming. The farms in the corn area of East Anglia, for example, are often referred to as the new factory-farms; and the scale and complexity of their organization seem to justify the term which makes the new farming more akin to the highly mechanized factory with its proliferation of machines and its reduction in human labour. This has caused the number of people employed in agriculture in the area to diminish to a very small percentage of the rural population. To a lesser extent the same process has happened in coal-mining, the other work which I have been interested in. Though the reduction in labour has been proportionately less than in farming, the main loss in manpower there has been in the mines that have been closed through coal-seams being worked out.

My upbringing in a mining valley made it almost inevitable that my writing should take a certain slant, and should be coloured and deepened by living in a community that was in crisis. My first published stories were about miners; and my reading during that period in the thirties had a definite political bias. As I have already stated, among the books I read was one that influenced me greatly: Friedrich Engels's *The Origin of the Family* (1884). Engels wrote this book towards the end of the last century after discovering the researches of Lewis Morgan, the American anthropologist who had lived among the Iroquois tribe of American Indians, studying their customs and particularly their system of marriages. Morgan was a true pioneer in finding out the structure of the family; and Engels gave material point to his work. The task of the family was two-fold: to produce the means of existence, food, clothing and tools; and, on the other side, the reproduction of human beings themselves. Morgan found that the kinship and marriage structure of this Indian tribe was essentially the same as the *genea* of the Greeks and the *gens* of the Romans. This came as a revelation to me for the reason that I had found the Roman *gens* a stumbling block when I was working for my degree: I could not understand it. To find now that the pattern – the whole structure of marriages – could be reconstructed among a tribe of nineteenth-century 'primitives', and would prove a key to unlock and explain such ancient texts, was to me a real discovery indeed. It also proved, moreover, that a primitive society was a well-balanced and intricate entity, not a haphazard collection of individuals. Although there was no writing and only the simplest form of signification, the tribe seemed to function efficiently. The knowledge of the tribe was preserved orally; and was in the keeping of the priestly class and handed down from generation to generation. The discovery was in line with a truth that registered with me for first time: because a people had no writing it did not follow that they could be 'written off'. Even the word to describe them, *primitives*, was a woefully inaccurate term. Far from being a pattern of the *first* or earliest men, the Iroquois, for example, at the stage of development when Morgan recorded them, had progressed for thousands of years from their ancestors, tree-dwelling and food-gathering savages.

Engels's account of Morgan's researches affected my thinking about society; and much later it was confirmed by the accident of my meeting a man who took and restored an old fifteenth-century open-hall house in Suffolk in which we had formerly lived. Hugh Paget, after graduating in history at Oxford, spent most of his life employed by the British Council. While in its service, he had been in many countries all over the world from Poland to New Guinea. In conversations with him, however, I was most impressed by what he told me about his experiences with the Aborigines of Australia. He spent a great deal of time with them and confessed that he preferred their company to that of present-day Australians. Long talks with them gave him an entirely new view of the Aborigines. He found, after stripping away the misconceptions he had about them, that they were reasonable and friendly and surprisingly, when he got to know them, he found them deeply contemplative. They were given to thinking about, for instance, the one topic that has concerned man down the ages: where do we come from and where are we going? Hugh Paget's observations were echoed by the experiences of an American anthropologist who lived with his wife and children among the Aborigines since the last war. Ronald Rose, whose work I researched during the sixties, wrote about his experiences in his book *Living Magic*.* Rose confirmed Hugh Paget's

*London, 1957.

regard for the Aborigines, and he was probably recording them about the same time.

Another book that influenced me in assessing the value of unlettered men was Robert Graves's *The White Goddess*. Graves devotes a great deal of his book to the poetic myths of Ireland and Wales. I had a fair knowledge of the Welsh myths and only a smattering of the Irish. Therefore I asked an Irishman at a Dublin conference his opinion of *The White Goddess*. He replied with devastating brevity: 'It's bloody nonsense.' He was clearly judging the book from what he accepted as the norm of academic judgement. Graves, for his part, was not writing from the same standpoint. He was using a completely different pen. He had studied and assessed the texts with the intuition of a true poet. He had not attempted to disprove or denigrate the academic approach but to complement it with an entirely new interpretation. This roused the ire of the inhabitants of Academe who are notoriously resistant to any different treatment by someone who does not accept unques- tionly the *received* way of interpreting the distant past. As they themselves interpreted them as moderns, they saw the early myths as pathetic attempts at conveying reality. Instead, the ancients carried over into mundane affairs the same type of thinking as they used when they tried to construct a credible explanation of all that they saw around them using their own limited experience, and not being in possession of our newly acquired science to interpret it. They thought in symbols, and with this type of thinking they explained, to their own satis- faction, the whole context of their lives. The primitives' myth is symbolic or intuitive truth, not our scientific truth. In myth the central core of meaning cannot be described in detail because myths are constructed out of necessity at a stage of society when factual, scientific detail is lacking. Therefore instead of pin-pointing the truth in exact referential terms, myth circumscribes an area where it is certain the truth lies.

From my own amateur excursions into anthropology, my researches into rural life over the last thirty years in Britain, and my questioning of the last survivors of those early com- munities who had basically the same work-techniques in their farming as did their ancestors over two thousand years before, and still held many of their old beliefs and still cherished some of their old myths and aphorisms, I am convinced that Graves in his book treats the ancient communities in Britain with the respect that they deserve. Overall he gives a truer account of the 'feel' of them than we get from the painstaking reconstruction of scholars many of whom look upon the ancient people they write about with the same patronizing condescension as the authorities treat the Aborigines today.

One thing I noticed when I first started writing about ordinary working men and women was the attitude of some people that I was wasting my time going to this usually unlettered class, especially to get historical information. The inference was 'This is not the class that makes History.' With a certain type of academic I sometimes detected a trace of condescension; nothing overt, but a certain intonation crept into the responses whenever my project of gathering historical information from older farm people was discussed. This may or may not have been due to hyper-sensitivity, owing to the exposed nature of my position: of someone embarking on an essentially historical scheme from outside the university, and not sure of its reception. But what was not subjective was the response I got when, on the advice of friends, I made application for a grant-in-aid to various bodies and I got no favourable reply. But this did not deter me: I carried on working as before. I was so convinced of the rightness of my approach that nothing now would stand in my way. Part of my conviction was that the accepted method of finding out about the past was not the only one. It was not simply the facts that needed to be investigated but the contemporary human context of the facts. To a surprising degree this could be partially recovered from the rural society in this century, from men and women born in the period 1870–1900. A detailed knowledge of these two generations: of their work and daily lives, their speech, their reactions, and their beliefs will give a clue. Where there had been continuity for a couple of thousand years, it is possible to get to the real soul of the tribe that is still discernible in these last generations.

I have also been encouraged to take an unfashionable view of researching the past by the experience of modern artists. During this century they have gone back to early man for renewal. Dismayed by the loss of faith in the superiority of our own modern culture they have embraced the values of early man as shown in his art. They sought for inspiration outside the formal discipline of the art school and became conscious of the early tradition of art. The discovery in France of the Lascaux cave paintings, especially the quality of the paintings of animals, which some artists hold has never been surpassed, was a big factor in this new appreciation of the quality of early art. Artists like Picasso, Braque, and Henry Moore, recognized that tribal art had an atmosphere about its sculpture and artefacts which was missing from the overworked naturalism of much present-day 'commercialized' art. The primitives still retained some of the vigour and mystery that had been lost in modern attempts to get perfect naturalistic representation. Artists have gone back to the primitive for inspiration and have found guidance. They resorted to the primitive for help in their rethinking (or more accurately re-feeling) a new technique to meet the challenge of the great modern *break*, as David Jones, the poet and artist, defined it in his book *Anathemata*. They attempted to present the new consciousness with a conviction that they could enshrine it in plastic form, giving it an entirely fresh mould reflecting an inkling of a new level of social awareness.

Southwell Minster

16

Country Dancing

In 1968 I attended a conference of the Soil Association who met at Attingham Hall in Shropshire. One of my fellow speakers was Douglas Kennedy, the folk dance collector. He was also living in Suffolk and we were already known to one another, and had a chance to deepen our acquaintance. He had been a friend of Cecil Sharp and a collaborator with him in collecting folk dance and song, and he succeeded Sharp as Director of the English Folk Dance Society when he died. Sharp had gathered a group of young men, mostly from the universities, and enthused them with the need to salvage the folk dance and song tradition which no one had recorded.

Sharp had discovered folk dance by accident about a dozen years before at Headington where there was a large stone-quarry about a mile east of Oxford.* He was staying with his wife's people at Headington; and on the Boxing Day of his visit he was looking out of the window upon the snow-covered drive and saw a strange procession of eight men, six of them dressed in white, decorated with pads of small latten-bells strapped to their shins, each carrying coloured sticks and white handkerchiefs. Accompanying them was a concertina player† and a man dressed as the 'Fool'. The concertina struck up an invigorating tune, 'the like of which Sharp had never heard before'. The dancers were tough, real country-men, and there was no suggestion of effeminacy about the dancing. The men danced with springs and capers, waving and swinging the handkerchiefs they held, one in each hand, the bells marking the rhythm of their steps. Sharp was entranced by the music and the dancing. It was the turning point in his life: he had begun his career.

He began almost immediately to collect up a phalanx of workers to teach and record folk dancers and music. But the First World War intervened and most of his young men volunteered. Of this group only Douglas Kennedy survived and returned to the Folk Dance Society. As one of the 'Sing-ing Kennedys' of Scotland, folk singing and dancing were in his blood; and his own pursuit was to continue in the family tradition, and at the same time to keep alive the work Cecil Sharp had begun. Douglas married a sister of Maud Karpeles who later went with Sharp collecting songs in the Southern Appalachians, songs that had been taken over by the early English settlers in America. He has been immersed in folk dance and folk song all his life, passing on the tradition to his son Peter Kennedy. He first became involved in folk culture through his sister, then a student at Chelsea Physical Training College for Women. Cecil Sharp was at that time, 1911, con-ducting classes in English Folk Dancing with a view to cre-ating a pool of teachers of folk dance.

It was fitting that Douglas Kennedy and I were speaking together at the conference. We both had a similar conception of rural society in England in that we felt the countryman had

*A. H. Fox Strangways, *Cecil Sharp*, Oxford University Press, 1933, p.26.
†William Kimber was the concertina player and became a leading figure in the folk song and dance movement.

been grossly undervalued. Douglas Kennedy had come to his belief through contact with Cecil Sharp and his own work among country people. Townspeople not so long ago used to look upon a country dweller as a kind of *natural*. The true position, however, is revealed in the remark of a farm worker, who was bothered by a rather 'superior' enquirer: 'If you want to find a fool in the country, you'll have to bring him with you.' Douglas Kennedy in one of his books* discussed the recovery of the ancient ballads, stories, and music when literary experts usually take the same attitude towards their origin:

> They postulate an unknown poet who was the writer of a particular story or ballad which ever since has been handed down from generation to generation by word of mouth, and, since the peasant never invented anything, must have been deteriorating each step of the way.

This, in spite of the example of the poet, John Clare, who was a perfect enshrining of a creative peasant. There was a tacit belief that no good could come out of 'Nazareth'. As I have said it used to be very hard for the countryman to gain acceptance in Academe whose occupants were hemmed in by disciplines and syllabuses. They had – perhaps still have – a wrong conception of him, and he received little notice at all. But now, since the emergence of oral history, and its partial acceptance as a text in the academic bible, the position has improved. The intelligence of the tribe, the long-standing communal nous which Douglas Kennedy refers to and is adumbrated by Jung's collective unconscious, has at last been recognized. It is an element, as a student of the rural scene will recognize, which binds the earliest times in history with the present. It has helped to loosen the procrustean bed that academic discipline has so prescribed. Discipline, it is agreed, is necessary in any context of study; but when there is little movement and discipline has been allowed to degenerate into regimentation, there is room for an altered approach. In

Folk Dancing: Today and Yesterday, D. Bell, 1914, p.15.

those universities where oral history has a footing there is at least an opportunity for a dialogue between conventional documentary history and the chronicling of the wisdom of the tribe.

The association of folk dance and folk song with a certain stratum of society inevitably gave them, if not political affiliations, at least non-establishment outlines. These were deepened in the infancy of the movement by Sharp's meeting with Charles Latimer Marson, an Australian curate. (Sharp's father, a London merchant, had suggested that after Cambridge, he should try Australia in order to make his way in life. He stayed for a while before returning to England.) Marson, who was rather a thorn in the side of his colonial bishop, made his views known out there at a diocesan conference addressed by an Eton divine who had been insisting, apparently with general approval, on the need for *gentlemen* as ordinands. Marson was stung to reply:

> The playing-fields of Eton have a large place in our history. It is there that most of our battles have been lost. But what the Church requires is bounders like Peter and Paul.

Marson soon followed Sharp to England, where he wrote books on Christian Socialism and became a rector at Hambridge in Somerset. There he took an important part with Sharp in collecting folk songs. In fact, it was while he was at Hambridge that Sharp got his introduction to live folk song. He was sitting in Marson's garden talking to Mattie Kay, a Lancashire girl with a beautiful, untrained contralto voice, when they heard John England, the gardener, singing as he mowed the lawn. The song was 'The Seeds of Love' which Mattie Kay made famous by singing all over England.

Recently I visited Waldringfield where Douglas Kennedy and his second wife, Liz, live. They have a cottage near the river and they spend a great deal of time on it sailing in their boat. I recorded Douglas Kennedy (born 1893):

> I left school in Edinburgh and went out to Strasbourg for a year. In order to learn German I stayed with a German

family. And to get a bit of life I could go to the university and hear lectures; and I belonged to the Students' Union. So that was a good experience. I had just come back from there and, also rather patriotic, I joined the London Scottish Volunteer Regiment in London. I was enthusiastic for my drills and so on. And my sister at the same time joined a Physical Training College in Chelsea which Cecil Sharp was visiting. He was hoping to pick up students there because they were all taught how to teach, and he could pick out some of the more skilful to help him in his work, in his work of teaching country dancing and folk dancing in schools. When I had heard about him my sister said:

'Why don't you come to Chelsea one night and hear him at work?'

So one night I left the drill hall at Buckingham Gate with my books and heavy rifle slung across my shoulder, and went to the Polytechnic where the Physical Training College was housed. I was put up in the gallery out of the way, and I was able to watch what was going on. Cecil Sharp was at the piano, and he was also talking to the people who were on the floor – attractive youngsters, you know, but there were a certain number of men – that surprised me – scattered among them. After they had been dancing for a while I heard my sister's voice saying:

'You ought to come down. We want an extra person to make up a set here.'

So I was hauled out of my gallery and clambered downstairs, and put in a set among the country dancers. I didn't know much what was going on, whether it was coming or going, but I did enjoy it. And at the end they said:

'How did you like that?'

'I enjoyed it.'

And a man came up and asked me whether I would like to learn some Morris dancing. I said I was willing to try anything. But I'd never heard of Morris dancing! The upshot was that I met Cecil Sharp there and then; saw what he was doing and was interested, as my sister said I would be. And I met this group of young men who were, unfortunately later lost in the battle of the Somme: George Butterworth, George Wilkinson, Percival Lucas, [E. V. Lucas, the writer's, brother], Reginald Tiddy. They were high-powered, artistic people, who were not only academic scholars but very musical also, believing in the fact that the collecting of English material for England was of vital importance. So I quickly got into the medium, and I used to go along with Sharp to some places, where he was going to lecture, along with a group of dancers with him, who included some of those from Chelsea. And we illustrated his lecture. This went on until the outbreak of the First World War. Then everything had to stop. But we had formed this Society in 1911: The English Folk Dance Society. There was an earlier society: The Folk Song Society which was still going but not exactly what Sharp was after. That was the beginning as I remember it.

While we younger people got caught up in the war, Cecil Sharp decided to accept an invitation to go to America where he was asked to produce a masque he had written for Harley Granville-Barker who was the producer of the Shakespeare Festival at the Savoy Theatre, [1914] just before the actual outbreak of the war. He decided to go to America: he took his life into his hands and started there doing whatever jobs he could get. Very soon he was teaching Morris dances and sword-dances out there. In fact he got so involved that he asked my sister-in-law to come out and join him out there. So she went out; and the next thing, he needed another girl. Could we find another girl? My wife had to deal with all this because I was away, of course. She found another girl to go out; and soon she got married – much too soon. And Sharp was very cross. This sort of thing went on during the war. Then the most interesting thing: he got the opportunity to listen to some folk song material that had been collected in the Appalachian Mountains.

As soon as he saw this material* he realized it was of great importance. So then began his going into the mountains of Kentucky and the Southern Appalachians. He got the most remarkable haul: hundreds of songs. So many of them were earlier examples – when I say earlier, simpler, more archaic than the English ones. Of course he was thrilled with this experience because he heard not just old people singing, as in England. (It was a question of getting an old person who had the songs.) But out there it was young people with lovely voices. When he came back after the war and lectured on this find he had quite a big job coping with the musical people who were so interested to find out more about this story. Because it was a tremendous story. He returned to the English Folk Dance Society, and took on the job of being Director again; and did so for the next four years, until 1924 when he died. Everything stopped there. Then I was confronted with the question whether I would feel like stepping into the breach. Because there was no one else who had been with this work before the war. I was the only survivor who had any experience at all. Most were killed in the battle of the Somme. So I had then to decide whether I would go on being a university student which I had been when I enlisted at the beginning of the war or take on this job of being head of this new Society. (So I and my wife got together and said that I would do this.) So for the next forty-five years I was completely involved in the organization, raising large sums of money to build Cecil Sharp House [the Society's headquarters in North London].

Yes, that was a remarkable seminal meeting with Sharp and the dancers at Headington. What was most coincidental was that they don't as a rule dance at that time of the year. But it was a hard winter and they'd wanted a bit of extra money, and they were out of work. So they came out on Boxing Day; and they were apologizing to the

*Cecil J. Sharp and Maud Karpeles, *Eighty English Folk Songs*, Faber and Faber, 1968.

spectators because they knew that the people of Oxford knew that you didn't do Morris dancing at midwinter on Boxing Day. The usual time was Whitsuntide. However, there were the tunes; and this marvellous concertina player, William Kimber; William Kimber's father – not the William Kimber he got so much dance material from. And there was this group of great big brawny men, kicking their knees up and behaving generally in a manner that made more self-conscious people smile. These were the people I've been interested in for all the rest of my life: Why do men do this particular thing and dance? The last people you'd expect. Most people associate folk dancing with women, but on the contrary it's anything but effeminate. All my life when I've had the opportunity of seeing different groups of men dancers in different parts of northern Europe, they all have this same wonderful remoteness from the fact that they are dancing. They don't have to explain why they are dancing. There's so much in what they do that tells you that they are making life. The whole thing is a vivifying process which was essential to the whole of life – a life preserver. And the curious thing is quite a number of them, in so far as the thing has gone on for so long, some of the aspects that could explain it more clearly are not so apparent now; and so we get a shadowy figure like the hobby-horse and the other kind of animal-men who were in the background so often. And of course with the change from the central character whose job it was to do the big thing of re-vivifying the world by dying and coming to life again which goes on through the whole surviving panorama of ritual dance. Groups of young men dedicated to the central character who promotes service of a life, as it were. *They* then become, as in so many cases, the dominant troop; and the central character who is supposed to be the god is neglected for the time being while they portray the marvellous, vivifying action of dance to bring in life, again. So with this mixture of central figures and an ever present *corps d'élite* whose job it is to groom and nourish the god.

225

When you see the Morris dancers at Headington and their simple English style, it's a bit of a mouthful to swallow all this. But take all the different aspects of this and the whole jigsaw becomes an impressive story.

Then you see, I had the difficulty, in the beginning, in dealing with the actual dancing in that the traditional dancers don't teach each other consciously. Youngsters in the village see it go on and they present themselves as apprentices; and sometimes don't even ask to come in but dance on the skirt of the teams' dancing; and by the time they've had a bit of experience about it, they are ready to join in. And if there's a gap in the team because somebody's fallen out, somebody of the younger generation is always ready to step in. And what was very interesting: the first occasion I was at Bampton which is another village near Headington that has kept continuity going since before the First War. There you'd see a sailor or soldier step out of the crowd and come into the team and go on doing this with the team without feeling his costume was out of step with the rest. So in view of the time, there was a *strain*: you grew your dancers as you did your plant. You don't have to *teach* village people. So the whole process of the impregnation of the feeling for music at that level is quite different from the people who want to teach it by rote. This was a very different business from the beginning, the appreciation of this. Children's games, for instance: they all wanted to get hold of Lady Gomme's book. There was the book of games! The teacher only had to get the book and teach the children to play the game. Whereas, the children didn't want to be taught in that way at all. And when it was taught that way, it was stilted; it wasn't real. They liked to go into a playground, where *Jenny Jones* was going on, and just tag on. And that's how they picked it up. And that's still the process of learning – actually doing.

The talk with Douglas Kennedy, who has spent his long life actively involved with folk dance and with an intimate connection with folk song, convinced me that they are legitimate subjects to include under the rubric of oral history. In the first place, they were communal activities which have their origin in the prehistory of the community. Secondly his observations about the symbolism of the troop of dancers and its division into a central character who in the pristine stage represented life, and who, in some versions, dies and is helped to his feet by his attendants,* ('Rise up and fight again'), reveal that in its origin it was essentially a religious rite. The dancers are the counterparts of the *animal-men*, men wearing the masks of animals who figure among the paintings on the walls of the palaeolithic caves that were discovered in different parts of the world at the end of the last century and the beginning of this: Lascaux and Altamira, notably, in the south of France and in Spain. Douglas Kennedy's mention of *animal-men* in the tradition of the English dance bears out their similarity with some of the men in the cave paintings. We have the hobby-horse and Mari Lwyd (the Grey Mare) in the dancers and actors in folk games, which put them on a similar footing with those cultures which anthropologists and nineteenth-century writers, such as Sir James Frazer, drew attention to overseas. No one except Douglas Kennedy, as far as I know, has yet referred to the vestiges of this early period in man's history that are still present in folk dance and folk culture (taking culture in its root meaning of the tending of the soil). I was emboldened by Douglas Kennedy's hints and the other material from this ancient period. I also refer to Mrs Jay of Blaxhall and her reminder that the gleaning of corn lasted in Britain to the beginning of this century. She took part in it and was aware that Naomi and Ruth were doing it in Biblical times.

An example of this continuity and a dramatic exposition of the importance to man's subsequent history of this remote period in palaeolithic times (the Ice Age), when men lived in the caves, has been recreated in recent years by a second-generation American, Alexander Marshack, who has placed

*H.I.F., pp.232–3, the old mummers' play.

his findings in a book.* Marshack, acting on an intuition, interpreted an incomprehensible series of dots, markings that he had discovered on a piece of bone found in a cave, as a record of bi-monthly phases of the moon. He requisitioned very up-to-date equipment which he took into the caves to confirm his hunch. He proved conclusively that the series of dots, or strokes, made by different incisors at different times, was man's first attempt at a calendar. This record was also marked on the rock itself. He also found these marks in palaeolithic objects taken from the caves, all evidence that the dots were a calendric notation, and all confirmed by his sophisticated equipment with microscopes, specialized lighting, and photographs. Marshack realized that this special lighting was necessary to distinguish clearly images and markings that had been made twenty thousand years before. And it was for this reason he used infra-red and ultraviolet photography to enable him to decipher the detailed markings. The magnification of the markings and especially the images on the cave walls enabled him to make another dramatic discovery. Many of the drawings or paintings had been redrawn and painted over again:

> To the eye, it looked like an animal, but through the microscope it looked as though the person had come back time after time to re-use the image. This kind of use and re-use posed a whole set of questions. Because if the horse, for example, is never really killed, or if the deer can be renewed by simply adding an ear or an eye, then obviously the image has a kind of constancy. It was the microscopic evidence that turned me to the art in the caves; and in the caves I found exactly the same thing.

Often, Marshack found that the original paintings had been retraced so many times that it was invisible to the naked eye but showed up clearly under special lighting. He believed that these people came into the caves periodically with a

*The Roots of Civilization, Weidenfeld and Nicolson, 1972. See also an article 'Thinking in Time' by Calvin Tomkins, in the *New Yorker*.

definite intent of revitalizing the image or associated religious myth, a ritual that renewed the images by their visit. This was the confirmation of the religious significance of their recurring visits, at definite times and for definite reasons. It also supplants the first-formed theory of the purpose of the cave-images: that the paintings were made as a form of sympathetic magic, to help them in capturing the animals depicted. Marshack summed up his new interpretation with the words:

> The image on the wall somehow helped to structure the life of the group. It's not the image of a meal – it's the image of a process.

The image is also of man, for the first time, making symbols as a means of communication, and taking one of the earliest steps in symbols to aid his developing intelligence which finally led him to appreciate their use in handling numbers and, ultimately, to describe this in a developing language.

A short time after recording Douglas Kennedy, and in continuing our discussion, he mentioned that he had actually visited the Lascaux cave before it was permanently closed owing to the partial deterioration of some of the paintings through contamination by the influx of thousands of visitors over the years they had been opened to the public. I had always been interested in Lascaux, and when the article about Alexander Marshack and his book appeared in the *New Yorker* I cut it out for further reference. And when Douglas Kennedy used the phrase *animal-men* in his recording it reminded me of the article and Marshack's book which I subsequently read. The result was that Douglas Kennedy agreed to record his memories of that visit, and his further involvement in the folk dance and song movement. Douglas Kennedy:

> My visit to Lascaux cave was in 1953. With my wife and my son Peter we were making our way through France down to the Basque country to attend a conference of The International Folk Music Council at two Basque centres in France and Spain. The IFMC had a conference in London in 1935. It was staged in Cecil Sharp House, a newly

opened memorial of the founder of the Society. And
every morning, sessions by various members about the
different backgrounds gave the general pictures of the
early days of man's behaviour through a large part of
historical time. Afternoon and evening demonstrations
were given at the Cockpit in Hyde Park, in Regent's Park,
the Open Air Theatre, the Albert Hall, and in the Garden of the Archbishop's Palace. For a week London saw
various types of dance from various parts of Europe.
One recurrent feature of the dances was the appearance
of a character dressed up to represent usually an animal,
a different type of person from other members of the
group. You might say he was an actor, but all the dancers
were actors because they were giving some representation of the relationship to meet some sort of religious
impulse behind what they were doing. And the recognition of one character – the animal-man – that had been a
superior creature to the ordinary dancers. The animal-
men appeared in so many dances of this kind. In England the hobby-horse, Yugoslavia a goat or a kid, and in
other parts of Europe a bear. The horse seems to be
fairly universal, and the association of the dancers with
the animal-man is something that the cave-paintings had
shown indications of before Lascaux was discovered.

But to talk about our experience in Lascaux cave. We
joined the queue, and we met some friends from London
in the queue who expressed surprise that I should be
interested in art. And I rather brusquely said:

'We are going to see something of more importance
than the elements of art which are shown.'

When we got inside the cave we took some little time to
get used to the semi-darkness although there was a little
extra lighting that had been put in. But for a moment it
was difficult for us to take in. The overwhelming scene
was gradually revealed to us. The animals, somehow
drawn or scratched in more or less semi-darkness. The
light must have been a simple form of wick-lamp, sent
out a kind of guttery kind of light, and yet there were the

creatures, beautifully so depicted, that they would be difficult for us to draw unless we were pretty good artists in proper lighted-up conditions. But here were these creatures – quite stunning; and for a very long time there wasn't a sound from the crowd who had been introduced to this new world – rather this very very old world – because we were given some facts mainly from the Abbé Henri Breuil who was a specialist in the paintings of these caves and of those in many other places. It was clear that these were an exhibition of a form of something – certainly it was wonderful art – but there was obviously something more to it. The period we were in was some 20,000 to 30,000 years ago. The end of the Ice Age and whoever had drawn these pictures were of this period, or possibly earlier, who lived by hunting; and the animals they hunted and had to live with – while they lived on them – were such creatures as the ox and the deer and the antelope and the horse. The stag and the bison were the big pictures that were near us and were incredibly alive. You felt that they were plunging and you could almost hear the noise that they could make, the whole place was simply a wild scene of animals – some of them no longer alive, extinct in fact. We just stood and gazed, and as we grew accustomed to the light it was noticeable that some of the paintings were brighter in places and there was no doubt that you could see that the pictures had not been left alone, that they had been touched up. In fact, you could see distinct layers of paint. And in those cases where there was an outline scratched, etched in the rock-face of the cave, you could see that the lines had been drawn several times, overlapping not always coinciding, a bit one side or the other. This indicated that there had been a constant retouching, a renewing of these creatures.

It was borne on me fairly early that something in its expression was trying to talk to us; that it was telling us something quite specific about the need for the picture to be kept going. The whole thing had to be kept alive and this was a clear indication that the animals were something more than just food. They were the friends of the hunters, who had to pick out now and then an individual or possibly murder a whole herd by driving them over a cliff. They had to have enough meat over the period, and however they killed the creatures there is no doubt that they did so not only with skill but with reluctance. And this relation betwen man and the animals on which he lived is the subject I'd like to expand on.

Perhaps before we talk about that we should discuss who had drawn these pictures of their friends on whom they lived in such a remarkable degree of vivacity and vitality and for whom they had an enormous regard – one might almost say affection. One of the theories that this was Cromagnon man at the end of the Ice Age who were the hunters, clever people from whom we are descended, always following the animals, keeping up with them even if they didn't herd them, killing them in a special kind of way. Trying all the time not to detach themselves from the big animal-world of which they were a part. When I say they realized, I think, the fear of man as his emergence as a thinking creature was one of anxiety as to how, if he got too detached, he would ever get back. But at the time, driving him on, was this thing that has made man so different from the animal-world that he has to go on finding out, go on discovering; and even in this stage of 20,000 years ago in the caves there are, it is believed, features – little marks besides all the outlines and shapes of the animals, little marks to indicate that man at that time was keeping in touch with the astronomical world. That is, he was following certain features that he was recording. One belief is that in the recordings in the caves, the marks, represent the phases of the moon. So he was obviously able to live in a world of his own mind, and in a world he was aware he was a part.

This to some extent makes a division in the human animal of a mental area and a physical area and when it comes to dramatic ritual, to acting, to dancing, to anything that leads to the arts, this is a very important picture to have. The cave-paintings reinforce that this was happening at the end of the Ice Age and in this beginning our world was growing into the world as we know it today. This idea, apologizing to the creature that he is going to kill and trying to make up to the prey for living on him and eating him and not being sick afterwards, is still prevalent in certain parts of the world. The Eskimo, who until quite recently was living on seals. We get the picture of a particular hunter standing over a hole in the ice, his legs astride, holding his weapon ready to harpoon the poor creature: he was singing a little song explaining to the seal that he hates to do this. He is very sorry about it; but he has to live and he can't do it without killing his friend. But he is still hoping that in some way he can be friends. This is the kind of attitude I can remember my father telling me about a ghillie in Scotland who worked for the Ogilvies at their place at the head of Glen Islay. This man had every now and then to cull some of the red deer that were kept in control. The young stags, numbers had to be regulated. Every now and then he had to shoot off some of these lovely animals which were his friends, his family. And he would say before he pressed the trigger:

'Do forgive me. I'm sorry I have to do this.'

This attitude of man towards animals is something that has gone on, and is still prevalent.

To return to the aspect of the continual renewal of the paintings by the hunters who felt that they had to inscribe outline on outline and paint on paint: to preserve life, not the life of the animals but the life of the continuous herd, of the living world going on living. And this drive – this is a religious drive in hand with the fear of man getting too far away from the animal and having to keep in touch, somehow by whatever means he could, of preserving life. And the hunters at this moment being life-preservers is reflected in these dance rituals because they are dancing to preserve life. Although it isn't so patent in the English Morris it is patent in other forms of dance performed by men in Europe. There is a dance 'The Calusari' in Romania, this continuous process of dispensing life to the community in order to cure sick babies, of making fertility to ensure that the girls will mate and have their babies. And there is this drive behind so much of the drama and the ritual that man has and we have clearly depicted in France and Spain, and indeed in other parts of the world: for the Stone Age people of Australia, of South Africa that have these pictures on the walls of caves – pictures of animals and hunting-scenes but which are no doubt part of this drive of keeping life going and keeping the contact of man with the living world. The life-preservers, as I call them, the life-preservers are a study I have made the most of my life, feeling so much of the understanding of the ritual drama, of the characters in the folk plays, of the purpose of dance itself, is only understood as something that makes life, rather than detracts from it. When you're talking about dancing, it isn't enough to have something which has a form of movement that just keeps time. People can dance mentally by keeping time and thinking they are dancing. But that isn't the dancing that keeps things alive. The dance movement is not a living movement unless it has this pulsation which has a drive which pushes the business on. To make life through the art of dancing the purpose of gesture, the purpose of the dance movement makes more life than was there before.

Now let me tell you about the Calusari. In appearance they are dressed in mainly white with the colouring ribbons, possibly with sun-hats with garlands around the hats, soft shoes with the bells hung on their legs. A general looseness about their costumes that they can be very free to move; and they carry a cudgel which is very much a part of their equipment. They can use them to make obscene gestures; and of course it's marvellous to beat or hit anybody with. Among this group there is one character who is not sprucely dressed. He doesn't look

like a prince or anything like that. He looks very much
like an old woman or a witch. His face is blacked and he is
dumb and doesn't speak to anybody. You can speak to
him; he can smile at you, wink at you, but he doesn't
answer back, and won't answer back. And he is so for the
whole of the forty days and forty nights of Pagan Lent
which is given up to this particular performance, and the
tour of the countryside which they do as medicine-men
who provide music for the dancing; and they carry a
short pole, a white pole that has been stripped of its
branches, bark, and leaves. At the top of this pole they tie
a small piece of garlic. Now this group before they begin
dancing has to be prepared. They have to be purged.
They have to have the Death beaten out of them so that
Life can enter in. The process of this is quite remarkable.
They have to take it in turn; but each man must lie down
on his back, have his legs held together by two other men
with their crossed cudgels; and, so pinned, another man
with a stick or a handful of sticks can beat hard on the
soles of his feet. You would have thought that with soft-
soled shoes that they couldn't stand up to that. But they
do; and then they are turned over on their face and given
a final whack on the backside. Every man in turn goes
through this process. Even the musicians have to go
through this, and they take it in very good part. Except
the Fool, this dumb man with a black face and who
doesn't talk and doesn't behave properly whatever happens. They have to run after him and catch him and hold
him down. But he just can't be held down, because he's a
bit of Nature itself, and is not to be commanded. And
having done all the other purges, the fiddlers strike up,
and then they begin dancing.

Their method of dancing is to walk round in a circle –
when I say walk – they have a wonderful bouncing
dance-walk, which is like an animal. They use their
walking-sticks while doing that. They walk with a wild
freedom calling out 'Calusar, Calusar'. Then they break
out with fast stepping. The music changes its note. It

goes up a bit and is very demanding and commanding. There's a tremendous excitement while they step. It's this alternative dance-walk and stepping that constitutes the making of the medicine which they dispense. They dispense it, too, by dancing around, and they go from place to place with this movement. When they stop in any particular palce they'll have a little rest, then they'll do some special kind of dancing for a special kind of purpose. One of the early things they do is for the sick children. The young mothers who were not satisfied with the state of health of their loved one brings him out and each dancer in turn takes the baby into his arms, dances with him just a little bit, holding him very carefully while he does quite vigorous steps; puts the baby down on the ground while he does various steps dancing round it and over it. The mother hasn't the slightest anxiety because she knows these are special people who will take great care of their loved one. Then the baby is lifted up and put in his mother's arms; and she goes away looking quite satisfied that she has had the best clinical treatment possible.

This goes on until the babies are all dealt with; and then they move on to another part of the community to do some general dispensing; or else towards the end of the day they will wait in the centre of the circle. They go to an open space where there's plenty of room, and to act there is a small circle in the middle; and the girls – they are the married girls – gather round ready for their particular part. This is very beautiful to watch. It is dusk by the time it happens, and it is not easy to see individuals. The girls are very shy in the ordinary kind of way; but are much braver when it is fairly dark. The dancers open out so that they are spaced very widely; and no matter how many girls there are they form a big circle and hold hands with the young men so that there's a continuous dispensing current going through the whole circle. They will dance vigorously, wildly, and excitedly until there's a climax, and they all break up and disappear into the darkness. And that ensures, and I think every girl feels quite certain, that she will meet her man and have her husband and her family; and generally not be surprised at the wonderful life that is brought by the life-preservers.

Douglas Kennedy then turned to examples of animal-men who have been celebrated in England and have been turned into minor gods. There is the horse in Padstow in Cornwall which is the central figure in a ceremony carried out by a group of players on the first of May every year. He is called ' 'Oss 'Oss'. The central figure is a dragon-like figure which you would not recognize as a horse except that he has a tiny horse's head stuck on the front of the contraption that the man inside has around him. He puts on a remarkable performance acting the death of life and its sudden revival as befits the season. This goes on all through the town with drum-beating, and singing. Douglas Kennedy visited Padstow in 1912 with Cecil Sharp. He said:

> The atmosphere was not altogether good there because the incumbent, who was to some extent responsible for regulating this annual festival didn't approve of it, and regarded the Mayers and their horse as a drunken, disreputable lot and he was sorry that this had to go on every year. But the locality insisted on it. But when we went back again – my wife and I – fifty years later the whole thing was just as before, but without the blemish of disapproval from on high. We were struck even more by the magic of the whole thing.
>
> The next county has a similar ceremony at Minehead, but not as spectacular as Padstow. With Cecil Sharp in 1912 we also gatecrashed in the Helston May Day ceremony.

He went on to indicate that this ancient tradition survived in many parts of the world, and he stated that he could not leave out those in Britain including the Abbot's Bromley Horne Dance in Staffordshire, a dance by a number of men carrying reindeer horns, in a procession with a hobby-horse and a Fool, and a Maid Marian who is an important man-woman figure in the concourse. This is a beautiful twining dance going on through the town into the surrounding country, visiting the various farms, a life-giving fertility dance which is of great importance to the locality.

> I was speaking [said Douglas Kennedy] to a couple of farmers who told me that they would be very sorry if the town-dancers didn't come and visit their farm because they would become anxious about their future crops.

Another dance that should be mentioned was the North of England sword-dance: both the long-sword dance and the short-sword dance – the coal miners' dance. There is, too, the Mari Lwyd ceremony in south Wales, already mentioned. Douglas Kennedy continues:

> There is one element without which the story is incomplete, that is the Green Man. He is a figure which all through the Middle Ages, and before, has been prevalent as a Folk Thought among country people and, indeed, among the whole society; for his face, the face, is seen in many carvings on the underside of choir-stalls and in the bosses of cathedral roofs. This face of a man, with vegetation growing out of his ears, nose and mouth, is quite ubiquitous. Many people have studied the Green Man and know about it. He is an important figure, and obviously he was more important in the Middle Ages than now; and we only see his relics either in the static form of carvings or in the Jacks in the Green which recurred quite recently in London. A man who was covered in greenery except for parts of his face and who danced about to what was called Rough Music, the clanging of iron pokers and unmusical noise that was bringing this life and expressing greenery into the community. Now this life has always had a double-barrelled application when it came to the greenery. Because the people who had run the Jacks in the Green were normally

sweeps who swept the chimneys and were covered with black. The association of fire with such important people as smiths and fire-makers – the charcoal-burners and so on – fire that was invariably followed by greenery; soot being a very strong fertilizer. So the Green Man might have been a sweep himself. I was talking to my grandfather in my early days and we happened to meet and talk with a sweep. I had to take my cap off and say:

'Good morning, Mr Sweep.'

I *did* use to do that, and almost always I gathered from the sweep that he understood it was an important piece of behaviour to someone like himself who was obviously a bit of a magic man. Now the sense of the greenness in the world can be found – of course, one might read into it sometimes when it wasn't really meant: irrepressible life coming back – had led to the idea that you could bury a person in the ground, and that person would rise up again. Like the story of John Barleycorn who springs up again and surprises everybody after he had been ploughed in.

Well, I can remember in an incident in Waldringfield [near Woodbridge] where I now live: when I was standing looking over the countryside at a fairly recently drilled field; and the farmer who was standing beside me suddenly pressed my arm and said:

'Look, Mr Kennedy: the mystery!'

And I looked up the field, and in four or five furrows in the top corner, there was just a hint of greenness in the corner there, showing on the surface of the whole brown field. And I thought afterwards what a very complete way to describe this whole story being realized right from the early 20,000 years ago; and indicated clearly by man in so many different ways that this was the vital factor that made us and our planet so important and different from anything else we have found in this world.

Huntingfield

17

Conclusion

About twenty-five years ago, as I have described, I began to hear the term oral history. I was involved in the folk life movement at that time and was collecting information and ideas from my neighbours in Suffolk, chiefly details about their work on the land. Much was rapidly changing: stories about their family and the part the whole family took in the farming year; their schooldays and their involvement with the farm even while they were still at school; the wives with the simple provisions for the family – the Three Bs: bread making, brewing and bacon-curing – and the climax of the year: the corn harvest. Sometimes these folk life studies were also referred to as social anthropology. And I was quite happy with either term. For although I used books and documents to find my way, I was getting the bulk of my information, like the anthropologist, directly from people. When the title, oral history, came from America I was very critical of its obvious shortcomings but could not think of a better alternative. I was, to a certain extent, reassured when I read one of the most thoughtful books* that has come out of America on that subject. It was written by William W. Moss, director of the John F. Kennedy Oral History Programme. In it he describes the first national colloquium in America, and how difficult they found it to define the scope and the boundaries of oral history, and failed finally to come up with a satisfactory definition. Neither were many of the charter members satisfied with the title oral history, but:†

> they felt constrained to use it because it had become habitual and none of the alternatives suggested were sufficiently inspired to last.

I solved my problem, as I have already explained, by not meeting it head-on but by walking round it, and by continuing under a provisional banner and not changing my original allegiance to folk life studies. I judged that it did not matter ultimately what the activity was called as long as the gist of what I wrote about was clear and had a close relevance to conventional history. I never let the finding of a more exact title for it deter me from working as I had always done. I was strengthened, however, in my affinity to folk life by a remark by an anthropologist of standing who said that some of the best books of history he had read were shot through with anthropology. I labour with this explanation for the same reason that it is necessary to discuss continuity in the study of history thoroughly, in that to understand the subject one needs to know not only how things are but how they have come to be.

All the time I was involved in collecting material and writing books on oral history I was continually attempting to justify the validity of the exercise. My main and ultimate

---

Oral History Program Manual, Praeger Publishers, New York and London, 1974.
†Ibid., pp.6–7.

conclusion was that history is a continuum first in *time* and also in *extent*. There are enough examples in the present book to illustrate that there is no retrospective limit in time to many of the customs and beliefs and practical activities which were widespread at the beginning of this century in the rural areas. Many of them were in existence well before the beginning of recorded history. There is nothing spectacular in saying this: it is only to affirm that farming the land preceded recorded memory, and similarity with the earliest farming practices is still traceable in common practices that were followed up to the recent break of complete mechanization. This is verification by *time* but it can also be proved by the argument from *extent* by the farming practices of less advanced peoples all over the world who now still use techniques that have lasted since prehistoric times.

There is another area of oral history that confirms its extent and also its universality. This is the folk tale whose provenance is ordinarily thought of as a particular rural area but whose theme is duplicated in many parts of the world. This was brought home to me by a simple folk tale that I was very familiar with in my boyhood in south Wales. On the hills above the valley where I was born there is a small hamlet called Llanwonno with an old church, probably pre-Norman. In the early nineteenth century a famous runner in south Wales lived in this parish. He was called Guto Nyth Bran: Guto of the Crow's Nest, the name of his father's farm. His grave is in Llanwonno churchyard, and on more than one occasion I walked over the hills to visit Guto's grave. There are many tales in the neighbourhood about his prowess as a runner. The most common one is of his contest with an Englishman named Prince in a race over the hills to the town of Caerphilly. The story, however, that best illustrates the theme of the university of folk tales tells of Guto's rounding up of his father's sheep. He was such a good runner that he didn't need a dog to help him; he could manage the sheep on his own. One day, however, he took a bit longer than usual in getting them in the fold. His father asked him:

'Did you have any difficulty?'

'No, except for a little brown one. It gave me a bit of trouble.'

The farmer found on going to the sheep-fold that 'the little brown one' was an exhausted hare. This type of legend travels a long way, and similar mythical tales are grafted on to many a prosaic local happening. This particular tale of Guto probably has its provenance in the Armenian epic of *The Saga of Sassoun* when David, the son of Mehair the Great, was sent out to herd the town's cattle. He did the job well: he rounded up all the cattle but included all the wild animals as well – bears, wolves, and foxes – much to the townspeople's dismay. A similar type of story is found in Norfolk where I now live. *The Pedlar of Swaffham* is also embroidered and taken from the treasure trove of mankind, modified by being given a local habitation and a name. This story has as its counterpart, possibly its origin, a tale about a Jewish Rabbi, Eisik of Cracow in Poland.* Scholars have studied this correspondence of local tales and myths all over the world and have shown that most tales derive, at least in part, from those in the common store.† It would be fitting for oral history to record such legends as myths in the area studied. The tales are vital components of any community and are one of the elements that welds a society together. Moreover, as they are told to children, they will continue in their present form as a long memory of their town or parish.

In connection with this sort of mythical tale it has often struck me that if only a few professional anthropologists in the late nineteenth century had, instead of going abroad *en masse* to study untouched, usually isolated communities, stayed and worked in the British Isles and Ireland, they would have found a harvest worthy of all their labour. The remains of a very early society lay on their doorstep if they had only looked for it. Yet they would have had to dig for it.

*Mircea Eliade, *Myths, Dreams and Mysteries*, Collins (Fontana Library) 1968, pp.245–6.
†Anti Aarne and Stith Thompson, *The Types of Folk Tales*.

This reminds me of a story I heard in Orkney concerning some of this ancient material. A writer, whose reputation was world-wide, had a house on one of the larger islands. He was once asked whether he knew anything about the Society of the Horseman's Word. He denied the possibility that such a society existed. Yet at that time there was a sworn member of that cult living only a stone's throw away from the writer's gate; and they were still carrying on their rites and having regular meetings while he was still living on the island. This incident demonstrates that had someone begun to inquire into these old beliefs, even at the end of the last century, he would have had a very difficult task in removing the veil that had purposely been thrown around this old complex.

But, apart from a special instance such as the above, there was often a queer reticence about earlier periods in our history. This may be that our own society, at particular times in our history, was going through a turmoil of changes in itself or even so preoccupied with its very existence, as happened during the last war, to pay much regard to earlier times. The remark of E. H. Carr, quoted earlier* has drawn attention to this marked periodicity of historical interest. I echo that thought. Through my studies in oral history over the last few decades, I gained a much better conception of the Middle Ages than when I studied the period at university level some time ago. We chiefly read about the medieval church and the religious orders; apart from the usual wars and the political history. But through my experience of living in Blaxhall, which had maintained an uninterrupted existence since the medieval period, I felt my way into it through the farming, where there had been continuity since medieval times, and even from a much earlier period. The men who described farming with horses to me before the break, took me back to another era that was confirmed for me by my study at the same time of Thomas Tusser's *Five Hundred Good Points of Husbandry*. The Blaxhall people were among my early mentors. The speech of most of them, who were either farm

*p.187.

workers or farmers, and their wives, was often pure dialect or else tinged with the East Anglian variety of enunciation. Owing to its survival in Chaucer's *Canterbury Tales* it was redolent to me of the Middle Ages themselves. To confirm some of the words I was hearing spoken for the first time, I re-read Chaucer's *Tales*. It gave me a fresh enjoyment, and a more exact understanding of medieval living and a fuller appreciation of domestic conditions. For example in *The Reeve's Tale* where the two northern students worsted the miller it was essential to know the lay-out of the miller's house – an 'open-hall' dwelling – to get the full impact of the story. It added another interest to conversation with my neighbours to find out what was a new word to me which I later confirmed in Chaucer's text.

While working on oral history in the field I have often been struck by the old method of presenting history by what could be called the time-chart device.* I have felt that, although it is a method of helping children to memorize the sequence of events or dynasties, it has a negative side. The division of history into charts, clearly delineated in vital segments, has a deterring effect in that the uncompromising lines tend to mark the past off irrevocably from the present. In fact the past, far from being moribund, is revived continually in connection with the farming of the land, for example where the old methods are coming up for reappraisal. More spectacular is the very recent reassessment of the men of the caves. They, in popular imagination, aided by cartoonists, figure as huge bully-boys trundling massive clubs. The truth about the cave man has only been recognized in our time by the realization of his advanced artistic skill and more recently by the discovery that he worked out the first method of recording time, giving to his successors an indispensable tool of his living. But he, like the so-called primitive, has been put right at the bottom of the time-chart and left to stay there in a permanent under-assessment. The division of history into clean lined

*H.P. & M., pp. 200–3.

layers which have all the implication of finality, to represent the past, puts the past farther away then it actually is. I speak from my own experience and reiterate that the artificial barriers we have set up about thinking about the supposed irrevocable past have been demolished for me through my pursuit of oral history during the last decades. This exercise has also proved a continuing enlightenment of the actual methods of assessing the past, and the posing of the question whether the rigid documentary method of the past is the only method of illuminating it. Should it not be supplemented by the oral history technique of what has happened in our own country, aided also by the information we get from anthropologists and archaeologists from other parts of the world? The vertical metaphor we employ in the time-chart method stills rules our historical consciousness, and we instinctively exclude looking for analogues to the event outside our own period and our own particular history. In estimating the value of oral tradition as a historical source we use the *vertical* or time-chart method and study it in our own history. Yet a *horizontal* trope, shifting the ground of the search to another part of the world, and to another era, could be equally enlightening as was Douglas Kennedy's calling the figures *animal-men* in the modern English country dance, and so pointing by implication, to the masked human figures – undoubtedly performers in a ritual – in cave art. The time-chart is an extremely useful device by which children can visualize development in historical time. Yet it must be pointed out that it is partly responsible for ankylosing our ability to imagine another more suitable metaphor or symbol which is less rigid – such as time represented as flowing like a river.

The family is an excellent starting-point for the development of oral history. One of my informants gave a memorable picture of listening to his father in a Suffolk cottage telling him stories and his experiences on the farm:*

*H.P. & M., pp.182–3.

> The owd boy [his father] used to tell me all manner of tales
> when we sat agin the fire at night.

A child introduced in this way to the oral tradition never
forgets it. It could well become a prelude to an interest in
history gained in the most evocative way – memorable and
unforgettable. He hears tales in a setting he knows intimately:
he can visualize and absorb them directly as a background to
what his father relates; and the images stay for decades. The
boy would react with incomprehension if he were told he was
listening to history. The abstract term would mean nothing to
him. Yet in spite of this the boy has both feet squarely in history
without knowing it. The family is the natural place to introduce children to history, particularly by starting with the work
of the father: (and mother if the mother, as in some families, is
working as well). The child easily identifies with the work
through hearing it discussed at home. He gets a novel idea of
history through looking into the work of his father whether it is
farming, mining, engineering, painting, fishing or seagoing. It
will not be abstract history concerning political power-
struggles he knows nothing about but concrete occupations
with which he is familiar and that are often spoken about. He
thus gets his idea of history in the best possible way: it is also
bracketed with his family loyalty which can become a useful
adjunct in the course of following his interest.

Family history, however uneventful on the surface, is an
excellent way to introduce an adolescent to the oral tradition
and its relation to contemporary happenings. It could, for
example, give a student starting on a course of history a sense
of personal involvement; and it could conceivably be the best
way that a history of the family could be salvaged. In collecting
this kind of personal history one realizes on what precarious
grounds the material exists at all: merely the chance of some
member of the family volunteering to record it with very little
inducement except personal satisfaction.

In my work, as I have already said, I have been concerned
chiefly with two generations, the people who were born after

1875, and the generation that followed: people who were born at the beginning of this century The older generation had the much richer lore and, in fact, appeared to have lived in an altogether different world. In some respects they did, a much older one; and it was my main thesis that this world is still recoverable in a historical sense from their testimony. Yet its outlines will be much less clear if the attempt is made using orthodox historical methods alone. We can often get the organic details only by adopting the anthropologist's technique of patient and careful study of the former environment, and a systematic recording of the survivors. In connection with collecting information I once engaged to give a talk at a Folk Life conference, and I was stressing the danger of concentrating solely on the object – like the archaeologist, who has little else besides the object – and the need to include the man who uses the tool or equipment. In reading through a transcript of the talk, I was struck by a glaring incongruity and I added a footnote when it was printed:

> With all this talk about the object aren't you being contradictory and a little bit glib? You warn us against dehumanizing the object and yet you yourself are committing a worse offence, using men and women themselves as objects – merely to take information from them, to read them as documents.

This is a valid criticism that any folk life or oral history collector has to face; and the criticism cannot, I think, be met with a convincing logical rejoinder. But all the sting can be taken out of it, if the collector is in direct sympathy with his informant: that is, if he does not consider his approach as just another facet of an academic technique or exercise, but as a man-to-man relation. Three of the most outstanding figures in folk life studies have emphasized this directly or indirectly. I refer first to Sigurd Erixon, the Scandinavian pioneer. Some years ago he advised students at a similar conference to listen to an informant's whole life story, if this is possible, rather than take away specific information which he happens to want at the moment. This undoubtedly is the ideal. Again Seamus

Delargy and Iorweth Peate have pointed out more than once the need for the collector to be in absolute sympathy with the people he is interviewing. No amount of technique can adequately compensate for the absence of this essential element in the relationship. Even if contact is only temporary or minimal, a lack of rapport will directly affect the result. This is equally true of collecting oral history or any other discipline that relies on getting information directly from people.

As for the future, I believe oral history's future is assured; for essentially it is within the reach of everybody to preserve the past – of small happenings as well as great. The outlook as a movement is also supra-national. It has clearly shown that it is looking outward to other nations. The International Oral History Conference has already held five yearly meetings and is thus helping to modulate the tendency to concentrate solely on the history of the mother-nation.

Index

Index